Praise for The Marten and the Scorpion

Shortt (*Wellside*) plunges readers into the underbelly of medieval Samarkand in this beguiling fantasy. // Clever, tightly written, and full of action, this thrilling novel is an epic wuxia film wrought in paper and ink. —*Publishers Weekly*

Robin Shortt's madly fast-paced, pungently vivid wuxia-influenced tale... //...a wildly colorful cast of characters... // ... the real fun of this breakneck paced story was discovering, along with Darya, the palimpsest of the jiang hu world—the world of the chivalric martial artist—overlying the real world of the Silk Road, bringing with it mysteries and even hints of magic. // ...I relished this novel from beginning to end, and I really hope that there will be more adventures with Darya and her friends. —Sherwood Smith, creator of the Sartorias-deles universe and Wren's world, Nebula award finalist

The Marten and the Scorpion is an extraordinary tapestry of mythologies, rich with adventure and secrets, and an urchin of a heroine, as ragged and tenacious as a broken blade. Shortt's sharp, eloquent words bring to life a unique and enthralling world of intrigue and danger, where Kung Fu masters from the furthest reaches of the Silk Road flit over the rooftops of medieval Samarkand, while the streets below crawl with assassins, cutthroats, poison and plague. I loved it. I devoured it. I want more. —Leife Shallcross, author of *The Beast's Heart*, winner of the Aurealis award

Also by Robin Shortt:

Wellside

THE MARTEN AND THE SCORPION

BY ROBIN SHORTT

Candlemark & Gleam

First edition published 2019

Copyright @ 2019 by Robin Shortt

For information, address
Athena Andreadis
Candlemark & Gleam LLC,
38 Rice Street #2, Cambridge, MA 02140
eloi@candlemarkandgleam.com

Library of Congress Cataloguing-in-Publication Data
In Progress

ISBN: 978-1-936460-90-8
eISBN: 978-1-936460-89-2

Cover art by Candra Hope

Editor: Athena Andreadis

Proofreader: Kelly Jennings

www.candlemarkandgleam.com

In memory of Jin Yong, Wang Dulu and Gu Long

Author's Note

I've used the Wade-Giles transliteration system in this book, rather than the more commonly used Pinyin. I'm aware that using a Western-designed system rather than a Chinese one may appear culturally loaded, to say the least, and I apologize to anyone I've offended. However, while Pinyin is unquestionably superior for learning (and typing!) Chinese, W-G is still the champ for giving a non-Chinese speaking Western audience an idea of how Mandarin Chinese is actually pronounced (if you disagree, listen to someone pronounce wuxia as "wuck-see-ya" then get back to me).

CHAPTER ONE

I n Samarkand we love a fight, or anyway we love to watch one. Anything from a shoving match to a stabbing is guaranteed to draw a crowd. So it's no surprise that the two men arguing in the Street of the Rope-sellers have an audience, a dozen or so pedestrians who've put off whatever errand they were running and gathered round. They're hoping the disagreement turns into a beat-down.

So am I. But not for the same reason.

The two men glare at each other across a brightly-coloured rug, one of dozens that make a patchwork tapestry of the street. Each rug is piled with merchandise—rope of course, but also leather saddlebags, immense clay pots, rolls of hemp. Behind each rug a merchant proclaims the quality of their goods (at the top of their voice) to passers-by.

Laid out on this particular rug are a dozen Kashani roofing tiles in brilliant green-and-gold glaze. The merchant squatting behind them is a lanky Ghurid with his round turban tied Indian-style. On the other side of the rug, the street side, is a Khwarezmian, almost as wide as he is tall, wrapped in a richly-patterned robe. He's trying to buy some tiles, but he isn't making himself understood; maybe the Ghurid can't follow his heavily-accented Persian, or maybe he just doesn't like Khwarezmians and is trying to piss this one off. The Ghurid is chewing betel and every so often he spits a red wad into the dust at the Khwarezmian's feet, and the big man clenches his fists every time it happens.

I'm just across the street, sitting on the cloth awning that shades a teahouse's doorway. Now I run my hand over my shaved scalp, back then forward. That's the signal. A short figure on the street corner with his hair in three stubby braids detaches himself from the wall he's slouching against and makes his way towards the two men.

The Khwarezmian snorts and turns away, shaking his head. Looks like there's not going to be a fight after all. The crowd starts to break up, but then the kid with the braids tugs on the large man's robe, who instantly slaps his hand down on the purse tucked into his belt. This is a Samarkand bazaar, and anyone who lets their mind wander while strangers bump into them is going to wind up broke in a hurry.

He looks down at the one who did the tugging, and relaxes a little—this kid doesn't *seem* like your typical pocket-picking street rat. He's wearing a commoner's salwar kameez, a long loose shirt and pants, but over it is a Turkish-style kaftan of fine make, although it's seen better days. A large scab decorates his nose. The Khwarezmian double-checks his money is still there, and then takes a careful step back from the boy, just in case he is a street rat after all. "What do you want?" he says.

The kid clasps his hands respectfully in front of himself and responds in Khwarezmian Persian, which makes the big guy raise an eyebrow. "If it pleases you, sir—I know something of this man's language." He nods at the Ghurid, who looks right through him. "I can translate if you wish." His accent's a little off—I could have done it better—but it'll do.

"And what's in it for you?" asks the Khwarezmian.

I drop to the ground and edge closer so I can hear better. My stomach cramps up, reminding me I haven't eaten in a day, but I'm in the current now and it's easy to ignore.

The crowd are a lot taller than I am—even the kids, I'm such a runt—and between their jostling bodies I catch a glimpse of the kid piously raising his hands to heaven. "Is it not written in the *Wisdom of Royal Glory*, 'Make life your capital and goodness the profit thereof, and tomorrow you shall have fine food and dress'? My family may have fallen into penury, but we beg no charity; feel free to pay what you feel I deserve."

I roll my eyes, but the Khwarezmian's glitter greedily, and anyone with half a brain could tell this kid what he's likely to get. "You are a credit to your family, boy. Now," he says, tapping one of the glazed tiles on the rug with his foot, "ask this man if he has ten thousand such tiles; my home in Gurganj needs a new roof."

The boy nods seriously and turns to the Ghurid. "*He asks if you have ten thousand of those tiles.*" My Urdu isn't as good as my Persian, but it's still better than his.

The Ghurid grunts. "*Is that all he said? He's been flapping his lips for the last half hour.*"

The boy hesitates. "*Well...*"

"*Well what?*" asks the Ghurid.

The boy glances at the Khwarezmian. "*He says the workmanship is poor, but he will order that many since a man who sells such must be a charity case.*"

The Ghurid's nostrils flare. He pops another betel leaf into his face. "*Is that so? Tell this fellow that I have ten thousand. Ask him how much he will pay me.*"

The kid turns to the Khwarezmian. "He says 'yes.'"

"Just 'yes'?" says the Khwarezmian, glancing at the Ghurid tile-seller who's glaring at him openly.

"He says—I am sure he did not mean this, but—"

"Just tell me," says the fat man, returning the tile-seller's glare now.

The kid clears his throat. "He says that he usually does not entertain such small offers, but he will make an exception for you since you have clearly fallen on hard times."

"He does, does he?" says the Khwarezmian through clenched teeth. "'Small', he says? Tell him that—in spite of his discourtesy—I will pay a thousand dirhams for ten thousand tiles. But his men must load the caravan for free, I will pay no extra for that."

The thinning crowd thickens again as the likelihood of a fight goes up. I tense up and my eyes scan the forest of legs, plotting routes in and out.

The Ghurid is looking expectantly at the kid, who clears his throat again, looking uncomfortable. The man spits a red clot in the dust and rises slowly from his squat. He's nearly a head taller than the Khwarezmian. "*Tell me.*"

The kid actually blushes. "*He says five hundred dirhams, no less—and you must get off your fat ass and load them yourself.*"

A minute later, the men are standing nose-to-nose, each yelling at each other in his own language, not bothering to wait for a translation. The crowd is cheering them on raucously. When the Ghurid raises a fist, I move.

All the two men see is a skinny kid dashing through the crowd, not looking where they're going, and crashing into the Khwarezmian's legs. The fat merchant barks in annoyance, grabs my shoulder and pushes me aside without even looking at me, sending me sprawling on the dusty bricks. I pick myself up, screeching curses at both men, and run.

That's the last I see of them, but the rest of the scene plays out in my mind as I sprint down the street. The Khwarezmian turns back to the Ghurid, his mouth open to deliver another stream of curses—and then his brain catches up to what just happened. His hand flies to his belt, and finds an empty space where his purse used to be. Wildly he looks around for his translator, who has also disappeared. He turns back to the Ghurid, his hand raised, trying to explain, when a fist crashes into his nose and knocks him on his ass. The crowd claps appreciatively, and neither man is thinking of anything much for the next few minutes.

CHAPTER TWO

The Khwarezmian's purse is a heavy weight inside my kameez as I cut through the Bazaar of Haberdashers, heading for the rendezvous with Masoud. I know no one's following, I can feel it, but I run anyway—I'm still riding the buzz that a clean lift gives me, and besides, the bricks will chill my bare feet if I stand still for long. Winter's supposed to be over, but you wouldn't know it.

I'm still in the current, hardly breaking stride as I dodge through the gaps in the crowd. They don't even see me. I'm just another Samarkand street rat, not worth even a moment of their time. Then I pass a street stall where an old man pushes chunks of fatty mutton around on a domed iron griddle, and the smell of it almost brings me to my knees.

I lean against a wall, hugging my belly as my stomach knots up, and wait for the wave of dizziness to break over me and ebb away. The old man glances at me, then back at the griddle. "No food for beggars."

Even though my guts are still twisting, I stand straight. "I'm not a beggar." He grunts, not looking up. "I'm. Not. A *beggar.*" I'll show him. I sneak my hand into my kameez, and feel the weight of the purse against my chest. Then I hesitate. A street rat with a bulging purse is something he'll remember. And if word gets back to Nina and Oleg that I've been spending their money...But I don't give a damn. I'm no beggar and I'll *prove it*—

"Be off," he says again. "Or are you going to make trouble?" He looks up, over my shoulder. "Sirs? Sirs?"

I turn my head. Across the street are three lean men with drooping moustaches and caps of green felt, dark braids down to their shoulders. They're ahdath, the city guards. They look up, and one of them begins to amble our way.

If they think I'm causing trouble, they'll grab me and pat me down. No way they'll believe the purse is mine; even if they do, no way they'll let me keep it. I imagine Nina's face when she learns I had my day's take confiscated.

I turn away, but not before I hawk and spit at the old man's griddle. A hearty glob of it lands among the chunks of meat, and sizzles. The old man's reedy curses follow me as I push my way back into the crowd.

What energy I had is well and truly gone. Every step is an effort, and the crowds are a confusing jumble. When I reach the Square of the Money-changers, my legs are trembling jelly.

The square is almost at the centre of Samarkand, in the looming shadow of the city courthouse. Up against the courthouse wall is a fountain, a stone bowl a few yards wide with a fat rim to sit on and a trickle of water running into it from a clay pipe. There are dozens of these fountains in Samarkand, built decades ago by the Black Khans to show the city's legendary hospitality. To a street rat, that last part is a joke. Samarkand is certainly hospitable—to khans, and landlords, and rich merchants, and anyone with money to spend—but if *we* slip up, even once, then down we go, and no one will help us up again.

Masoud is sitting on the rim of the fountain. He's turned his kaftan inside-out to show the lining, which is patched and shabby, not worth a second glance from anyone. As I approach he peels the old scab off the healthy brown skin of his nose—he'd glued it on with spit—and slips it into a pocket to use again. The only traces of the translator in the bazaar are those braids of his, but of course he's way too proud to ever undo them.

I can't help running a hand over my own scalp. The skin is rough with nicks and scratches; Nina shaves my head every two weeks, and she's not too careful with the razor.

"That was a terrible lift," Masoud says as I walk up to the fountain. "You barely gave me time to get away." Like he's lecturing some baby straight out of the orphanage, even though I've been lifting just as long as he has. My stomach twists again, and this time it's anger as well as hunger doing the twisting.

"Piss off, Masoud," I snap as I sit beside him. "I'm faster than you and you know it. All you did was run the scam, just—" I raise a hand, fingers and thumb opening and closing miming *blah-blah-blah*, while my other hand reaches into my kameez and takes out the Khwarezmian's purse.

"Faster, huh?" His hand shoots out without warning and grabs my wrist before I can react. "Yeah. Right. And you still can't climb. We see you practicing, it's pathetic." He pulls at my arm. I resist, or try to, but I can't even hold my hand still, much less pull it back. I look at Masoud's own hand, with its healthy layer of fat under the skin, a sharp contrast to the skin-and-bone of my own. Masoud is one of Nina's favourites, and he always has enough to eat.

A tiny grunt of effort escapes my lips. Masoud smirks and plucks the purse out of my hand. He lets go of my wrist and I snatch my arm back. The skin is hot. I'm going to bruise.

"See? Weak. Even little Nasr's stronger than you now, and he's almost as fast." He loosens the drawstring of the purse and peers inside. "What if that Khwarezmian had grabbed you? Or some do-gooder in the crowd? No way you could have gotten loose."

"That slow-ass old man couldn't have caught me in a million years," I retort. "Why didn't you ask Nasr to be your lifter, then, if he's so good?"

"I did," says Masoud. Coins clink as he rummages in the purse. "Oleg has him running some errand all day. Anyway, he made the climb yesterday, didn't you hear?"

"Nasr made thief?" Masoud smirks, and I feel a little cold inside. Nasr was the only pickpocket in the Martens who had my back. With him gone, I'm alone.

All that's left of the rush from lifting the purse is a tremble in my hands and a tight knot in my chest. A wave of exhaustion breaks over me, washing away any desire to keep the argument going. After all... he's right, isn't he?

While Masoud counts the coins I lean over the fountain and scoop up a double handful of water to splash on my face. The cold makes me gasp, but it snaps me fully awake again. I look at my reflection as it wobbles in the water, and scrub at myself until the pale dust I'd caked on my skin is gone.

I'm a mongrel, like Masoud and all the rest of the Martens. Most of them, like most of the rest of Samarkand, are a mix of Turk and Persian, but I'm darker, like the merchants from the kingdoms in the south. My nose is like theirs too, a little...but guessing is pointless. What am I going to do, go looking for my real family? I *think* I remember my parents, but I'm not in any hurry to catch up with them.

Masoud holds a coin up in the sunlight, a silver mu'ayyadi dirham. Even if the rest of the purse is only coppers, it's still enough to make quota. I'll eat tonight. The knot in my chest loosens a little. Then Masoud opens his mouth again.

"I don't get it, Darya," he says. "You're a *girl*. Why not just work in the orphanage, wash the floors and cook and stuff?" He's dancing the dirham across the knuckles of one hand, showing off. "It's not like you're ever going to make thief—"

"That's not up to you," I snap. Masoud gives me an unpleasant smile. The dirham stops neatly and reverses direction, rolling over the back of his hand.

"Get real. I'm going to be running the thieves soon, and you know it. So then what are you going to do? You can't lift and scam forever. Just...give up. Go be a girl. Until Nina sells you off to a whorehouse—"

Almost before I know I'm going to do it, I grab the coin. Masoud yanks his hand back—far too late—and glares at me furiously. He sticks his hand out, palm up. "Give it back."

"Take it back. I'm not that fast, remember?" He reaches for it again, but I sway back and his hand grasps empty air.

"How much did we get?" I say.

"Enough." Another grab, which I avoid with ease.

"Let me see," I say, standing up. This lift has been the first good luck I've had in more than a week and Masoud better not pocket any of it before we reach the courtyard. The less we hand over to Nina, the less I'll have to eat tonight, and the more time and energy I'll have to spend hustling to make it up. Energy I might not have.

He ignores me, his eyes still on the coin. "Let me *see*," I repeat, and I grab for the purse, which is a mistake. His hand closes on my wrist again and the coin tumbles to the ground, rolls away from the fountain on its edge. Masoud can't help glancing after it, leaving himself open, and I clench my fist, intent on giving him a fat lip for that whorehouse line.

The flat slap of a foot on the bricks makes me turn my head. Someone's stepped on the rolling coin.

"Well," says a drawling voice, "look who it is."

CHAPTER THREE

There are five of them, spread out in a half-circle around the fountain, fencing us in. They must have snuck up on us while we were scuffling over the coin. They're about sixteen, the same age as Masoud and me. (I assume. No one's ever bothered to keep track of my age.)

"Martens," says one of them, "they're Martens." I keep quiet. I don't know them to look at, but they're clearly in a beggar crew, and I don't want to make any assumptions that could get me beaten up. Or killed.

"Well that won't do," says a taller guy behind them, the one who stepped on the dirham, as he bends to pick it up. Then he straightens again and I see his high cheekbones and his blank grey eyes, and my guts plummet all the way down to my toes. It's Ali. These kids are Wolves.

The Wolves have been pushing hard this whole winter, taking corners from the smaller gangs left and right and even going after bigger ones, like the Foxes and Bears. They're acting crazy, and it's supposed to be down to Ali. They say he dropped three of the Foxes' beggars into a midden-hole last month, left them to tread water in human waste and garbage until they drowned. Looking at those eyes, I can believe it. They're perfectly clear, unclouded by any kind of doubt or pity. The eyes of someone who's broken in the head.

"Where did you lift that?" says Ali now, jerking his chin at the purse Masoud is holding. Masoud's way with words has deserted him. He just looks sick and scared.

"Bazaar. Street of the Rope-sellers," I say, pitching my voice low. They won't spot I'm a girl, though. Girls don't lift purses; I lifted a purse; therefore I'm a boy. After people make up their minds about things like that, nothing their eyes or ears tell them matters.

Ali shakes his head slowly, regretfully, although I doubt he's ever felt anything like regret in his life. "Everything in the bazaar is ours. You're poaching."

"The hell it is," I say. I probably shouldn't talk like that, but my blood is still up from Masoud's taunting. "Everything south of Bookbinders belongs to the Martens. Always has."

Ali's expression doesn't change. "Not anymore." Which is interesting. The Wolves are making a move on the Martens—that's a juicy piece of gossip, if I live to share it.

Ali holds out his hand. "Give it up now, and we'll just beat you. Maybe cut you a little." He sounds almost bored, like there's no way we won't go along. And he has a point—all through our conversation my brain has been working like mad, plotting escape routes through the ring of Wolves around us...and there aren't any. They'll dogpile us before we make it ten paces. I don't like the sound of *maybe cut you a little*—depending on where he wants to cut, he could even find out I'm a girl, which is its own set of problems...but it'll be worse if we resist.

I open my mouth to say "Fine," and I'm surprised to hear myself say "Go to hell" instead. Masoud lets out a little moan. Ali's eyes widen with the first emotion I've seen in them—sudden, white-hot anger. I've got his full attention. I meet his eyes, my own anger rising and burning away the fear a little. Then something over his shoulder catches my eye, and I tense, ready to make a move.

As Ali opens his mouth to tell his Wolves to take us, a shout rings off the walls of the square. "Thief!"

The Khwarezmian stands against the wall of the courthouse. His robe is torn and dirty and he holds a cloth to his bloody nose. "Thief!

My purse! Thief!" he yells. He's pointing right at me and Masoud. No one around him is paying any attention, but it's only a matter of time before some do-gooder takes an interest. Or worse, the ahdath.

Some of the Wolves turn to look at him. It's a reflex; they're street rats, and in their experience, when someone yells "Thief!" it's usually them he's talking about. They step back, ready to flee if they have to, and the half-circle around us opens up just a little. Just enough.

My foot kicks back against the fountain, throwing me forward at a gap between two of the Wolves. One of them manages to bring up an arm to stop me but I keep low and his hand skids off the back of my kameez. Behind me I hear a grunt and a thud as Masoud shoulder-charges another Wolf and knocks him aside. Then the merchant's shouts are drowned out by Ali's wordless scream of rage, and the Wolves are after us.

CHAPTER FOUR

Go to a bookseller (in the Street of the Bookbinders, say, if you don't mind getting charged foreigner prices) and buy a map of Samarkand. It'll show you the city wall, pierced by its many gates—Lion's Gate, Monk's Gate, China Gate, all the others. Inside the walls you'll see the great central plaza, the boulevards radiating from it like the spokes of a wheel, the marketplaces and bazaars, the ancient fortress of Afrasiab on its hill, the Old Mosque, the minarets and mausoleums the Black Khans built, back when they ruled Samarkand in their own right.

Everything else—a full seven-eighths of the map—will be blank, or maybe filled in with random lines that suggest narrow lanes, crisscrossing and twisting.

That's the Maze, where the common people of Samarkand live in their tens of thousands. No one's ever made a real map of the Maze. It would take you months, and by the time you were done, with all the houses knocked down and rebuilt and extended in the meantime, it would already be hopelessly out of date.

The houses are mud brick and wood, two storeys at the most, clustered in groups around tiny courtyards, and between them is a labyrinth of skinny lanes and side-streets, dead-ends and blind alleys, laid out according to no plan whatsoever.

And now the Wolves are chasing us through it.

They're close enough I can feel the impact of their footsteps through the bricks as we run through the backstreets. Masoud is stronger and faster and at first he pulls ahead...but then the current has me, and he's eating my dust. If we're caught we'll be maimed, crippled, killed, but none of that matters in the current, and I can feel a grin spreading across my face.

I call it the current because that's what it feels like, like something is circulating inside of me, like the water flowing through the canals that crisscross the fields beyond the city wall, flooding my whole body with energy. And there's another current, this one outside—one with the whole city caught in it, all the people and things moving through its streets. When the two fall into sync, the chaos of a Samarkand bazaar becomes something as predictable as the beating of a drum or the dripping of a water-clock. The current is why I'm so good at what I do, why Oleg and Nina let me run with the Martens even though I'm a girl. When I'm in the current, I feel like I could steal the black sable lining from the Khan's own coat. While he's wearing it. In the middle of a parade.

So while Masoud and the Wolves lumber along, clipping pedestrians and slowing themselves down, the gaps in the crowd seem to open just for me, and close behind me as soon as I sprint through. Two men are carrying a bundle of planks—I duck beneath them, half-skidding along the ground before rolling and springing up, already running again. More men are tossing barley-sacks from a cart into a low pile in the street—a skipping step and I vault over them. Masoud jumps them too but lands heavily and almost falls. I don't even have to glance backwards, I can tell what's happening just from the sounds. Behind him one of the Wolves hits the pile and then the ground, bursting one of the sacks and scattering its contents. His friends keep up the pursuit.

Footsteps, gaining. I duck a little and fling out a hand like I'm trying to keep hold of something, and at the same time I break my stride with a quick double-step that sounds like something hitting the ground beside me. The Wolf breaks his own stride for a second, thinking I've maybe dropped the purse. Long enough for me to dart between two overloaded donkeys and widen the gap between us. He realizes his mistake soon enough—he should have realized even sooner, it's the oldest trick in the book—but I've bought myself some time.

A small dispassionate voice at the back of my mind tells me that I can't keep this up. Current or not I've had three hours of sleep in the last twenty-four, and no food, and soon our pursuers will wear me down. I can stay ahead of them for a while, but I can't lose them, and I know I'm screwed. A midden-hole is in my way; the wooden cover is askew and the stink of sewage rises into the air. My legs wobble just as I leap, and I barely clear it. My feet hit the far edge and I have to windmill my arms for balance to keep from falling in.

"This way!" It's Masoud, to my right, gesturing at the narrow mouth of an alley. I run through my mental map of Samarkand, but I can't find it there. It could lead us into a dead end, or circle around and spit us out into a pack of Wolves.

"Come *on!*" Masoud gestures again, frantically. Maybe he knows the way. Maybe he doesn't know the way and he's just panicking. Anyway, I have to decide.

I decide to trust him. We're both Martens, after all, and Martens don't leave Martens—that was the oath we swore. Without slowing down, I change my course, just a little, aiming for an open doorway. Just before I reach it I leap and kick off from the wall beside it, reversing my momentum and heading for Masoud. A Wolf hurtles past me, so close I could touch him, too fast to stop himself. He crashes painfully into the wall while I sprint for Masoud, who's already disappearing down that alley.

A pile of rubbish blocks the narrow entrance. I leap it, and the one behind it. The alley twists and turns, with more piles of crap to vault.

I stay on Masoud's heels but I'm not liking this at all. Littering in a thoroughfare gets you a hefty fine from the ahdath. This much rubbish means no one uses this alley to get anywhere. Which means it's...

I turn a final corner and see the dead end. I mean, technically the alley goes on, but up ahead two houses have been built right up against each other, leaving a space between them that looks from here to be about six inches wide.

Masoud has already reached the end, and I see now what his plan was—there's a window set high up on one wall of the alley, just before it narrows. As I watch, he crouches, tenses, and a standing leap takes him up to the window. He grabs the windowsill—just.

I'm shorter than Masoud, and weaker, and exhausted, and I know I'll never make a jump like that. As he hoists himself up, grunting with effort, I skid to a halt below him. "Masoud!" I hiss, trying to be quiet, hoping maybe the Wolves didn't follow us down here, but even as I say it I hear them up the alley, shouting to each other and kicking aside the litter.

"*Masoud!*" My only hope is Masoud reaching down and pulling me up, but I have a nasty feeling about that. I raise my arms anyway, standing on tiptoe. In a moment the Wolves will turn the last corner and see me. Masoud turns to look down and my heart leaps with hope, but all I get is a single frightened glance and then he reaches above him for the edge of the roof. He hauls himself up and over and he's gone.

Rage drives every other thought from my head. Not fear—I forget all about the Wolves—just burning fury at Masoud, and at myself for being tricked like that. My hands curl into claws, and in my mind's eye Masoud dies a hundred bloody deaths while I laugh and laugh. Maybe he thinks gang honour will keep me from ratting him out. Maybe he thinks that once the Wolves are done with me, I won't be *able* to rat him out. Still, I can't quite believe he's done it. Martens don't leave Martens. *But then you're not a Marten, are you?* says a voice inside my head, a voice that sounds like Masoud. *You're a girl.*

It's not far to the window at all, really—any real thief could make it no matter how tired or hungry they were. I tense my legs and jump, and my outstretched fingers barely brush the bottom of the windowsill.

The footsteps slow down, stop just around the corner. I hear whispers, commands. The Wolves know it's a dead end. They're getting ready to rush me. I look around. There's nothing to do, nowhere to go. I don't have a hope.

Except...

As the first of the Wolves round the corner I turn my back to them, take a couple of long strides and launch myself at the end of the alley, at that narrow crack between the buildings. A hand grabs my kameez and tugs me backwards but I'm already moving too fast, and I break away easily. Turning sideways right before I hit the wall, I throw myself into the narrow gap.

It's wider than I thought at first, but it's still not all that wide, and I clench my teeth in pain as the rough brick grinds against my chest and back and elbows. Quickly I work myself further into the crack. I can see it gets even narrower up ahead. Fingers brush the skin of my arm and I shudder, but I'm already too far in for them to get a grip on me.

I can just turn my head, although it scrapes up my nose. Behind me, arms reach into the gap, hands opening and closing uselessly as they try to grab me. Above them I see a flash of grey—Ali's eyes, narrowed with venomous hate.

"Someone get in there after him!" I hear him snarl. I don't want to turn my head away again, but I do. I squeeze my body further into the gap, sidling along with my legs, gripping the bricks with my fingers, dragging myself along. I can't hear anyone volunteering to follow me, and I can guess why; they're all too big. Just this once I'm grateful for being the scrawniest pickpocket in the Martens.

But...I'm not a little kid anymore, and the gap is getting narrower. The walls either side of me angle in toward each other, and moving forward is already getting harder.

"Find a way around!" The echoes in here make Ali's voice tinny and strange. "Wait for him on the other side."

I was afraid the Wolves would have that particular brainwave. Their footsteps ring hollowly off the bricks as they rush away. Have they all left? No—I hear a cough from behind me. They've left a sentry. I can't go back, and now I only have a little time to get through.

My hands scrabble for purchase, brick scouring my fingertips till the blood comes. I can feel my heart thumping in my ribcage and I try to take a deep breath, calm myself, but my chest can't expand, the gap is already that narrow. Now the poorly-laid bricks bulge inwards, only a little but for a second I think I'm not going to make it. My ribs creak as I force my body forward. For a second I'm stuck fast, my shoulders on fire as the walls grind against them through my kameez...

And then the gap widens a little, I'm past the bulge, and able to breathe a little. For a moment I'm relieved, but only for a moment, because I realize that there's no way I'll be able to get back, even if I want to.

Ahead is a vertical line of bright sunlight, impossibly thin and distant. It occurs to me that I might not be able to make it forward *or* back. I might be stuck here forever. I imagine the Wolves working their way up to the roof and dropping stones on me. Or drizzling down lamp oil, and following it with a lit candle.

A harsh sob escapes my crushed lungs and I'm moving again, frantically, scraping my cheeks raw. One hand emerges into open air—I half expect a Wolf to grab it, but no one does—and then my elbow is out and I can brace my forearm against the wall outside to pull myself forward. A moment of utter, blind panic as my hips catch...

...And I'm free. I collapse on the ground outside, whooping for breath.

I savour the cold spring air as I suck it into my lungs. Every one of my muscles is jelly, and my ribs feel permanently bent out of shape. I would love to just pass out, but the threat of the Wolves gets me on my knees again, looking around.

I'm in a courtyard faced on all four sides by the rear walls of buildings. After my ordeal it seems enormous. There's a heavy wooden door set in the wall to my left, and a narrow archway opposite me leading to a covered alley—an escape route, thank all the gods there are—but otherwise the dusty bricks are bare except for a pile of rags in one corner.

If I haven't totally lost my bearings, the alley should take me to the Boulevard of Roses. Once across the boulevard I'll be deep in Marten territory, and safe—safe as a pickpocket ever gets in Samarkand, anyway. If I rush (which is a joke, I can barely stand) I could even make it back before sunset, in time to report to Nina with my takings—

Takings. Masoud still has the fat man's purse. A hot coal of anger flares in my belly. I take a limping step towards the archway, and then Ali's voice rings out in the courtyard. "Hey! *Hey!* You down there!"

He's on the roof of the building behind me. He must have climbed up the same way Masoud did, but he can't make it down again—the wall on this side is smooth plaster with no hand-holds, and if he jumps he'll break an ankle at the very least. I look up at him, wondering if I have the guts to gloat, but then I see he's not even looking at me. And he's grinning.

"Hold him!" yells Ali, struggling to hold back laughter. "Two jars of wine if you hold him for me and my crew!" He's looking at something behind me, and almost before he's finished talking I hear cloth rustling.

I turn, only a small part of me able to believe this is happening. The pile of rags in the corner isn't rags at all. It's moving, shifting, and as I watch it rises up, and up, until it towers over me. It lets the ragged blanket drop from its shoulders, and a pair of ice-blue eyes regard me from a sunburned face.

It's the Teuton.

CHAPTER FIVE

Samarkand is home to a lot of broken soldiers—flotsam from all the wars in the world, washing up here on a tide of blood. They drink, whore, kill for money, until they pick the wrong fight or drink themselves to death. They're scumbags at best, monsters at worst, and the Teuton is quite possibly the worst of them all.

He's from the west, the *far* west, and its endless wars. His skin is cracked and peeling from sleeping in the sun but underneath it's pale, almost dead white. Masoud says the Teuton's land is so far to the west that the sun gets tired before it makes it all the way out there, so the Teuton's people live in darkness. Whatever; Masoud is full of crap. Regardless, even by the standards of Samarkand's killers, the Teuton stands alone.

He's wearing what he always wears, a ragged once-white tabard marked with a sun-faded black cross, over a rusted shirt made of lots of little metal links. Hanging from his belt is the scabbard of a huge double-edged sword; he's about the tallest person I've ever seen but the tip of the sword still almost touches the ground.

He brushes his lank blond hair off his forehead and regards me with those eyes, pale like blue cloth left out in the sun for a summer. His hand rubs his dry lips and the almost-white stubble on his chin. My eyes flick to the corner where he's been sleeping, and I see the empty wine-jars scattered about. There isn't much the Teuton wouldn't do, especially if he's been without booze for a while. Snapping my neck for two more jars isn't nearly out of the question.

I let myself look scared, so scared I can't even think, which isn't that hard. I back up until I hit the wall of the courtyard. Then, instantly, I kick off it and fling myself forward. My only hope is to catch the Teuton by surprise, rush past him, and for an instant I think I've done just that. Then his metal-sleeved arm shoots out and I run straight into it. It might as well be an iron bar, and it knocks all the air out of me. He shoves me back, sends me skidding across the courtyard. My feet go out from under me, my head bounces off the ground and I slide to a stop with stars bursting behind my eyes.

I gasp for breath and look up past the walls of the courtyard at the blue sky. Ali has disappeared, maybe working his way down to street level to claim my corpse. My mind is just clear enough for me to think, *This isn't fair.*

The Teuton's shadow falls over me. He looms in my vision, backlit by the setting sun, his blond hair like a fiery halo around his head. The closest I'll ever get to seeing an angel. Maybe he'll kill me himself, maybe he'll just hold me 'til the Wolves come for me, but either way I'm done.

I look up at him and wait for the end, and instead I hear a voice say, *"Nin hao."*

The Teuton and I both turn to look. Four people—I blink and my vision clears—*two* people stand in front of the archway leading out of the courtyard. They're young, not much older than myself. One wears a long white robe, threadbare and patched in places, slit up the sides to the waist, with immense sleeves and long black lapels crossed left-over-right, over a thin tunic and loose trousers. He must be freezing his ass off, but he stands perfectly relaxed and still. On his head he wears a black cloth, folded complexly to make a kind of cap.

The other—this one's a girl, I realize—is dressed a little more practically, a couple layers of cloth under a jacket of tanned leather, cinched with a belt and decorated with bronze buttons and tiny shells. Her trousers, tighter than my own salwar, are tucked into thick felt boots that come up almost to her knee, not like the little black slippers the guy wears. Her hair is braided into narrow strands strung with strips of red cloth and bright beads that rattle as she casually rolls her neck. Her eyes never leave the Teuton.

Her face is similar to the guy's—the same high cheekbones and eyes upturned at the corners, kind of like the Khitai horsemen who rule the lands around Samarkand—but not the same. The girl's features are longer and she's taller than the guy. She holds a long spear, its butt planted on the ground beside her. A red-dyed horsetail dangles from the shaft just below the spearhead, which is covered with a leather bag. The guy is unarmed, but he carries something strapped across his back, a long thin oblong of black lacquered wood, writing in gold up the sides.

The Teuton looks them up and down. "*Nin hao,*" says the guy again, and bows slightly, giving the Teuton an odd salute, his hands up in front of him, the right in a fist pressed against the left's open palm. The girl doesn't move, just watches the Teuton, her eyes sparkling with curiosity. None of them look at me.

Where did they come from? There are drifts of dust on the bricks around the archway, but I don't see any footprints behind them at all. Still, I'm not going to miss an opportunity like this. I tense myself to make a break for it, but as soon as I move the Teuton's boot comes down on my already-bruised ribs, slamming me back against the ground. I grunt in pain.

The guy and the girl glance at me, then back to the Teuton. The guy says something else, in a tone of polite inquiry. I'm not too far gone to notice how good-looking he is. The girl leans against her spear with easy grace.

The Teuton growls something in his own harsh language, and his hand comes to rest on the hilt of his sword. The guy and the girl look at each other and exchange a few words. Their language sounds like music, the vowels rising and swooping. I don't understand a word, but I have a pretty good idea what they're saying.

After you.

Not at all. After you.

The girl smiles—it lights up her whole face, and for just a moment she's stunningly beautiful. Then the spear blurs to life in her hands, whirling above her head before she snaps it back, the covered blade pointing at the Teuton's chest and the girl's legs braced in a combat stance.

Up to this point I'd been entertaining the hope that these two might be able to help. Now my heart sinks into my guts. Her moves are far too flashy, and she hasn't even taken the cover off her spearhead. She's a hero—but the Teuton's a killer. And if she thinks he'll go easy on her because she's a girl...

The killer grins unpleasantly, and his sword leaps from its scabbard with the whisper of steel on leather. Not giving the spearwoman a chance, he sends the blade slicing through the air at her neck. I wince—I saw one of the Teuton's fights, last autumn in the bazaar, and I still remember that sword cleaving a Karluk Turk from shoulder to navel. I wait for the *thunk* of steel into flesh, the gout of blood.

Instead there's a blur of motion and the sound of wood on steel, and the Teuton is stumbling backward, hissing in pain. His sword is a blur, vibrating from the impact with the spear, and he can barely hold it in his hand. The girl with the spear grins wider. The flexible shaft of her spear is still shivering from blocking the Teuton's sword, the horsehair tassel trembling.

Now she points the spear at the Teuton and with a flick of her wrist she sets the covered point to dancing, circling fast, the horsetail whipping around so much I can't even tell where the point is, let alone where it's going. Then suddenly the shaft slithers through her hands as she thrusts it at the Teuton's chest. He knocks it aside with his sword, then sidesteps and brings the blade down suddenly, hacking at the spear's shaft, trying to cut it in two. But the spear leaps to life and somehow deflects the blow, hitting the flat of the sword and twisting it almost out of the Teuton's hands.

I doubt I could even lift the Teuton's sword, but the big man wrestles it through the air in a dizzying series of chops and feints and slices, reversing its momentum again and again and sending it on a new and deadly course each time. But as fast as he is, the spearwoman is faster. Steel thuds on leather as she deflects an attack with the spear's covered point. Then it whips up and slaps the Teuton across the face, making him grunt and stumble backwards momentarily before he rushes forward again. The rhythm of the blows picks up speed as the two go at it.

My chest is on fire from the Teuton stomping on it, and I can only manage a thin wheeze. I can't even get to my knees. I can only watch. The guy in the robe watches too, leaning back against the courtyard wall with his arms folded in his sleeves, smiling a little.

After another bout of slashes and parries, the two break off, circle each other. There's a kind of medallion, an ornate spiral, picked out in vibrant red thread on the back of the girl's jacket. The Teuton holds his sword across his body in a defensive stance, but her spear is whirling in the air, describing complicated loops and figure-eights. She's not just holding her own against the Teuton. She's having *fun* with this.

The Teuton charges, sword and spear strike each other—and stop. The Teuton and the spearwoman hold still as each tries to force the other's weapon aside. The Teuton is red-faced with effort, his muscles bulging. The spearwoman doesn't seem to be making any effort at all, but strangely her spear is holding the sword at bay, not giving an inch. She glances back at her friend, grinning, and the Teuton takes advantage of the distraction. One hand leaves the sword's hilt and lashes out, an armoured fist driving straight at the girl's throat.

It sends her flying across the courtyard, and for a moment, as clear as day, I see her face turn purple as she tries to breathe through a crushed windpipe.

Then I blink and I see she hasn't got a mark on her. She's almost *floating* backwards through the air, like gravity has looked the other way for a moment. She lands on her feet, softly enough that the impact doesn't even raise any dust, and smiles.

The Teuton narrows his eyes. Then he shows the spearwoman his ugly smile and reverses his sword, driving it at the guy leaning against the wall, who doesn't move as the sword's point stops an inch from his neck. The Teuton looks at the girl and jerks his head, motioning her to move away from the archway. The meaning is clear—either she lets the Teuton walk away, or he'll skewer her friend.

My head is swimming and my vision is blurry with fatigue and pain, but it seems to me that the guy's ironic half-smile doesn't waver, even with a sword at his throat. She cocks her head, then spins her spear around until it's upright and leans it against the wall beside her, and then steps aside, giving the Teuton one of those bow-salutes the guy did earlier. My heart sinks further, all the way down into my feet. I know what the Teuton is going to do. "No," I half-moan.

The girl hears me, turns her head ever so slightly, and winks. The Teuton doesn't see it. He turns to face the guy in the white robe and drives the point of his sword at his neck.

It never makes it. Another blur—he's just as fast as his friend, maybe faster—and his hands are up and grasping the flat of the blade between his palms. Like the spearwoman, he doesn't seem to be putting any pressure on it at all, but the Teuton can't push or pull his sword out of his grip. Then he slides one hand along the blade almost down to the hilt, and with one swift movement he pushes with his palms and bends the thick steel sword almost in a right angle.

It falls to the ground, clattering on the bricks. The Teuton must be as astonished as I am, but he doesn't skip a beat, just sends his mailed fist at the smaller man's face.

Except he isn't there. The Teuton's fist smashes into the wall as the guy swings his torso down and around, the wooden box on his back not slowing him down at all. His arms sweep in a graceful circle, his forearms meet the Teuton's and fling them aside. Then he's up in the Teuton's face and striking, striking, his hands like birds pecking at the much taller man's shoulders, elbows, neck, driving into the metal shirt with a force that should break his fingers. After half a dozen blows the Teuton's arms hang uselessly at his side. Another half a dozen and he can't move at all, just stands there swaying.

The guy takes half a step back and leaps, straight up, his body spinning, and the sole of his shoe whips around and slams into the Teuton's chest. He falls backwards like a chopped-through tree, hitting the ground with a crash that echoes off the courtyard walls.

Movement in the archway. It's Ali and his Wolves, spilling into the courtyard. They take in the prone Teuton, and the two strangers who've apparently taken down one of Samarkand's most vicious killers. The girl kicks the bottom of her spear and catches it as it falls into her hands, snapping it around to point at them, and the Wolves turn and run.

I manage to struggle up onto my knees. I want to thank these two, ask them who they are, ask them how they *did* that, but I can barely think the words, let alone say them. I nod to them instead; that will have to do.

The guy smiles, and it looks like he's going to say something, but now the alley beyond the courtyard echoes with the sound of stomping boots and clashing steel, and a deep voice barking orders. I know what *that* means, any Samarkand street rat does. Maybe these two do too; from the way they glance at each other they seem to know it's not something they want to stick around for.

I don't think they'll have a choice. There's only one way out of the courtyard, not counting the tiny gap I came through...but it turns out that doesn't matter, because the two in the strange clothes *leap*.

No, that's not the word. Once again, they *soar*, like they've decided to just ignore the pull of the earth, and the earth has let it slide. The guy flies up and over the tall wall of the courtyard, an impossible height. The spearwoman's leap isn't quite that high, but then she's running, vertically, up and over the edge of the wall, as light as a feather. They turn to look down at me as I stare up open-mouthed; then they're gone, and the courtyard is filled with noise as a dozen men come trooping into the courtyard, and once again there's a sword pointed at my face.

Chapter Six

The point of the sword wobbles. I manage to take my eyes off it and look up into the frightened eyes of a boy who can't be any older than I am. His Adam's apple bobs as he swallows nervously. He's wearing the green felt cap of the ahdath.

"Mehmet!" booms a voice, and the sword wobbles again as the boy looks behind him. "Put the damn thing away," continues the deep voice's unseen owner. "If you're going to point it at anything, point it at *that.*" The boy's eyes cut sideways to the Teuton's unconscious body.

"Better yet," comments another voice, this one sounding like its owner gargles gravel every morning, "slit its throat. That's the Teuton, that is."

"No," says the first voice, the deep one. "He has friends. Unlikely as it seems. Now. You."

A hand grabs the back of my collar and yanks me up until my feet are dangling six inches off the ground. I look up at the hand's owner—a huge Karluk, a captain's badge on his cap, his triple braids swept over one shoulder. "What do we have here? A little Marten? You look more like a half-drowned rat."

I don't reply, just dangle at the end of his arm.

He grunts. "Well, little housecat, let's get you out of here before *that* wakes up." He nudges the Teuton's body with the toe of his heavy leather riding boot. He sets me on my feet and I sway a little but manage to stay upright.

I can see a third man now, with a luxuriant moustache. He bends to look at the Teuton. "He's really messed up, boss," he says to the captain. His voice is the gravelly one, and as he looks at me I can see the old scar crossing his throat. "Mind telling us how?"

The least I can do for my saviours is keep them out of the ahdath's way. "It was me," I say. "He was giving me a hard time."

The captain grins. Then he cuffs me behind the ear; not hard, by his standards, but his hand is the size of my head and the impact on my already bruised skull nearly drops me. "That's for giving *me* a hard time."

The captain's name is Uthman, and he leads me through the archway and down yet another winding alley. Once we're far enough away from the Teuton, he jerks his head at the skinny recruit—Mehmet, he called him—who searches me for anything I might have stolen. And not to return it to its owners, either.

"Sorry," Mehmet mumbles as he pats me down. He has kind eyes; I have no idea how he ended up an ahdath. I shrug. I don't have anything on me anyway, and I know Uthman's not going to arrest me. He takes protection money from Oleg (and half a dozen other beggar gangs) and he has a solid reputation among the street rats. Tough but fair; not a fanatic, not a sadist; he'll take a cut of whatever he finds on you but he'll leave you enough that you make your quota. Give him crap and he'll knock you around, but it won't be anything personal. One of the good guys.

"There's a fat Khwarezmian in the Street of the Rope-sellers squealing like a stuck pig about his missing purse," Uthman says mildly as we emerge from the alley into bright light. "But you wouldn't know anything about that, would you?"

"What's a Khwarezmian?" I say.

"Funny," says Uthman, and raises his hand to cuff me again. I flinch, but he doesn't follow through; maybe he can't find anywhere to leave a mark among all the other bruises and scrapes. "Careful, little housecat," he says. "This particular Khwarezmian has pull. There's a whole herd of Ferghana horses at China Gate he's fixing to move back west."

Ferghana horses are the best in the world. One of them is worth a hundred of me. Uthman nods, seeing that I get it. "Serious money. He could make trouble for you and your friends."

"What friends?" I mutter, thinking of Masoud. I look around: the setting sun lights up a half-dozen food stalls, cloth stretched over wooden frames, selling tutmac for the most part. My stomach lurches, and it's not just the beating I've taken or the fragrant steam rising from the bubbling pots of noodles. It's almost sundown. If I don't make it back to the warehouse I'll miss curfew, and that means the tree.

"I have to go," I say.

"I'm not *finished*, housecat," says Uthman. "You tell Oleg no more scores like that for a while. Okay?"

I nod, although I have exactly zero intention of telling Oleg anything of the sort. It's not healthy to be the bearer of bad news around Oleg.

"I was outside the city wall today. Up at a dihkan's place," says Uthman. I nod again, already plotting my route home in my head. The dihkans, the landlords around Samarkand, have nothing to do with me.

"We were up there," continues Uthman, "because the dihkan's wife woke up in a bed full of blood. Husband lying there with his throat opened up. Family, slaves, guards—no one heard a thing, all night."

That gets my attention. I look up at him, wide-eyed.

He nods. "There's quite a few people in this city who're a little *on edge* right now, and they're looking for someone to take it out on. A beggar gang like yours would be just the ticket. So keep a low profile, yeah? Off you go."

"Sir?" It's skinny Mehmet again. "Shouldn't we question her? That big guy was really—"

Uthman's brow darkens. "Funny," he growls, "I don't see a captain's badge on you. Am I wearing yours by mistake?"

Mehmet blushes and swallows again. He looks away from Uthman, and his eyes meet mine. I smile at him and he ducks his head, blushing harder. Nice guy, but he *really* needs to find another line of work.

Then Uthman waves a hand, dismissing me, and I take off.

CHAPTER SEVEN

Somehow, despite how banged up I am, I manage to run all the way back to the warehouse, although I have to stop twice to lean against a wall and retch. Nothing comes up but foul-tasting spit. By the time I arrive my head is pounding like it's about to split open.

The warehouse is buried deep in the Maze, almost right up against the city wall. Next door is the orphanage, and I stare up at its towering windowless wall while I catch my breath and struggle not to faint. The blank brick brings up a lot of memories, almost all of them unpleasant.

The sun is still glimmering on the horizon but I force myself to stay there until I'm breathing slow and even. I've got a few minutes to spare, and it's worth spending them to get a hold of myself, if I'm going in front of Nina.

She sits in the warehouse's small front room, on an overstuffed cushion behind a low counting-table. A blue dish sits on the table, a peacock design worked into the glaze, piled with plump dates.

The other pickpockets would have handed in their takings long before. There's only one Marten ahead of me in the line, and unsurprisingly it's 'Uj—huge and slow, small eyes peering from a lumpy mass of zits, a head and a half taller than anyone else in the Martens, although he's one of the youngest. All the street rats are younger than me now. *You can't do this forever*, Masoud whispers in my head.

As I walk in, trying not to wheeze, 'Uj holds up one clublike fist, showing off the handful of dented silver spoons he's holding. There's no way he lifted them; he would have taken them off another pickpocket, by force or threat of force. Probably one from another gang, although he'd be just as happy to do it to a Marten. That's how 'Uj makes quota.

Nina spits a stone on the floor beside her and taps one yellow fingernail on the table. 'Uj drops the battered spoons on the wood and Nina hunches to squint at them, her whole face scrunching up and her cold eyes glittering as she assesses their value. A trickle of syrupy spit dribbles from her lips. It's disgusting, but the dates' sweet smell still makes my stomach growl.

'Uj just stands there, immovable as a mountain. He's named for a giant from ancient times. I don't know if it's a nickname or not. If 'Uj ever had another name, he's probably forgotten it himself. Finally Nina nods and waves him away. 'Uj has made his quota. I don't see any relief, or any other emotion, on his lumpy face, but he'll eat tonight, and he's safe from the tree. Unlike me.

Then I'm stepping up to the table, while 'Uj lumbers, through the doorway behind Nina, into the warehouse proper.

"Late," says Nina, looking me over. Nina is about a thousand years old, face wrinkled like the dates she's eating, wearing a shapeless sack of a dress and a headscarf. She's from Rus, far to the north, and her eyes are an unnatural blue. She spits another stone on the floor. I watch it bounce and come to a stop, shining with saliva.

"I am *not* late," I say finally. "It's not even sundown."

Nina's lips curl in a cruel smile. She jerks her pointed chin at the doorway behind me and I look over my shoulder. A tower, a slender minaret belonging to one of Samarkand's mosques, is blocking the sun. Yesterday, or tomorrow, the sun would have missed it. Luck.

I turn back to Nina, whose eyes glitter triumphantly. "Your quota doubles," she says, "when the sun is gone. Or it's the tree for you. So? Well? Where is it?"

"Masoud," I say, although my mouth is suddenly dry. "Masoud had it. We lifted a purse, he must have showed you."

Nina's eyes narrow. She twists her neck around and snaps "Masoud!" into the doorway behind her. She doesn't wait for an answer. She hasn't had to wait for a long time. She grunts as she rearranges herself on the cushion, looking me up and down. Then, without warning, her skinny hand shoots out and grabs the front of my kameez, giving my chest an experimental squeeze.

Very clearly, I see myself bring an elbow up into Nina's chin. I see myself drive a fist squarely into Nina's nose. I see myself lunge across the table, sweeping those goddamn dates aside, and bring Nina down with my hands around the old bitch's throat.

But I don't do any of that. I think of Maryam, who ran the orphanage next door while I was there before Oleg and Nina's takeover of the Martens. I didn't know about the takeover—spectacularly bloody, even by the standards of Samarkand organized crime—at the time, of course. All I knew was that Maryam, who was no bowl of rose petals but who'd occasionally sneak us a treat from the kitchens or sing to us when we had a fever, was putting us to bed one night when the door burst open and two men dragged her screaming out of the room by her hair. And the next day, Nina was running the orphanage instead. No more treats or singing.

Finally Nina's hand retreats to her side of the table. She sniffs. "Still a few months of passing for a boy in you, I think," she says. "As long as you don't gorge yourself like a little pig, get curvy, yes? I will make sure you do not stuff your face so much."

Again, I say nothing, but inside I despair. Any less food and I don't know if I'll even be able to work. Which means I won't make quota. Which means less food, which means...

Then Masoud's in the doorway behind her, a book in his hand, 'Uj looming behind him. Our eyes lock for a moment, and I see his widen with shock and guilt. Then he recovers, and leans nonchalantly against the doorframe, returning my gaze blandly. "Yes, Grandmother?"

That's what he calls Nina. It makes me sick.

'Uj remains behind him. He defers to Masoud, most of the time. Most of the Martens think 'Uj is stupid, but that's not it. He just never bothers to think, and why would he? He does just fine with bulk and strength. He'd only use his brains to figure out who he was going to hit next, and with Masoud to pick out his targets he doesn't even need to do that.

Nina smiles at Masoud—most of her teeth have rotted right through, and her expression is ghastly, although Masoud returns it with a warm smile of his own. "Our little scholar," she says fondly. She points at the book with a crooked finger. "Attending to your lessons, yes?"

"Of course, Grandmother." Masoud puts on his pious face and the clever-clever tone he uses when he's quoting something. "'The realm is won by the sword but held by the pen. The sword runs red to take the land, the pen runs black to take the gold.'"

She claps delightedly. I think I'm going to retch. Nina is teaching Masoud to read, so he can help her with running the orphanage and the warehouse, and Masoud never misses a chance to lord it over the rest of us. Over me.

"This one says you worked together today," says Nina. So Masoud told her he lifted the Khwarezmian's purse by himself. He didn't expect to see me again, not alive and upright anyway, so as far as he knew there'd be no one to contradict him.

Now, though, he's got a choice. Admit he lied and that we lifted the purse together, or stick to his story and sell me out. He's careful not to look at me but he hesitates for a moment, and I think he might be wavering.

Then that pious look drops over his face again, like a door slamming shut, and he shrugs again. "She was there, yeah. In the bazaar. Just hanging around, though, I lifted the purse myself."

My eyes go wide. "He's lying!" I say, before I can stop myself. "He's a damn liar! I—"

Nina's hand whips around, slapping my face with a crisp *crack*. The impact twists my head around, and the cheek Nina struck instantly goes numb, then just as quickly explodes with burning pain.

"It's not her fault she goofs off," Masoud says generously. He leans over Nina's shoulder table to take a date, pops it into his mouth. "'Women have no constancy; where their eye looks their heart follows,'" he says with his mouth full.

He's covering his ass. He doesn't want to admit he ran us into a blind alley, and then ditched me, and then lied about it. Maybe, if I was standing over there, I'd be weak enough to do the same. I still want to bang his head against the wall until it caves in.

"Filthy little girl," said Nina. "Without us you would be dead on the street, or worse. We stick by you—do you stick by us?" She snorts and spits a wad of phlegm, slimy with sugar, on the floor by my feet. My hand twitches, wanting to fly to my face and cradle my throbbing cheek, but I ball it into a fist before it can. Damned if I'm going to show any weakness here. Nina looks around. "Any more latecomers?" she asks rhetorically. Then she sniffs. "Very well. In we go."

She scoops up a handful of dates in one withered claw, and heaves herself off her cushion. Masoud solicitously allows her to lean on him as she limps into the dark doorway at the back of the room, and she ruffles his hair. 'Uj falls in behind them and I bring up the rear, willing myself to put one foot in front of the other.

"And remember," says Nina over her shoulder, "nasty girls, lazy girls who tell lies, you know what happens to them? You know who pays them a visit, in the middle of the night?" One finger draws a line across her throat and she grins her hideous rotten grin at me. "And all they find the day after is a bedful of bloody sheets."

Of course I know. I hear Uthman's voice in my mind: *Woke up in a bed full of blood.* I shudder, and her grin widens.

The Assassins.

Chapter Eight

I n the orphanage, the Assassins were a mainstay of Nina's bedtime stories, told to a dozen terrified four-year-olds at a time as we huddled in our freezing dorm.

A flickering candle in her hand, illuminating her wrinkled face hideously from below, she told us about Alamut. The Eagle's Nest, a fortress in the West where the Old Man of the Mountain sat on his throne and dispatched his faceless killers to every corner of the world. Once the Old Man marked you for death, the Assassins would find you, no matter where you were; they could climb any wall, creep through the narrowest window.

If we made her life difficult, she'd tell us, if we ate too much or wet the bed or screwed up in a hundred other ways, she would personally send word to the Old Man of the Mountain, and his Assassins would come for *us*. We would simply vanish one night, and no one would ever see us again. And once in a while a kid wouldn't be there for the morning or evening head-count, and Nina would leave us in no doubt as to what had happened to them.

And we knew they were real. We heard grownups talking about them, grownups who were as scared of them as we were. We'd hear that another rich and powerful man—an imam, a dihkan, a qadi—had been struck down by an Assassin in the middle of the Friday sermon, or in his bedchamber in the dead of night. That you never knew who around you might be an Assassin, until the dagger cut your throat or spilled your guts. And we knew that if we asked for a second helping, or didn't make our beds, their next target would be *us*.

I visited Alamut in my nightmares a lot. Still do. I see a mountain range like jagged fangs, a towering needle-sharp peak at their centre, and at the top of that peak squats the Old Man. His face is a little like Nina's but his limbs are grotesquely long, splayed like a spider's at the centre of its web. With his spindly fingers he plucks clots of living darkness from the mountain's shadows and sends them in every direction, silver blades gleaming in their claws.

I've learned since that the Assassins aren't monsters. They're just men—Nizaris, fighters for a persecuted sect of Islam. They aren't made of shadows, they don't live under our beds, and they've got bigger things on their minds than kids who tell fibs. The ones who went missing from the orphanage just ran away, probably, or Nina sold them to slavers.

But knowing that is one thing, and the fear is another. And if what Uthman said is true, the Assassins are in Samarkand right *now*.

I follow Nina and Masoud and 'Uj into the warehouse. There are other Martens in here, the ones who made curfew. They fall into step as Nina passes, all of us heading deeper inside.

We make our way through stacks of rugs and tiles taller than 'Uj. We file past row upon row of free-standing shelves whose tops are lost in darkness, each shelf loaded with fragrant sacks of spices, bolts of cloth, jars of incense and dye...every kind of thing that passes through Samarkand and that you can sell for a profit, which means every kind of thing in the world.

Not all of this is the Martens'. The warehouse belongs to a merchant, some little Bulgar I don't even know the name of, and he lets our crew use it as our headquarters, and stash the stuff we steal here. I don't know what he gets out of the deal. Maybe nothing. It's not like he's going to tell Oleg "no", not if he wants to keep his guts on the inside.

Something rustles in the shadows that fill the warehouse. Probably just a pigeon or a rat, but I'm still thinking about the Assassins, and I shudder again. I'm glad it's too dark for the other Martens to see me. At least the fear is taking my mind off my empty stomach.

The next shelf is stacked with books, spines cracked and covers faded from the hundreds of miles of hard road between Samarkand and wherever they came from. I run my hand over the battered leather bindings and wonder what's inside. Masoud acts like all the wisdom of the world is within his grasp, just because he can read. Masoud is full of crap, as I may have mentioned, but there has to be *something* in there worth learning, otherwise why would people do it? The funny thing is, I think I'd be better at it than Masoud is; I pick up languages naturally, I can get by in half a dozen of them just from hanging around in the bazaar and listening.

No one's ever going to teach me to read though, so who cares.

At the back of the warehouse a doorway leads into a tiny courtyard, open to the sky. I shiver, and it's not just the cold out here. This is another place I visit in my nightmares.

Just beyond the doorway, up against the warehouse wall where we have to walk right past it, is a cage made of mismatched wooden slats. Inside is an actual marten, Nina's pet or mascot or whatever it is; supposedly it made the journey with her from Rus, and it's why she chose the Martens for taking over in the first place. Lucky us. Its sleek ferretlike body—it eats better than any of us—twitches as it follows us with its eyes. We keep well clear; get too close to that thing and you'll lose a knuckle.

Besides the cage, the courtyard's only contents are a rough wooden shack up against the back wall, and a dead tree. The tree stands in the centre of the yard, trunk twisted like a broken neck, bark warty and lumpy like diseased skin. Its bare limbs spread all the way over the courtyard's walls, enclosing it like the crooked bars of the marten's cage. Looking up I see the darkening sky cut up into irregular patches by the crisscrossing branches.

Beside the tree is a brazier full of glowing coals. Sticking out from the middle of the coals, where they're hottest, is the iron handle of a poker. My gaze settles on it, and my heartbeat quickens.

We're the last of the Martens to arrive. Nina hobbles over to a bench near the doorway and sits down, and the rest of us spread out along the walls, staying as far away from the tree as possible. We naturally cluster into groups, sorting ourselves by age and size as neatly as if we'd been shaken through a sieve.

First are the littlest kids, barely out of the orphanage. They're the runners, the Martens' scouts and messengers. They all look terrified, as well they might; all of them are on probation, and the slightest screwup means they'll be beggars on street corners for the rest of their lives.

Next to them is the largest group, my group—the pickpockets, the lifters and scammers. Older than the runners but young enough that if we get busted the ahdath will let us off with only a beating. I'm nearly the smallest, although I'm the oldest. I stand a little apart from the rest, and they don't look at me at all. The only one of them who ever talks to me (unless we're running a scam together) is little Nasr, and I don't even see him here. Running an errand for Oleg, Masoud said. What's that all about, anyway?

Masoud's still a pickpocket, but he's standing with the next group over, and as I look at them my heart clenches with jealousy. These are the thieves, the burglars and smash-and-grab artists, the ones who supply most of the stolen goods for the warehouse. All of them have grown their hair out and plaited it into three braids, Karakhanid-style. *Every man a Khan*, as Oleg says. I know it doesn't mean anything— Oleg's buying their loyalty with words, and saving his money—but at the same time I want those braids so badly.

Masoud also wears the braids, even though he's not a thief yet, but that's just because he's Nina's favourite. He's right among them, talking in low tones with Farid, their leader. My gaze, as usual, lingers on Farid. He's a head taller than the rest of them, broad-shouldered, arms corded with muscle. He sees me and gives me a slight nod; I nod back, feeling warm inside despite the cold. Farid's always given me respect, and Farid's respect goes a long way in keeping the others off my back.

The rest of the Martens are ranged along the wall opposite, big guys in their late teens and twenties. They're the muscle.

The Martens, like the other beggar gangs, lay claim to a number of crossroads and street corners throughout Samarkand. We put our beggars there, to collect money from passers-by. Sometimes the good ones—the ones with a lot of traffic, where a beggar can expect to do well—are disputed. Other gangs will try to kick our beggars off them, put their own in their place. Our muscle—big thugs like Sanjar and Kazan over there—are there to stop that happening. They'll probably form their own gangs one day, affiliated with the Martens but answering to no one. I barely look at them. They're twenty feet from me but they might as well be on the other side of the world; I'll sprout wings and fly before I stand over there. 'Uj will probably skip the thieves and go straight into the muscle, and sooner rather than later. He's only thirteen and he's already the biggest one here.

The beggars themselves never come to the courtyard. They live in the orphanage, they're led out at dawn each morning into the city to work and they're taken back at dusk. Pickpockets never have anything to do with them if we can help it. It's bad luck, and if your luck gets bad enough—like mine is getting, right now—you might get to see their lives from the inside, and for the rest of yours.

I'm the only girl here.

The sun has set and the temperature is dropping fast. Many of us are shivering and hugging ourselves. But, although there's more than one furtive look at the brazier, no one gets closer to its warmth.

I glance again at the thieves. They lean casually against the wall, talking and joking in low voices. *They* never have a quota to make, they only go out on special jobs. They never get the tree.

I want to be among them so much it twists my guts. I want to stand with them (*with Farid*, I think). Joke with them. Belong. Thieves stick together. Thieves have a code. So do pickpockets, supposedly, but I found out just how much that was worth when Masoud left me in the alley today. Thieves have each other's backs. None of the pickpockets have mine.

But I'm also fiercely proud to be standing alone. Because even though no one has my back, even though I'm hungry and afraid, I'm still standing. I haven't let Oleg and Nina and Masoud and Samarkand itself beat me, not in my heart where it counts.

Then pure fear washes all my thoughts away, as I hear the voices coming from behind the door of the filthy shack at the back of the courtyard. We can't hear what they're saying, but there are two of them—one barely a whisper, the other loud and deep and booming with anger. Everyone here knows you never want to hear that voice angry.

The voices fall silent for a moment, then the door of the shack springs open, swinging out and around on its leather hinges and crashing against the wall. Oleg shambles out.

He's huge, and even though he must be in his forties, most of his bulk is still muscle. Even his fat isn't flabby; his stinking furs hang open and he's naked to the waist beneath them, and the hairy belly above his ragged trousers is drum-tight.

Like Nina, he's a Varangian from Rus, and the rumour around Samarkand is that he used to belong to the Varangian *Guard*, swinging an axe for Constantinople. He might have spread those rumours himself, but they're easy to believe. I was in the orphanage during his rise through the Samarkand underworld, but the stories the Martens tell about it are unbelievably gruesome. I know how it is with those stories—every drunk who gets a blade slipped into his kidneys while he's passed out in an alley becomes the hero of an epic, full of deadly combat and dying curses—but if even a tenth of the ones about Oleg are true...

It's been twelve years since then, and Oleg's immense red beard is streaked with grey, but he still fills the courtyard until there's no room for air. (Nina looked about a thousand years old back then and she still does; I half-believe the old bitch will never die.) The booze-stench rolls off him in waves, his eyes are bloodshot, and crusty dried vomit streaks his beard. If he was another man, that might make him seem weak, pathetic, but it makes Oleg all the more frightening. All the Martens know that when Oleg is drunk—or worse, hung over—he's capable of anything.

Today, though, he just casts a surly look over the assembled Martens and turns to Nina. "Well?"

Nina spits a date stone and nods. "Five."

Five pickpockets, including me, who haven't made our quota. Five of us to line up under the tree. A one-in-five chance that I'll be the one Oleg makes an example of.

His eyes flare. Five is more than average. I don't even know why he cares about the money, all he ever spends it on is cheap tavern food and cheaper booze. The stinking furs he wears are probably the same ones he came down from Rus in.

Nina doesn't have to call out names. The Martens who didn't make their quota are already heading to the tree; dragging your heels just singles you out for punishment. For a moment I think my feet are going to betray me, stay rooted to the spot, and I feel sheer stark terror—but then I'm moving to join the others.

We line up under the tree. Sweat creeps into my eyes, partly from the heat cooking off the brazier but mostly from the fear. I want to wipe it away, but once again I curl my hands into fists to stop them from moving, and let the sweat sting.

Only when we're all lined up under the lifeless branches does Oleg lumber toward us. He hawks and spits a huge wad of phlegm into the brazier, and a foul smell rises as it hisses and pops. I look straight ahead but in the corner of my eye I can see the pickpocket next to me. He's around ten, barely out of the runners, and although he's as silent as I am tears are streaming down his face. I feel a surge of hope that maybe Oleg will pick *him*, and then an even more powerful surge of disgust at myself for thinking it.

Oleg's voice is a deep rumble that echoes off the courtyard walls. "You know why you are here?" he asks. His heavy accent is even worse when he's drunk, and I can see everyone straining to pick out the words. You don't want to make Oleg say something twice.

He doesn't wait for an answer. His red-rimmed eyes sweep over the pickpockets standing along the walls. He hasn't even looked at the five of us at the tree yet. "You know why?" he repeats. "Why we let you rats wander over town, not begging on one corner all day, locked in the orphanage all night?

"Because you make us money. More money than by begging. But if you don't—"

In a single motion, unbelievably fast for a man of his bulk, he whips around, grabs the handle of the poker and wrenches it from the brazier in a flurry of sparks and an avalanche of glowing coals that spill onto the ground. One rolls towards my bare feet, and stops an inch from my toes. I manage not to flinch. Oleg still isn't looking at us, but he's waving the poker in our direction, back and forth in long slow sweeps. Its cherry-red tip leaves a glowing trail in my vision.

For a second I really, honestly think I'm going to piss myself. Nineteen times out of twenty, if you're at the tree and Oleg picks you, it's just a beating—a vicious one, but not so vicious you can't go out earning the next day. Oleg has to protect his investment, after all. That twentieth time, though, when standards are slipping and he needs to make an example, or he thinks we're not afraid enough of him, or he's been drunk enough for long enough to get crazy...

That's when you get the poker.

"Maybe you *do* make more money as a beggar, then. Or maybe not. Maybe no one gives you money. They see you are lazy little nothings and feel no sorrow for you. Maybe I need to *make* them feel sorrow. And who do they feel for, who makes me the most money?"

The tip of the poker blurs and it's pointing straight at my eye, Oleg's face right behind it, inches from mine.

"*Blind* beggars," he hisses. The stench of his breath is unbelievable, sour vomit over old booze, and below that something else, like meat that's been in the sun all day. Nina cackles, a harsh caw like a crow's.

I strive to look straight ahead, keep every muscle still. That means looking past the poker, not at it, even as it seems to fill the whole world. Sweat drips from my nose. I don't know how long I can keep this up. The glowing iron moves closer and I clench my jaw so hard it aches. I can feel my eyebrow hairs curling and crisping—

And then the poker's gone, and Oleg's pressing the tip to the cheek of the boy who was crying.

The kid screams, a high thin whine like a rabbit in a trap. He tries to jerk away but Oleg reaches out and grabs the back of his head, pushes it onto the poker. A horrible smell rises in the cold night air.

"Little crybaby," Oleg says, and then lets the boy go. He collapses and curls up in a ball among the tree's exposed roots, pressing his face into the earth to cool it. He tries his hardest to hold the shrieks inside but still they burst out of him, one after another, muffled by the dirt. Oleg stands over him, raising the poker—

"*Enough.*"

It's barely a whisper, but somehow it cuts right through the boy's cries. I turn my head to see who has spoken, my determination not to move forgotten. All around the courtyard I see Martens doing the same, even Oleg and Nina.

Someone is standing in the doorway of Oleg's shack. I don't know how long she's been there. She's older than me, at least twenty, wearing dusty black leathers. Her hair is black too, short and ragged like she cut it herself. She's armed—two swords are strapped to her back, the hilts coming up over her shoulders, wrapped with well-worn leather. Her face is almost a girl's, fine-boned with a small pointed chin, delicate-looking even with its leathery road tan. The high cheekbones and upturned eyes remind me of the two from the courtyard...was that seriously only a few hours ago?

"I got this," says Oleg, but he lowers the poker.

"You're wasting time. Tell them." Her Khitai is strangely accented, and she doesn't raise her voice but it has a *force*, a pressure that hurts my ears. How is she doing that? Not that it matters, because whoever she is, she's just crossed Oleg. I see the other Martens tense up, waiting for the sudden burst of violence. Maybe he'll use the poker on her.

Instead, incredibly, he turns away, buries the poker in the coals of the brazier. He turns to glare at all of us, like he can scare us into forgetting he just backed down. To a woman. In his own home.

No one's going to point that out, though. Everyone is carefully looking somewhere else. Finally he grunts. "This is Crow," he says to us, nodding at the stranger. "She wants—"

"I'm looking for a box," says the swordswoman, Crow, speaking right over the top of him. "Black. Picture of a bird on it." Oleg's face goes a dangerous shade of red at the interruption, but he doesn't interrupt her back. The woman's hand goes to her shoulder and she draws one of her swords, then lowers the point and draws swiftly in the dirt. It's a long sword, the blade curving like the kilij the ahdath use,, and it looks heavy but she handles it like she's holding a peacock feather, each stroke light and precise.

"This is on the box as well," she says as she writes. This woman hasn't threatened anyone, hasn't even looked at me, but I'm almost as scared of that sword as I was of Oleg's poker. Although she's slender and almost petite—most of the muscle dwarf her, even Farid is a head taller—the courtyard seems too small to contain her. Like there's a lioness in here.

I focus on the characters she's writing, so I don't have to focus on her. She's not using an alphabet like Persian or Greek; it's more like the picture-words the Khitai use among themselves, I can even pick out the pictures-within-pictures that make them up, although of course I can't read them—

"We are going to find this thing," says Oleg, bringing me back. "Okay? We think it came from the East, maybe a month ago. Thieves?" He turns to Farid, who straightens and nods professionally. "You look for this box until it's found. Nothing else. Just this. You have contacts—fences, warehousemen. Use them. You find it, you don't open it, you don't do *anything* with it but bring it to me." Another nod from Farid, and Oleg turns to face the pickpockets.

"You look for the box too. But quietly. Let anyone but us know this thing is out there, and..." He looks meaningfully at the brazier, like the threat can fix the damage all this has done to his rep, but it's not enough and he knows it.

Nina spits a date stone. She's staring daggers at the woman in black, "Crow" Oleg called her. Crow leans against the courtyard wall, her shoulders drooping like she hasn't slept in days. Her eyes flick over the five of us in front of the tree, and I can't hold her gaze for even a moment. I study the dirt between my feet until I'm sure she's looking elsewhere.

What is going on?

"What about our quotas?" says a voice from the pickpockets.

"Half quota. All this week," says Oleg. Nina hisses something under her breath. He continues: "And if one of the pickpockets find this thing? He has no work for a month, and drinking money."

If Oleg had promised us a chest full of silver dirhams it would hardly seem more extravagant. But Oleg's not finished. He turns to the muscle next: "This goes for you too. You see anything, you hear anything, you follow up. At once."

The muscle look at each other. Kazan, strong as a bull and fearless (because he's almost too stupid to breathe), raises a hand. "What about our *corners?*"

In Kazan's defence, it's a fair question. If all the Martens are out looking for this mystery woman's mystery box instead of holding down our corners, what's to stop the Wolves, or anyone else who wants to, from taking them?

"You get a lead, you follow it," says Oleg, "forget your corner," and for the effect this has, he might as well have flapped his arms and flown up into the tree like a bird. The courtyard goes silent. Everyone's thinking the same thing—this is going to make the Martens look like crap. Even one day that goes by without us keeping up our claim to what's ours is going to encourage every two-bit crook in Samarkand to start pushing.

A rumble of protest spreads through the muscle. Oleg glowers back at them, and I don't want to be here for whatever's coming. But then there's a shout from the doorway and everyone turns to see.

Little Nasr the pickpocket comes limping into the courtyard. His face is bright red and he's wheezing for breath. He looks like he's hauled ass all the way from Monk's Gate, and he's clutching a package wrapped in coarse cloth. Wrong: he's not a pickpocket. Masoud said he made the climb. He's a thief now. My last ally is gone.

Nina half-rises from her bench like she's going to tear strips off him for being late, but Oleg waves her away and she sinks back down again. He gestures impatiently, and Nasr promptly tosses him the bundle. Oleg almost fumbles the catch, then pitches it to the woman, Crow. She catches it neatly, without even looking at it, and pulls at the knot that ties the cloth together.

"I didn't...They didn't..." Nasr manages to wheeze. Here's a first: Nasr, little pickpocket with the big mouth, is lost for words. "Didn't have it all. I had to go to..." He trails off. Oleg isn't listening.

Oleg turns to Crow, asking a question with his eyes. Crow examines the contents of the package. It looks like bundles of herbs, and the smell that spreads through the courtyard is way too bad to be food, so they must be medicine. Crow doesn't look up, but she gives the slightest nod.

"Get out of here," snarls Oleg. For a moment it looks like some of the muscle are going to stick around, argue the point about our corners, but then he roars "*Go!*" and everyone does. As we jostle in the doorway I turn back for a last look at Crow, but she's gone like she was never there. I think again of the two in the courtyard, who saved me from the Teuton. They moved like that, too.

CHAPTER NINE

I dream.

 I'm standing in the Square of the Money-Changers. The courthouse looms over everything, its shadow plunging the whole square into gloom. The tree is here, the one from Oleg's courtyard, grown huge and monstrous with a trunk the width of a house. I look up and see its twisted branches reaching out over the whole dome of the sky, disappearing over the horizon, trapping the whole world in a cage's crooked bars—

 My eyes snap open. My heart is racing. I sit up.

 The loft is as quiet as it ever gets, which is to say not at all. The thieves and muscle get to live in a squat down the street, but all the pickpockets share this long low room just under the warehouse's high roof. There's barely six inches of space between each dirty cot, and the cobwebbed ceiling is only a few feet above our heads; even I have to crouch when I stand. Bedding rustles as the street rats toss and turn, scratch at bug bites, grunt and snore and fart. Other rats, the regular kind, scamper between the cots.

 Someone is whimpering next to me. It's the kid Oleg burned with the poker; it turned out none of us know his name. The skin of his cheek is an ugly inflamed red around the stripe of blackened, cracked flesh where Oleg pressed the red-hot iron.

 It's only been a couple of days since Nina picked him out of the runners and gave him a shot as a pickpocket, and it looks like it's not going to work out. He might live, if a fever doesn't set in, but a scar like the one he'll have means he'll stand out in a crowd, and that's death when you've just lifted someone's purse and you're trying to disappear. At best he's got a lifetime as a beggar to look forward to.

None of the others have even talked to him. Only Nasr—little Nasr, who sang Maryam's old songs to this kid for half an hour, even with his lungs burning after running from one end of Samarkand to the other on Oleg's mysterious errand.

Nasr can afford to sing to the kid, though. He made the climb; soon he'll be a thief and leave us behind. No one else here can afford to get close to the kid. It's a kind of superstition: if you're too close to someone when they go down, they'll drag you right down with them. I know that's crap...but I haven't talked to the kid either.

At least I have food in my stomach. I was half-expecting Nina to turn me away when I lined up in front of her big iron pot, but she grudgingly splashed a ladleful of tutmac into my bowl. Just a few noodles floating like dead worms in a weak broth, but it was the first thing I'd eaten in a day and my guts have quieted down a little.

I'm at the end of the room closest to the door, where it's coldest and draftiest. We've each of us added to our one thin blanket with clothes we've stolen from the bazaars and rags we've picked up in the street. Even wrapped tight in my own collection, I'm cold as a corpse, and although I'm bone-tired I doubt I'll get to sleep again. At least that means no more nightmares tonight.

I take a deep breath, and my sides pulse with pain. It feels like squeezing myself through that narrow gap to escape the Wolves has bent my ribcage out of shape for good. Remembering being stuck like that makes my back prickle with sweat, so I try to remember something else.

So my thoughts turn to my two saviours from yesterday.

I've seen fights before, even been in a few of my own, but there's more than one kind of fight. The ones I was in were street rat scuffles, the kind you don't even realize are happening until they're over—it's just a blur of yelling and the thud of flesh on flesh and sudden lancing pain, and suddenly it's done and you're nursing skinned knuckles and bruises, as the rush fades away and leaves you weak and trembling.

Then there are the fights the real killers get into, the Teuton and others like him, the Khan's off-duty troops and the Khitai horsemen. Those fights are short too, deadly little skirmishes in taverns and alleys. There's skill there—you only have to see how the Teuton uses that sword of his—but it's applied brutally, viciously, and the results are appalling: the winner staggering out the tavern door drunk off his ass, while the loser sits on the floor trying to talk with his brains coming out of his ears, or screaming for his mother as he holds his guts in with his hands.

But those two strangers, in the courtyard today...

It's not that they fought gracefully, even beautifully. I've seen plenty of wannabe heroes try to pull flashy moves in a fight, to rattle their opponent and impress whoever's watching. But what that usually gets them is their face bashed in...only today it didn't. The woman especially—I can't even remember what moves she pulled, they were so fast they blur in my memory into a whirlwind of spear-thrusts and footwork, a storm of beauty. And then that leap, that took them straight up to the roof. If I could do that...

Well. I can't. But I'll do what I can.

I ease out of bed. The kid who got the poker has slipped into an uneasy sleep; he moans and stirs as my cot's frame creaks, but doesn't wake, and neither do any of the others as I pad to the doorway. At the other end of the loft is 'Uj, sprawled across two cots because he won't fit on one and he refuses to sleep on the floor. It's less room for the rest of us, but no one's going to say anything to 'Uj about it.

From the doorway you descend a rickety ladder to the floor of the warehouse. This isn't the first time I've snuck out after curfew, and I skip the rungs that I know will creak.

As I reach the bottom a flicker of candlelight catches my eye, and I duck behind a shelf of clay bottles. No one's supposed to be in here.

Nina lives in the orphanage, Oleg has the shack out the back, and the Bulgar who owns the warehouse never posts guards—no one's going to cross Oleg by ripping this place off. Has someone left a candle burning? They'll get a thrashing for wasting the wax.

One corner of the warehouse is blocked off by rolls of woollen cloth, making a roofless little room where the Bulgar keeps his ledgers, and that's where the light is coming from. Is he here now?

Through a narrow gap in the rolls of wool I can see a low table, cushions to sit on, books stacked against the wall. There's a candle in a dish on the table, and someone's kneeling in front of it, but it's not the merchant. It's Crow.

Her back is to me. She's still wearing her leathers, but her curved swords rest against the wall in their scabbards. Something is on the table next to the candle—something round, like a shallow bowl, covered with a white cloth. The cloth is moving.

Once, when I was a little kid, I saw a bird lying in an alley. I thought it was dead, but then I saw it twitch, ever so slightly. I prodded it with a stick, then flipped it over, and I saw that it *was* dead. The skin of its belly had rotted down to a thin membrane, which rippled obscenely as the things inside it gnawed at its flesh. That was what had made it move. I screamed and ran.

The cloth is rippling just like the dead bird's skin did. I shudder convulsively, and I see Crow turn her head, just slightly, showing the delicate line of her jaw. I back up slowly, until the shelves block me from Crow's line of sight, then I turn and walk out as quick and quiet as I can.

Sometime back before I was born, the warehouse must have been hit by an earthquake, or the ground settled under it. Whatever happened, a shallow crack spread up the east wall, reaching almost to the roof and splintering the smooth brickwork on either side.

Now I stand in the tiny alley that separates the warehouse from its neighbour, flexing my fingers and looking up at the crack. It stops only a few feet from the top of the wall, where moonlight glimmers on the edge of the roof.

The roof.

The rooftops of Samarkand are their own world. Most of the people who throng the streets below know nothing about it, but for every thief in the city, it's home. It has its own 'streets'—the climbing routes, the plank bridges laid between buildings that let those who know them cross almost the whole of Samarkand without touching the ground. It has its own monuments—even from down here I can see the clusters of spidery shadows marking the top of the wall. They're tags, stylized Turkic runes spelling out names and nicknames. Every thief in Samarkand, even if he knows no other letters, knows his own tag, and carves it wherever he climbs. There's a never-ending race to tag higher than the other thieves, and destroy their tags where you find them. I wouldn't be surprised if even the minaret of the Old Mosque, the highest point in Samarkand, has one or two tags at the summit that the muezzin knows nothing about.

The warehouse's east wall isn't the only way up to this other world, of course; I could name a dozen of them without thinking, some of them easy enough that even I could make it up. But even if I did, I wouldn't *belong* up there. Each gang of thieves in Samarkand has their own special climb, and whenever a pickpocket wants to make thief, they have to beat it.

For the Martens, it's this wall. I imagine Nasr standing here, ready to make the climb. I don't know what happened, exactly—the thieves don't allow spectators, and pass or fail, you're sworn to secrecy. I know you wear weights, to show you can climb even carrying loot, but I don't even know how much they weigh. The pickpockets swap stories, of course, solemnly swearing they know for sure it's twenty, fifty, a hundred pounds, but stories are all they are.

I've never even made it *without* any weights. But I want to, so badly it hurts inside. Because it's my only chance. Because I can't be a pickpocket forever, and if I can't make thief...

I bunch my fists, popping my knuckles, and my ribs flare up again as I take a deep breath. I expel it through my nose and feel myself falling into the current, like a swift river that carries me away. I see the whole wall, the hand- and footholds popping out at me, the paths up to the roof seeming to glow with their own light like spidery bolts of lightning. I place a foot into the crack a couple of feet from the ground, and begin to climb.

The first part is easy. The current guides my limbs, making every move deft and sure. I'm scrawny and short, and that means I have less muscle—but it also means less weight to haul up the wall. I wedge my fingers into a gap between the bricks where the mortar has flaked away; swing my body a little until my foot can reach the hole where a brick is missing entirely; reach up to grab the protruding edge of a brick and lodge my other foot in the crack...

And then the crack runs out, and I'm looking up a few short feet of smooth brickwork to the top of the wall. I wince a little as I push up with my foot, feeling it slip down the baked mud, stinging even through the thick calluses on my sole—I lunge upwards—

—And grab the edge of the roof—

—And there I stay.

My back knots as I try to pull myself up. Just one pull-up, that's all I need. The worst thief in the Martens could run a mile and still do it. Just one—

Grunting with effort, I heave myself up, arms burning. My eyes clear the edge of the roof and I see it, laid out in the moonlight, the flat expanse of the warehouse roof and beyond it all the other rooftops of Samarkand, a new world—

Then my back and biceps give out, and I drop.

I only just manage to stop myself falling off the wall entirely. As it is, my descent is more of a barely-controlled plummet, grabbing handholds when I can to slow myself down, and when I hit the ground the shock numbs my knees and I go sprawling, scraping up my elbows, back and butt even more than they were already.

I lie there, looking up at the moon, and feel a scream building in my throat. I'm back in that tiny crack between the buildings I wormed through yesterday, and now someone's bricking up both ends, sealing me in forever.

I do this almost every night, and I'm no closer to making it than I have been for weeks. I probably shouldn't even be trying—it burns energy I can hardly spare—but if I don't try, I can't hope, and then I'm done. Tears sting my eyes. My lips tremble, trying to hold back the scream, and then I hear the footsteps.

I struggle silently to my feet, and creep along the wall, staying in the shadows. When I reach the corner, I see a silhouette detach itself from the darkness inside the doorway, and head for the midden-hole across the street.

Masoud.

The midden-holes are all over Samarkand, deep circular wells with covers of wood or earthenware, for all the city's liquid waste. Shivering in the morning cold, Masoud kicks the cover aside and fishes in his pants.

As he pisses into the hole, I pad up behind him, one soft footstep after another. Has he even heard me? I see it so clearly—planting a foot on his ass and shoving, watching him half-turn to look at me, face white with shock, and plunging into the pit—that for a moment I think I've already done it. Then Masoud says "Darya?" without even turning around, and I realize I haven't moved.

The casual way he says it, without a hint of remorse, boils my blood. He finishes up and rearranges his clothes, and I step forward and push him with both hands on his back. Of course I'm too weak to move him, and he barely shifts his feet. He turns around and I flinch, but he doesn't bother hitting me back.

"Something to say?" he says calmly.

"You *left me!*" I hiss. I want to scream it, but I'm not angry enough that I don't care about bringing an ahdath night patrol down on us. "You left me and you *lied*. I nearly got the poker because of you!" He flinches a little at that, and I draw breath to really tear shreds off him, but then he says something that throws me:

"Are you a Marten?" he asks.

Last night, while I tossed and turned in my freezing cot waiting for sleep to come, I was turning over ways this conversation could go. This isn't one of them. "What do you think?" I say, with the feeling I'm being led into a trap.

"Really? A real Marten? And not just a Marten—you want to be a thief, right? One of Oleg's burglars, just like me?"

"You're not one yet," I retort. Masoud shrugs. He's still so calm. So I let rip with something I've been saving up ever since Uthman let me go: "*You're* not a Marten. 'Martens don't leave Martens,'" I say, quoting the oath we all took when we left the orphanage. "You *left me.*"

"Think about that, Darya," says Masoud. "'Martens don't leave Martens,' fine. And I left you. That only means *one* of us isn't a Marten."

"No," I say, shaking my head again, but it's like the ground is shifting beneath my feet. Masoud holds up a fist and I clench my teeth, expecting a blow, but instead he unfolds one of his fingers. "First thing," he says. "You're getting older. You've got maybe one more season as a pickpocket in you, and then what?"

"I'll be a thief. I will." I say it defiantly, but I've lost my footing here and we both know it. In my head I was going to lay into Masoud, full of righteous fury. Now I'm defending myself against him, as he stands there so hatefully calm. What happened?

"That's the second thing." Another finger. "You can't climb."

"Horse shit!" I hiss, but I can feel the lingering ache in my knees from my fall just now, every prickle of pain calling me a liar.

"If you could climb, you would have gotten away yesterday. You think we haven't seen you practising? You were practising just now, weren't you? Can you even do one pull-up?"

I'm clenching my teeth so hard I think they'll shatter.

"What if you have to carry heavy loot, or hold a rope to lower something out of a window? And third, Darya,"—finger number three—"you're a *girl*. You're okay at what you do, that's why you're in the loft with us, but you'll never be a real Marten. Nina's going to sell you off to some dihkan's household and you'll spend the rest of your life as a kitchen slave. And is that really so bad?"

I say nothing. Suddenly I just feel so *tired*.

Masoud drops his hand. He pushes past me and I let him. "How many times do I have to say it, Darya? Just *give up*." He walks back into the warehouse. "Stay in the game and you'll get caught and beaten, or worse. Give it up and act like a girl."

I could tell him to go screw himself. But I don't. Because he's right.

I'll go to Nina. Tomorrow. I'll tell her I'm done, I can't do this anymore. The old witch will get such a kick out of it she probably won't even make fun of me too much. She'll sell me off to some rich man just like Masoud said, and I'll wash dishes and empty chamberpots until I'm as old as she is. Maybe even work my way up to head slave, get to push some other girls around. It'll be easy—well, not easy, but I won't have to *fight* all the time. I'm done. I can't keep making quota on less and less food every day... Making quota...

And the idea is sitting right there in my head, fully formed. It's a bad idea, I can tell that right away. It's stupid, it's probably suicide, and it almost certainly won't even change anything.

I should forget it. Go back to bed. But I don't.

Chapter Ten

When I steal back into the warehouse, everything is dark. I'm tempted to dismiss what I saw, the candlelight, Crow, the thing on the table, as part of my earlier nightmare. But I know it wasn't.

Masoud is already asleep when I get back to the loft. I slide my hand between my thin mattress and the frame of my cot, and scoop up the half-dozen milk curds I hid in there a few days ago, just in case my hunger got so bad I couldn't work. It hurts to lose my entire stash, but I'll need the energy to get all the way out of the city and back.

As I pass the nameless kid's cot on the way out, he stirs and lets out a long, low groan. I pause, then take two of the curds from my pocket and press them into his hand. His skin is hot—bad sign—but his fingers curl around the curds. I don't look into his eyes. He presses his hand to his mouth. He doesn't thank me, and I don't want him to. The curds I've kept are to buy off my body, to shut the hunger up so that I can function. The ones I gave the kid are just the same, only it's my conscience I'm shutting up. That's all.

He's sucking on the curds in his sleep, like a baby, as I head back to the ladder.

I can just make out the eastern horizon as I walk through China Gate.

The ground is still frozen from the night before; I've wrapped rags from my cot around my feet, but every step still chills them to the bone. More rags pad out my kameez, but I'm still hugging myself against the cold.

Outside the gate is a scene of torchlit chaos. A caravan came in yesterday from the East, and they're still unloading everything. Donkeys and two-humped camels stand patiently under loads taller than they are, while handlers pull bales of silk and crates of porcelain off their backs and stack them on the ground. A merchant with a brush and a pot of black paint marks them for distribution, some to warehouses and bazaars throughout Samarkand, some to other caravans that will take them even further, to the furthest reaches of the world. Maybe even the Teuton's land, or further.

Other piles of goods wait to be loaded for the caravan's departure back east, glassware and dates and wine and a hundred other goods from those same western lands. In the distance I can see a small caravanserai, lodgings for the beasts and men of the caravan, the porters and animal handlers, the guards who protect it from bandits.

It's only a mile or so down the road, but tired and hungry and cold as I am it seems like a thousand times as far. And that's where I'm headed.

I make my way through the crowd outside the gate. Merchants are milling around the piles of goods, occasionally feeling the texture of a fur or a bolt of silk, talking in low voices with each other. I see Ghurids, Persians, Arabs, Africans...they must be from every country in the world. They bargain over gold and ivory, vibrant red-dyed Armenian cloth, feathers and furs and wax.

Over all of us loom the city walls of Samarkand, dark but growing lighter by degrees as the sun struggles up to the horizon. There's not a city on Earth like Samarkand. Not that I've seen any others, but how could there be? *Two hundred thousand people*—it must be the biggest city in Creation—and right in the centre of the Silk Road, the web of trade routes along which moves everything worth anything in the world.

And the crowd outside China Gate are the ones who do the moving. Those rugs in the bazaar, where men bicker over a dozen tiles or jars of wine? They're a sideshow, somewhere small-timers can pretend to be players. Out here are the *real* players, and they don't do any flashy haggling; they bargain in low voices, and a simple handshake seals a deal that will build an empire, or ruin one.

Being here, watching it, I can *feel* the flow of all those people and goods, like the currents of traffic in a city or of the strength in my own body. I'm just a pickpocket who barely even belongs to a gang, but right now I'm dipping a toe in the rivers of money and power that shape the whole world.

Above the gate something glimmers with reflected torchlight. A silver tablet is set into the wall up there, too high for me to see the writing on it (and I couldn't read it even if it weren't) but I know what it says. The Khitai horsemen gave it to the Black Khan, as a sign of his authority to rule Samarkand in their name.

The writing on the tablet is nothing like flowing Persian, or angular Turkic runes; it's more like pictures, each character a complicated combination of strokes. That's the language the Khitai use. The same language that Crow drew in the dust last night, showing us what's written on this box she's looking for.

The same language I saw, picked out in gold leaf, on the box the white-robed man was carrying, as he broke the Teuton's sword.

Samarkand sits on a plateau, and once you're outside the city walls there's barely a hill between you and the wind that comes roaring in over a thousand miles of steppe. Soon I'm shivering too hard to walk a straight line. The view, though, almost makes it worthwhile—more and more light is creeping into the sky now, and from here you can see east for miles, over the plateau and the fields beyond (full of earth and stubble now, but they'll soon be dusted with green as the crops' first shoots come through). An irrigation canal, emerging from a stand of fruit trees, sparkles in the last of the moonlight. It feels like the whole earth is laid out just for me, in delicate pre-dawn shades of blue and grey.

It's beautiful enough to penetrate even the cold and hunger and fatigue. I pop the last milk curd into my mouth and suck it slowly, savouring it. I'm a little over halfway to the caravanserai now, but trudging over the frozen earth is wearing me out faster than I'd like. If this doesn't work out, if I go a few more days with barely any food, I might just have to lie down and not get up again. Kids turn up dead of hunger in the Maze all the time. They usually just chuck them into a midden-hole. No one cares. I have to account for every scrap of energy I use up. So my progress is slow, and I have plenty of time to think of all the holes in my plan.

Hole number one: doing this on my own is a mistake. Even if my hunch is on the money, this could end up being a two-person job. At least. What if I have to go back and tell the others that, and when we return our chance has gone? Or what if I try to do this myself anyway, and I mess up and get caught? We're not supposed to rip anyone off outside the city walls. The caravanbashi pay protection money to the ahdath—a lot more money than the beggar gangs do—and the ahdath, in return, come down like a ton of bricks on anyone who tries anything out here. If I'm caught, assuming the caravan guards let me live, Oleg won't.

Hole number two: whether this works or not, I'll be pushing it just to make it back to Samarkand without dropping of exhaustion and hunger. No way I'll be able to run any scams or pick any pockets today. If I come back empty-handed, it'll be the second day in a row I don't make quota. The tree again.

Hole number three: my conscience. I owe those two. They saved me from the *Teuton* for all the gods' sake. If I rip them off, living with myself is going to be very hard for a while. But then I think of what I was prepared to do a few hours ago: grovel to Nina, scrub some rich man's turds out of a chamberpot for the rest of my life. As long as there's a chance to—

"You there!"

I freeze, like a frightened rabbit, not a thought in my head. Because I know that voice.

There's a wooden fence, just off the road to my right. Inside the fence is a herd of the most beautiful horses I've seen in my life. Outside the fence, sitting astride another horse, is a burly man in rich robes. He's pointing in my direction, and his face is crimson as he bellows at the top of his lungs.

The Khwarezmian. The one whose purse I lifted yesterday. He's going to chase me on his horse and trample me into the ground and leave my broken body for dead—

But just as I'm about to bolt, I see it's not me he's yelling at. It's another man, one of his servants maybe, kneeling on the ground in front of him. The merchant is shouting something about the horses—I can't hear, exactly, but I think the servant didn't give them enough feed, or maybe too much. He hasn't noticed me at all. If I'd bolted, he probably would have, and I *would* have been run down.

Half a dozen Khitai horsemen are coming down the road from the city. Moving as casually as I can, I sidestep until they're between me and the Khwarezmian, blocking him from view. The Khitai are moving at a slow trot, looking at the horses in the field, and I can keep up with them easily.

I stare at the horsemen keeping me out of the Khwarezmian's line of sight. Mostly because I'm jealous of their hats and heavy riding coats. They look warm as hell, thick felt trimmed with furs, tiger and leopard and something else that I'm pretty sure is marten, and I hope that's not an omen.

Partly, thought, I'm just curious. You don't see Khitai around here all that much, even though they rule Samarkand and everywhere around it. They're nomads, and they mostly stay out of the cities, leave them alone as long as the tribute keeps coming. I speak Khitai pretty well, it's one of the common languages people in Samarkand use to talk to each other, but these guys are using a lot of technical horse words (what the hell is a 'fetlock'?) to describe this or that animal in the herd and I'm pretty much lost, although I can tell they're impressed.

I'm impressed myself. The horses you see in Samarkand belong to farmers, bringing their crops in for the markets. Bony, terrified of city sounds and smells, always ready to bite or to kick out at pickpocket-head-height and break your skull. These horses, though, are all silky manes and sleek coats over lean muscle. They must be the Ferghana horses Uthman told me about, the ones the Khwarezmian bought. They're from a valley somewhere out east, and they're supposed to be the best horses in the whole world. Half a dozen riders, more of the Khwarezmian's servants, patrol around the fence, checking on the herd.

Then we're past them and I let the horsemen go on ahead as I survey the caravanserai. It's four buildings, long ones with close-set half columns marching along the brick facades, each building making up one wall of the large central courtyard. There's only one gate, with a constant traffic of men and beasts. If what I'm looking for is in there, I'm in trouble. No way they're going to let someone like me through the gate; what possible reason would I have for being there, besides stealing stuff?

Fortunately, the caravanserai isn't big enough to hold everyone, and those from the caravan who didn't rate a room inside have set themselves up around the buildings in tents and yurts. A lot of Turks and Persians, a fair number from the Indian kingdoms to the South, some Arabs from the West, and a few Easterners with their straight black hair and upturned eyes, but I don't see—

A shout, from somewhere to my left, followed by a roar of laughter. Some of the laughter is female, the voice high and full of fierce joy. I've never heard the spearwoman laugh, but I'm sure as anything it's her.

There's a fight going on behind one of the tents. A circle of burning torches surrounds the two people going at it, and a looser circle of spectators surrounds the torches. The spearwoman is one of the fighters; the other is a lanky Indian with a bristling moustache. I shrink behind an empty tent and lean out cautiously to watch.

She's not using her spear this time. She and the Indian are unarmed as they circle around each other, eyes alive, looking for openings. Then they close in a blur of blows, striking with a vertical fist or the heel of a palm, blocking with forearm and shin. Just as quickly they separate and circle again. The crowd murmur appreciatively. They're obviously caravan guards, mercenaries, covered with road dust and toting all kinds of weapons. This isn't a real fight, these two are just sparring, testing their skill. Just as she did with the Teuton, the girl seems to be dancing more than fighting, her moves full of extravagant flourishes and heart-stopping grace.

Now the Indian goes into a deep lunge, fist snapping out at the girl's solar plexus. She leaps, and her feet kick out once, twice, three times while she's in midair. The third kick grazes the Indian's temple and he staggers sideways. The spearwoman lands on the ground, light as a feather. The Indian shakes his head to clear it and resumes his stance, grinning. The girl is grinning too. I feel a smile spread on my own face; it's that kind of a grin.

I look around for her friend, and see him sitting cross-legged by a campfire in front of a yurt. Her spear leans against the wall next to the entrance. There's a cooking pot over the campfire, and he must have been doing laundry because his long white robe is stretched out on the outside of the yurt, tucked between the ropes that hold the round felt wall together, and it steams as it dries. He's wearing a sleeveless tunic, despite the predawn cold; he's a skinny guy, and not tall, but I can see every single muscle on his arms, etched in the skin like they were carved out of wood. He's not wearing that cloth cap and his long black hair hangs loose on his shoulders as he pokes casually at the ashes with a stick.

I realize I've been spending a little too long looking at him. Heat rises into my face and I quickly look away, back at the woman. She and the Indian seem to have wrapped up the fight, and now they're comparing notes. She's showing him a feint-and-strike combination in slow motion.

I need to get moving now, while they're both outside. This is going to be tricky: there's a dozen yards of open ground to cross between me and the yurt. The guy has his back to me, but if the girl glances over here...I'm not going to get a better chance, though. I take a deep breath, expel it in a long low sigh and feel myself drop into the current.

The fatigue and hunger melt away. They'll be back, sooner rather than later, but right now I feel like I could sprint all the way back to China Gate and not break a sweat. I take off like an arrow for the yurt, and I could swear my feet only touch the ground once or twice before I'm crouching there. No one calls out, no one comes looking. Okay. Next.

The yurt is the steppe nomads' kind, a circular hut with a thick felt wall wrapped around a latticed wooden frame, and more felt draped on the conical roof. Some of them can be huge, more like palaces than tents, but this is a little one, for only two or three people. There's a hole in the very top of the roof, to let out the smoke from the fireplace inside, and since there's no back door, that's how I'll have to get in.

I press my foot into the wall of the yurt. With effort, I push the felt into the wooden lattice behind it with my toes. It's so thick I only make the barest dimple, but it's enough for a foothold. I take a deep breath and boost myself up as lightly as I can. The wall creaks as I put my weight on it, but I manage to reach the edge of the roof and scramble up and over it.

More creaking. I breathe shallowly, trying to spread my weight around as much as possible, and the noise subsides enough that I can creep up to the hole in the roof and peer inside, spread-eagled so I don't break through the frame and fall.

Light from the still-hidden sun dyes the clouds rose-petal pink. Right now, if anyone looks my way all they'll see is a dark shape against the slightly less dark felt of the yurt, but once the sun comes up, a casual glance will pick me out easy. I have to do this fast.

I bracket my eyes with my hands to block out the light and look down into the yurt. There's not much in there—a couple of narrow straw mattresses with cloth-wrapped bundles beside them, presumably the possessions of the spearwoman and her friend.

I lean out further, and there's a tiny creak from the wood beneath the felt. I freeze, but now I can see it—the black oblong the guy was wearing on his back. It's wood, lacquer shining in the light coming through the door, and it could well be a box. It could well be *the* box.

I judge the distance to the yurt's floor. There's no fire in the firepit—lucky—but still, if I drop straight down I stand a good chance of twisting an ankle. On the other hand, if I hold on to the edge of the hole and swing myself forward before I let go, I'll land on one of the mattresses, which should break my fall. Of course, I won't be able to make it back up, and I can't exactly stroll out the yurt's only doorway, but here's some more good news: near the back of the yurt there's a gap between the ground and the wall's wooden lattice. The felt wall outside the lattice hangs all the way to the ground, so I couldn't see the gap from the outside. It's easily big enough for me to squeeze through with the box without being seen. Carrying the thing will be a hassle, it's almost as long as I am tall, but if I get enough of a head start without being seen—

Beside me, almost too soft to hear, comes the sound of cloth tearing. I turn my head and see a shining steel blade sprouting from the felt roof, and before I can react it sweeps towards me, so sharp it parts the felt and the wood underneath like a fin through water. It opens up a long slash right across my stomach, then disappears as it's yanked back down inside.

Nothing happens for just barely a moment, that moment right after you slam your bare toes into a wall, just before the pain comes crashing in. Only in this case I'm waiting for my guts to fall out of the gaping hole in my belly and land in a steaming pile on the floor of the yurt.

Except they don't, and I have another moment to realize the blade didn't touch me—didn't even touch my clothes—before the roof gives way beneath me and I tumble to the ground in a shower of felt and splinters.

CHAPTER ELEVEN

When the Teuton slammed me to the ground yesterday I'd thought I was as winded as a person could possibly get, but lying on my back on the yurt's dirt floor I discover I was wrong. I stare up into the ragged patch of sky I can see through the hole I just fell through. After a few moments' struggle, I manage a thin wheeze that gets a trickle of air into my lungs.

"Are you all right?"

Someone is kneeling beside me, and as they speak (Khitai, they're speaking Khitai) they lean over me, cutting off the light from the sky. It's the guy. He's still sleeveless, and his loose hair hangs down around his face. He has cheekbones for *days*. Below my field of vision I feel his hand take mine, and his other hand circles my wrist, three fingers pressed against me where my heartbeat pulses.

I turn my head slightly to look at him directly, and behind him I see the girl, holding her spear at an angle so it doesn't poke through the roof. She's sliding the leather cover back over the point, which evidently is what she just used to almost cut me in half. She says something casually, without looking at me, in their own language, all liquid vowels and swooping tones.

The guy ignores her. "Can you sit up?" he asks me.

I'm breathing a little easier, although when I try to speak I only manage an embarrassing squeak. I try again. "I think so," I croak.

He helps me with a hand on the small of my back. I feel keenly how close he is; his shining black hair brushes my cheek. He turns his head to look at the girl. "Was that strictly necessary?" he asks.

"She was going to rip us off, Yu Hao," she says, as she takes her spear out of the yurt, angling the long shaft carefully so it doesn't hit the walls. She's speaking Khitai now too, with less of an accent than the guy. She has a deep voice for a girl, throaty and musical.

He looks around the yurt, at the thin mattresses and the two tiny bundles that must be all their possessions. Then he looks up at the gaping hole in the roof. "You did more damage than all our stuff is worth," he says mildly.

She shrugs as she steps back inside. "It's the principle."

"Well, that will be a comfort the next time it rains," says the guy, Yu Hao, still looking up at the hole.

"Jerk," says the girl. "Still, you have to admit it was pretty slick, right?" The toe of her felt boot gently prods my chest. "Didn't leave a scratch on her." She looks at me curiously. "What *were* you trying to rip off, anyway?"

I'm still groggy from the fall and I can't stop my gaze from flicking to the lacquered box leaning on the wall of the yurt. It's only for the tiniest fraction of an instant, but the guy sees it. He looks at me with interest. "You play?" he asks.

I have no idea what he means, and it must show in my face because he stands up and walks over to the box. The girl groans. "You had to do it, didn't you?" she says to me. Her eyes are bright and I realize how drunk she is, she's probably been drinking all night.

I stare at her in absolute confusion, then I see the guy is sitting down again, the box on his lap. The top of the box is studded with pegs at either end, with silken strings stretched between them. He shakes out his arms, and reaches down and plucks a string, the hollow tone reverberating through the yurt.

It's not a box at all. It's an instrument.

He plays. One hand hovers by the instrument's head, the other over the centre of its body. His fingers plucks the strings deliberately, and now a thumb slides up a vibrating string with a rasp, making the note swoop and slide. The notes sound alien, with different pitches and rhythms than the music you hear in the bazaars.

I let myself fall back and lie there, staring up at the sky again. I'm done. They're going to turn me over to the ahdath, and Uthman will let Oleg know that one of his pickpockets has been ripping off a caravan, and Oleg is going to leave me a scarred blind beggar for the rest of my short life, and it wasn't even over the right box.

The girl doesn't shout for the guards, though. She cocks her head as she looks down at me. She looks very tall from down here. "You don't play, do you?" she says. "Of course you don't. So what's your *damn it Yu Hao will you knock that off?*"

The melody stops. "I tuned it," says Yu Hao, sounding a little hurt.

"It's flat. It's *been* flat ever since Tun-Huang, and I've *told* you it was flat ever since Tun-Huang and it's *still flat*. Whoever sold you that thing screwed you hard." An elegant finger points down at me where I'm still lying on the ground. "*She* could tell you it's flat, and I'm going to go ahead and assume she's never seen a ch'in in her life."

Yu Hao looks at me. He doesn't look surprised at that "she", which means both of them are sharp enough to know I'm a girl. Too sharp to fast-talk, in other words. It's over.

"Perhaps introductions are in order. My surname is Yu and my personal name is Hao. My associate goes by various names, but she is most commonly known in the circles in which we move as *Ch'ih Hsüan-Feng.*" He thinks for a moment. "'Crimson Whirlwind'."

The girl wrinkles her nose. "It sounds crap in Khitai. Call me Red."

"Why?" I say. "You want to make friends before you turn me in?"

"We're not going to turn you in," says Red, exasperated. "We don't go around throwing little girls in jail, even if they are thieving shits."

"I'm not a 'little girl'," I snap. Anger gives me enough breath to struggle to my knees.

"Do you *want* me to turn you in or what—" Red snaps back, and

Yu Hao raises a placating hand.

"My associate and I are merely curious about your reason for coming here," he says. Red rolls her eyes but doesn't say anything.

I look at him and half a dozen lies pop into my head, arranged in order of plausibility, although none of them are what you'd call plausible. I pick one anyway. "I wanted to thank you," I say. "For saving me from the Teuton."

"The 'Teuton' would be Blondie from yesterday?" asks Red. "With the metal shirt?" I nod.

"That was nice of you," says Red. "You always thank people by crawling around on their roof before dawn, then? That a Samarkand thing?" I press my lips tight and glare at her. She may be beautiful and she may have saved my life, but she's kind of a jerk.

She sees she's not going to get anything more out of me. "Fine," she says, throwing up her hands, and strides out of the yurt.

Yu Hao indicates the back of the yurt, where the wall's wooden lattice doesn't quite reach the floor. "You can get out through here, I think," he says politely. "Someone will notice the hole in the roof presently, and you had better not be here when they do." He looks out the door and raises his voice a little. "When they ask, I will tell them that my associate did it while drunk. Which is, technically, the truth."

"Just a minute, Yu Hao," Red calls from outside the yurt. "You're not sending her out like that. Look at her, she won't make it halfway back to the city wall."

I look out the entrance. From here I can see the cooking pot hanging from a low frame over the fire. Red kneels beside it, holding a wooden bowl. "I can make it," I say.

She shoots me an amused glance. "Yeah," she says, "maybe you can, you're a tough little bitch. But you're not leaving here without something in your stomach." She takes the lid off the pot, releasing a flood of fragrant steam. It's rice, it smells so *good*, and saliva floods my mouth as Red scoops a generous helping out of the pot into the bowl with a dented iron ladle.

"No charity," I say, although it costs me all the willpower I have.

"This is not charity," says Red. "This is hospitality. You're our guest." She holds my gaze, and finally I nod. It still feels like charity, but it's enough of an excuse that I can't fight the hunger anymore.

Red nods too, and sets the bowl aside. Then she plunges her hands into the still-smoking ashes of the fire. I wince in sympathy, but she doesn't seem to feel a thing. Her hands emerge covered with fine grey ash and clutching something, a large lump of baked clay.

Am I supposed to eat that? My question is answered when she strikes the clay with the heel of her palm, the blow almost too fast to see. The lump quivers, then neatly cracks in two. It's hollow, and I'd thought the smell from the pot was good but the aroma that now rises from inside the clay shell just about makes me weep.

"Beggar's Chicken," says Red, grinning at me, and lays couple of chunks of juicy white flesh onto the rice in the bowl. She rises to her feet in a single smooth motion, more graceful than a dancer in a parade. Back into the yurt, she presents the bowl to me, cradling it in her cupped hands. "Appropriate, yes?"

"I'm not a beggar," I say fiercely, and although I think I'm going to faint from the smell, I hold her gaze until she laughs her throaty laugh and says "Fair enough," and only then do I take the bowl.

I force myself to take small bites and wait between each one, so I don't overwhelm my shrunken stomach. Red and Yu Hao don't rush me, they step out of the yurt and leave me to it.

For a while, the bowl of chicken and rice is my entire universe. From far away, I hear raised voices; Red arguing with someone about the hole in the roof, turning them away. I don't even raise my head, just measure out the mouthfuls so I don't get sick and waste any by throwing it up.

When it's more than halfway done and I come up for air, the idea is there, sitting in the back of my head. I shoo it away, like a horsefly, but like a horsefly it just circles right around and bites me again. I can't dismiss it, and I know the reason. I ought to know, it's the only thing I own, the only thing I ever owned. My pride.

Because this *is* charity. Red may have called it hospitality, and hospitality to guests is such a huge deal in Samarkand that it got me eating. But it's charity, and if I take charity I might as well be one of Nina's beggars, being led from orphanage to street corner and back again every day, scarred empty sockets where my eyes used to be.

I don't want these two thinking of me like that, as just another ragged beggar at a caravan stop. Particularly, if I'm being honest with myself, Yu Hao. I steal a glance at him as he talks to Red in the doorway, absently brushing his long hair behind his ear as he makes some point or other.

This idea is a way around all of that—except it's stupid. It's more dangerous than the idea (the *bad* idea) that brought me out here in the first place. And on top of that, it goes against the oath. Going through with this would mean turning my back on the Martens. *You're not a Marten*, Masoud whispers in my head, and more than almost anything I don't want to prove him right.

But there's something else. Hunger, like I've felt every day since forever, brings your horizon closer. While you're hustling for your next meal, the future and all its unknowns are over that horizon, distant and unreal. Now, though, I'm as full as I've been for weeks, and I can see a lot further. Because Masoud *was* right about something—I won't be a Marten for long no matter what. Unless I make thief. But I'm not good enough a climber for that. Unless...

Red and Yu Hao are looking at me. I run my finger around the inside of the bowl to collect the last few fat white grains of rice. I know I'm stalling for time.

"You enjoyed your meal?" Yu Hao asks politely. He has the manners of a scholar (and it occurs to me how out of place that is in a Silk Road caravan guard), but it's clearly a dismissal.

"Just a second, Yu Hao," says Red. She's looking at me with her brown eyes, piercing but not unkind. For a moment I believe she can see a little of the turmoil inside me.

No, I suddenly decide. I'm not going to say anything. I'm going to walk back to the city, giving thanks with every step I take that I'm getting out of this with my skin intact. I feel a sudden rush of relief; I can't believe how close I came to crossing Oleg—

And then my memory spits up that kid, burned and whimpering in his bed, maybe already getting sick. Nina's never going to pay for a doctor. He'll spend the rest of his life a beggar, lying on a street corner in the cold wind as his fever rages and Nina and Oleg use his slow death to milk a few coins out of charitable strangers, and when he finally goes under, he'll end up in a midden-hole.

Anger flares inside me. No, not anger. This is pure, focused *rage*. And suddenly the thought of crossing Oleg and Nina and their new friend Crow fills me not with fear but something fierce and vicious and almost like joy.

"I thought it was something else," I say. I nod at Yu Hao's instrument. "That. I thought it was...something else." Even now I've decided, I struggle to get the words out.

"Namely?" he says, polite but indifferent.

"Crow told Oleg to have the Martens look for a box," I say. And then the words come gushing out. "No quota for the pickpocket who finds it. No muscle for the corners either, so we're going to look like punks, so it must be something good. I thought that was it."

They look at each other. "All right," says Yu Hao finally, "why don't you start with who 'Crow'—"

"—And 'Oleg'—" adds Red.

"—And 'the Martens' are," he finishes, "and we'll go from there."

When I'm done, my throat is dry and my head is pounding and the sun is well up in the sky outside. I should be filled with shame, and I am, but strangely I also feel a lot better.

Red is looking at me, both eyebrows raised sky-high. Yu Hao is staring at nothing. He's put his robe back on, disappointingly.

"What?" I say.

"I don't think we learned your name," says Yu Hao.

"Darya," I say. It feels good to tell him.

"Darya. This 'Crow'," says Yu Hao slowly, "can you describe her?"

I shrug. "Not that tall, black leathers, two swords—"

"Hair?" says Red.

"Like yours. Black. Shorter."

"Skin?" says Yu Hao.

I shrug again. "Like yours too, maybe? More of a road tan?"

"And this box she wanted," Yu Hao continues, leaning forward. "Do you remember what was on it, Darya? What she wrote?"

"I don't read Khitai," I say. I don't want to admit I don't read at all. Yu Hao has 'scholar' written all over him—although I've never seen a scholar with muscles like that—and I'm not about to tell him I'm an unlettered street rat before I absolutely have to. Not that he hasn't probably guessed.

"It wouldn't have been Khitai," he says, "it would have been Chinese."

I shrug. "Same thing, right?" He winces. "Actually—"

"Save it, Yu Hao," says Red. "Anything you can remember, Darya." She points to the dirt floor of the yurt.

I look at the dirt, wrinkling my forehead. I remember the swift strokes Crow made with the point of her sabre. I can't remember every single one, but each picture broke down into a few smaller ones and if I remember enough of those—

I'm halfway through the second one when Yu Hao puts his hand on mine to stop me. "Allow me," he says, and sketches in the dust below my own writing, his strokes deft and precise:

陰氳真經

I run my finger over what he's written. "Could be. Yeah. I think so—*ow!*"

That last because Red has whirled around, her hair-beads clicking as they whip around her head, and her foot has swept out and across the dirt in front of me, knocking my hand aside and wiping the writing away.

"*Ow.*" I squeeze my stinging fingers in my armpit and glare up at her, but she's not looking at me. She's looking out the yurt's entrance, checking if anyone saw.

"Are you all right?" asks Yu Hao. I have his complete attention now, not just the abstract curiosity he was showing before. His high-cheekboned face is intent, and his eyes are full of something like respect. I could get used to that look.

I flex my stinging fingers. "I guess." I'm way better than all right, though. I was on the money about this—whatever the box is, they want it too. They're even a little bit scared of it. Anything important enough to be scary is important enough to be worth money, in my experience, and whenever greed and fear are in the ring, my money is on greed every time.

"Why are you telling us this?" asks Red, still scanning the caravanserai's grounds outside of the yurt.

Right to the point, then. "Me and my friends"—'friends' is pushing it but I don't know how to say *backstabbing creeps* in Khitai— "we're supposed to find this box for Crow, like I told you." Here it comes. I take a deep breath and force the words out; they aren't the only ones who are scared.

"I could find it for you, instead."

There's a pause while the two of them digest this. "What," says Red finally, "just give it to us? Just show up here with the *Yin*—" She catches herself before she finishes whatever she was going to say. "With this box under your arm, just like that?"

I shake my head. "I can't promise that. If my friends find it first, give it to Crow, there's nothing I can do. But I can tell you what we find out, how close we are. Help you find it yourself."

"Interesting," says Yu Hao.

Red doesn't seem to find it interesting. "So this is payback? For helping you out with Blondie yesterday? You're clearing a debt? Because—"

I shake my head. "Not just that. I do this, you'll owe *me*."

"This is worth more than your life, is what you're saying," she says.

My eyes meet hers. "I'm a Samarkand pickpocket. How much do you think my life is worth?", and she can't stop her lips quirking in a grin. I think they're going for it. I feel dizzy, like I'm standing on the edge of something high, looking down.

Yu Hao turns to me. "All right. For the sake of argument. What will we owe you, exactly?"

"Yesterday," I say. "What you did. I want to learn how."

"You want to fight?" asks Red, and I shake my head.

"I don't care about fighting," I say. "I want to..."

The Khitai word for *climb* escapes me. The hunger is gone, fully gone for the first time in weeks, but in its place is bone-deep fatigue, it's like being submerged in blood-warm water, and the word drifts away before I can grasp it. And I don't really want to 'climb', anyway. I want to do what they do. I want to—

—and the right word comes to me after all. I say:

"I want to fly."

CHAPTER TWELVE

The words hang in the air for a moment, and just for that moment it feels like I've jumped off the minaret of the Old Mosque—I'm weightless, my stomach floating up into my throat. Red says something to Yu Hao, two dismissive syllables. Yu Hao just holds up a hand. He's thinking.

Red wasn't expecting this. Her head snaps around and she stares at him, says something low and emphatic. Yu Hao replies with a single syllable. Red says something else. Yu Hao replies calmly, but Red talks right over him, gesticulating with her slender hands as she speaks. The word *ch'ing-kung* keeps coming up. I don't understand that or any other word she's using, but I know exactly what she's saying anyway, because someone's been saying the same thing to or about me my whole life—I don't have what it takes. Time spent on me is time wasted. I stare at the ground and clench my teeth.

After Red winds down, Yu Hao doesn't say anything for a while. He looks at the floor, his chin in his hand. Red nods and folds her arms, like she's just scored a point. It's hard not to hate her right now. If they send me away, after all this...

Finally Yu Hao looks up at me. "I think we may have an agreement."

Red's jaw drops. Then she explodes. She talks so fast I probably couldn't have understood her even if I did speak their language. She stands over Yu Hao, and she's jabbing a finger over and over at me as she speaks but it's him she's looking at. She's not mad at me, I get that. She thinks Yu Hao is screwing up somehow, by doing this.

When she's done, she crosses her arms and glares at the dirt floor while Yu Hao raises an admonishing finger to me. "Understand that I make no promises. Not everyone has the ability, regardless of training."

I nod. "Sure, fine. Just teach me."

The finger stays up. "Another thing. Where we come from, to 'teach', to take on a student formally, is not a light matter. I will not be your 'teacher'. This is a trade. Provide us information on the...box. In exchange, I will help you as much as I can."

"Yeah, fine, okay." Whatever hair he's splitting to make himself feel better about this, it's meaningless to me. Red is doing a slow burn as she watches us. She looks like she's going to draw breath for another tirade, then suddenly she throws up her hands and turns her back to us, stalks out of the yurt. Well, screw her.

"An exchange," says Yu Hao again. "We expect information, every time you come to train."

"I *said* yes." As ever, my mind is going over escape routes, making sure I'm not being backed into a corner. I don't think I am. If I don't like what Yu Hao has to say, I can just walk away. He won't find me in Samarkand, and in a week or two he'll sign up with another caravan and I'll never see him again. And it's not like he said how good the information has to be.

"So," I say, "when do we get started? I can—"

"Now," says Yu Hao. He stands. "Up, please."

I struggle to my feet, the chicken and rice weighing down my belly pleasantly. I stand there as he strolls in a circle around me, looking me over. Then without warning his foot shoots out and knocks my left foot aside. I stagger, lopsided, and he takes the opportunity to kick my other foot out. My arms fly out to the sides as I try to stay upright. Yu Hao's hand bears down on my shoulder. I feel its warmth through my kameez, but the thrill from this unexpected contact is quickly eclipsed as he forces my torso down until my thighs are parallel to the floor of the yurt.

The muscles of my legs begin burning almost immediately. "Hey!" I protest.

"Horse stance," Yu Hao says, and facing me he takes the same stance, although a lot more easily than I did. I've never ridden a horse, but I suppose this is what it might feel like. I clench my teeth and try to pay attention. I can take a little pain, if it means being able to move like he does. "Now," says Yu Hao, "breathe."

"I am."

"Like this." He demonstrates, breathing through his nose, slow and deep, in a particular rhythm. Again, I try to copy him, but evidently I'm not doing it right, because he raises that finger again. Then he reaches down and puts his hand on his stomach just below his navel. "Into here," he says, "breathe into here," and then something I don't understand, "*tan-t'ien.*"

I try again, feeling the breath in my stomach muscles. "Good," says Yu Hao. "Keep it up."

I struggle with the rhythm for a moment, then something clicks and suddenly it's the most natural thing in the world. Warmth spreads through my torso from the place Yu Hao called the tan-t'ien. The pain in my thigh muscles recedes until it's almost bearable. With surprise, I realize I'm in the current, it's pulling me along.

He must see something in my face, because he says "What is it?"

"Current," I say, without really thinking, absorbed in the sensation.

He cocks his head, his shining hair following the motion, brushing the shoulder of his robe. "Explain."

So I explain, as best I can, which is hard. I've never really thought about it in words, especially not Khitai words. I talk about the feeling of something surging under my skin, like blood but different, more potent, and the answering surge of the world outside me. How if I can get them in sync, everything becomes clear. How I see what I have to do, or not do, to glide through it all...

I trail off when I see how Yu Hao is looking at me. There's a keen light in his eyes that wasn't there before. "*Wu-wei*," he says softly. Not having any idea what that means, I say nothing.

He purses his lips, taps them with a raised finger. Then he seems to make up his mind about something. Still facing me in horse stance, he brings his hands up to chest height, palms horizontal and facing each other, slightly curved like he's holding a ball by the top and bottom. "Follow. Like a mirror."

I bring up my own hands. He reaches out and takes my wrists, adjusting their position minutely before resuming his stance. My skin tingles from his touch, but I don't have time to dwell on it because now he reverses his palms and pushes one up and the other down, like he's keeping earth and sky apart with his hands. Then he reverses the motion, bringing his hands together like he's holding that ball again, and turns it over before pushing his hands apart again. I copy all this as best as I can.

Am I really learning something here? Or is this all just a scam? Excitement and suspicion chase each other around the inside of my skull, and then the pain in my legs flares up again and I force myself to concentrate on my breathing, to keep everything at a distance.

Gradually I realize that although the ball I'm holding is made of nothing but imagination and air, it's giving off a gentle heat that makes my hands tingle. The tingling spreads through my body, up my arms and down through my torso. Before now, when I've been in the current, it's always been just a vague sense of movement and rhythm, but this warmth seems to follow set paths within me, like rainwater coursing through the canals outside the city wall. And as it flows it seems to dig those channels a little deeper, until my body feels awash with—

"Enough." Yu Hao is standing in front of me, bending at the waist slightly to peer into my face. "Darya? Enough." I shake my head to clear it. My arms feel weird, floaty. I stand up straight and topple forward on numb legs, right into Yu Hao's arms.

Well, this is embarrassing.

He lowers me neatly to one of the straw mattresses. I wonder if it's his. I'd expected him to smell like a scholar, like chalk and ink and paper. Instead it's sweat, and leather, and road dust. I can't help breathing it in a little bit, and immediately wonder if he caught me doing it. His touch is delicate, but I can feel the muscles of his arm braced under my back; with those arms he could have caught me if I'd fallen off a two-storey building. As he lays me down I get a flash of sunlight in my face, coming through the hole Red sliced in the yurt's roof.

The sun is up that high already? How much time have I let go by without knowing? I realize I don't care. Yu Hao looks distant, like he's turning something big and complicated over in his head. He's still holding me.

Finally I clear my throat. It takes him a second to come back to himself, then his eyes widen and he blushes, actually *blushes*. He quickly lets go and steps back from the mattress.

"Forgive me." It's the first time I've seen him rattled at all. "I did not mean to—" He takes a deep breath, and once he's exhaled he's back in control of himself.

"Are we done?" I ask. Despite the fatigue in my butt and thighs, I feel...well, I feel *good*, for the first time in I don't know how long. Whatever it is we've been doing, I could stand to do a little more.

"Not yet," he says. "Lie down."

"I am."

"Not like that," he says, and drops smoothly to the floor next to the mattress. He lies on his side, arm tucked under him in a certain way.

"I don't see—" But he raises a finger, heading off my objection. "Okay, fine," I mutter, and, still irritated, I do my best to copy him.

"Now," he says, "breathe."

I nod and draw breath, but he shakes his head again. "Not like before. Like this." He demonstrates; it's almost the same pattern of breaths as before, but with a slight twist that makes it hard for me to copy him at first. He pats his stomach below his navel. "More in here. Fill the tan-t'ien first, and everything else follows." I nod and concentrate on following his lead, and it doesn't feel like I've got it, but Yu Hao nods and in an eyeblink he's on his feet again. "Keep breathing." He turns to leave.

A final question forces its way out of my lips. "Why? How is this helping?"

He turns back to me, that finger raised once again, then he reconsiders. He bends at the waist, hands clasped behind his back, and looks at me. "*Kung fu*," is all he says, and then he's gone.

I lie there, knowing there's no way I'll be able to get to sleep now, with questions chasing themselves around the inside of my head. "What the hell is 'kung fu'?" I mutter, and then, with nothing better to do, I begin to breathe through my nose, into my tan-t'ien, slowly, over and over.

CHAPTER THIRTEEN

I t feels like only a moment later that my eyes snap open, but the evening light slanting into the yurt tells me I've slept most of the day. Yu Hao and Red are nowhere to be seen. I'll have to run like hell if I want to get back to the warehouse by sundown. Not to mention I'll be coming back empty-handed for the second time in two days.

And for some reason, none of that bothers me. For weeks I've been lost in a fog of hunger and fatigue, groping through it clumsily every time I wanted to string two thoughts together. Now the fog has blown away, and as I look around the yurt, every detail seems to jump out at me with crystal clarity. It's not just a bowl of rice and a few hours' sleep that did that. What's going on?

I tease the doorway's felt curtain aside. No sign of Red or Yu Hao out there, either.

Even if they haven't told the guards about me, it's still not a great idea for a street rat to be skulking around a caravanserai. I lift the felt wall at the back of the yurt and slip out through the gap under the lattice, and head for the road, being careful when I pass the herd of Ferghana horses not to bump into the Khwarezmian. I walk more briskly, then break into an easy, loping run, eating up the distance to the city, and I find myself falling naturally into the breath-pattern Yu Hao taught me as we stood there in the yurt, feeling it in my stomach again, flooding my body with air. I feel like I could run like this forever, and when I reach China Gate with the sun still a hand's breadth above the city walls, I'm hardly even out of breath.

I'm halfway to the warehouse, dodging through the evening crowd outside the Jewellers' Souk, when I see it. A donkey loaded with thick rolls of wool is lumbering towards a merchant's stall laid out with trinkets of polished bronze. The donkey's handler is trying to rein it back but it's on a collision course with the stall. I can see the whole scene as if it were frozen in time, like a picture knotted into the weave of a carpet.

I run faster, the air scorching my lungs, and reach the stall just before the donkey does. As I run past, without breaking stride, I reach out and pluck a copper disc from the goods laid out there. The merchant sees me out of the corner of his eye, and he's smart enough to turn his head to check if anything's missing from his stock. Right then, though, the donkey clips the edge of the stall, making the whole structure shake and knocking the merchandise all askew. The donkey lumbers on obliviously, its handler grimacing as he continues to wrestle with its bridle, and the merchant freezes for a moment, trying to account for everything...and in that moment, I'm gone.

This time yesterday, running for the warehouse, I was staggering like a drunk, having to stop and suck air before I could goad my legs into moving again. Today, even after running all the way from the caravanserai, my feet pound the bricks with a steady rhythm, my lungs barely ache, and, clutching the copper disc and reliving how I lifted it, I even have the breath to laugh.

I'll reach the warehouse with time to spare. So I duck into a side alley that twists and turns and spits me out onto the Street of the Pepper-Sellers, just a few streets over from the warehouse.

Pepper-Sellers is where the Martens' thieves and muscle hang out. They share a house here, a squat really, a falling-down old one-storey shell. Judging from its size, each of their rooms can't be much bigger than one of our cots, but every runner and pickpocket dreams of making it here.

A mix of thieves and muscle are hanging out in the doorway. They've got a dice game going, and a little knot of pickpockets hang back and watch. All the actual pepper-sellers are at the other end of the street, nearer the market, but there are a few stalls selling street food here. I see thick yakhni stew steaming in a pot, and for once it doesn't make my stomach cramp with hunger.

Farid is at one of the stalls. I slow down as I approach, knowing how red-faced I must look, and wipe some of the sweat off my stubbled scalp; I wish I'd taken a minute around the corner to get myself together, but too late now.

I slow down even more as I see he's buying a cup of rosewater jūlāb. I doubt it's for himself, and sure enough, he crosses the street to where a group of girls stand in a doorway. One of them, a pretty one in a headscarf and a servant's smock that doesn't do much to hide her curves, steps forward to accept it while her sidekicks giggle. I change course, hoping to put the yakhni stall between me and them, but it's too late, he's seen me.

"Darya," he calls, and beckons me with a nod. Any other time I wouldn't mind that at all, but now my feet drag as I cross the street towards them. Farid gives the cup to the girl and she presses up against him for a moment. He gives her his easy grin, looking down at her and murmuring something as she tilts her head to hear, showing off the graceful curve of her neck.

I imagine being where she is, being that close to him. I could lean my whole weight against him and he wouldn't give an inch, not built like he is. Close enough to smell, too. The guys in the pickpockets' dorm just stink of sweat and dirt, but Farid prays five times a day and washes each time; I bet he smells great.

The girl stands on tiptoe to whisper her reply into his ear. Her friends are still giggling, and the sound sets my teeth on edge. They're serving girls from some rich man's house, maybe even from the Khan's palace—they're dressed well enough for it. Farid's girl's headscarf is a beautiful Persian weave, colours as vivid as the day they were dyed. Maybe Farid stole it for her, or even bought it himself. I imagine him giving a scarf like that to me...then I shut that line of thought down *hard*, because it's never going to happen.

Not that I couldn't get Farid into bed, if I wanted to. From what I've heard, he's got about as much self-control in that area as any other guy. But if I did, it would all be over. All the thieves listen to Farid, and if you want in you'd better hope he backs you. He'd back a girl, maybe, but there is no way in hell he'd back a girl he's slept with.

Because for guys, sex is something you *do*, but for girls—in guys' eyes, that is—it's something you *are*. And once they see you that way, that's *all* you are. The closest I could get to the thieves after that would be as a girlfriend, arm candy like Headscarf over there.

All this goes through my head in the time it takes me to cross the street, and when I reach Farid and the girls, I'm surprised at how wound-up and angry I am. I've always understood all this, but never really thought about it before; thinking, with no sleep and no food in your belly, is like threading beads on a string with shaking hands. Now, though, it strikes me with full force just how un*fair* it all is.

I tell myself to cut it out; if I got angry over everything in my life that was unfair, my head would have burst years ago. Fair and unfair are for people who know where their next meal is coming from. For the rest of us, there's only true and not. But it still hurts.

Farid raises a hand as I approach. "Darya."

Headscarf raises an eyebrow. "'Darya'? This is her?" They've been talking about me. Fantastic.

Farid nods. "Darya's the best pickpocket we've got. Good lifter, good dodger, good eye for loot. Darya, this is Mahnaz."

I arrange my face into what I hope looks like a smile. Literally any other time, Farid saying all that would put a foot-wide grin on my face, but all I can hear is what it sounds like to Headscarf. I'm a street rat. A pickpocket. A parasite.

"*This* is her." She looks me up and down. Not just curves but big eyes, full lips, delicately pointed chin. Her clothes would be drab by some people's standards I suppose, but they're untorn and freshly washed. My clothes are so worn they're colourless, or rather the same colour as everything else in Samarkand—brick dust and mud. Great for blending in, not being noticed. They don't save me here though. "This is a *girl*," she says with exaggerated doubtfulness. One of her flunkies gives a high pitched giggle.

"Mahnaz is a house slave, for the Inalids." I've heard of them, of course. One of the biggest trading clans for miles. Houses and warehouses all over Samarkand. Even their slaves are somebodies. As opposed to me.

Mahnaz curls her lip ever so slightly as she takes in the bruises, the fresh scabs, the scraped-up cheekbones. "What did you call her, a 'lifter'?" Her eyes meet mine and her sneer turns into a smirk. "She looks like a street rat." As if on cue, her girls all chime in.

"She *does* look like a rat. A shaved rat."

"*Ugh.*"

"I've seen rats *bigger* than her."

I remember when I made it out of the runners, became a pickpocket. I remember my first night in the warehouse loft, sleeping in my own cot instead of on the orphanage floor. It was winter and the loft was frozen solid but I hadn't even noticed, not with the pride glowing in my belly like a hot coal.

I should keep my mouth shut, of course. That would be the smart play— "At least I'm not a house slave. Cleaning the shit out of rich men's chamberpots all day."

"Darya—" says Farid.

Mahnaz turns to her friends with a can-you-believe-this expression, then back to me. "I may have emptied a few chamberpots but at least I don't *smell* like I *sleep* in one."

I manage to hold her gaze but I can't help the blood rushing to my face. Of course I don't have a comeback. I've barely even talked to other girls—unless Nina counts—let alone trade insults. They probably sit around practicing their snark on each other over breakfast every day. Must be nice. I've never even had breakfast.

My hand bunches into a fist. I can get in a good hard shot to her nose, no trouble. After that, the fight's hers—she's bigger, and well fed, and she can slap me stupid. But I can bloody up those good looks some. She can't make me look any worse. So I win.

Farid steps in before I can take the shot, though. "I'll see you later, yeah?" It's a dismissal, but he's clearly only doing it to save me from her verbal mauling. She gives me a lazy smile and Farid a kiss on the cheek, and off she goes with her friends, who glance at me as they pass like I'm a fresh dog turd they just missed stepping in.

"Mahnaz is okay, really," says Farid.

"I bet," I say.

Farid lowers his voice. "Any luck with the box?"

I don't trust myself to speak. Instead I just shake my head, trying to look serious. All I feel is shame at having backed down with his girlfriend just now. Shame, and something else, that's been growing in my chest all the way from the caravanserai. Guilt. I can make my peace with selling out the rest of the Martens—maybe—but Farid...

"The thieves neither," he says. A couple of the Martens' muscle are leaning against the wall a few yards away. Farid pitches his voice low so they won't overhear. "Oleg's had the word out since last night, and we've got a couple of leads. Fences, black-marketeers. We've been hitting them all day. Working in broad daylight, it's nuts. But Crow wants that box, like, yesterday." He's as close to me as he was to his girlfriend. He does, indeed, smell great.

"Who is she?" I ask, just to keep him that close, keep the conversation going.

He shrugs. "Don't know. She's from the East, though, like this box is. I know she didn't come in a caravan, though. Rode into Samarkand alone." I raise my eyebrows. All the great empires that used to keep the Silk Road safe fell ages ago, and riding alone these days, with all the bandits and slavers out there, is suicide. "Maybe she had connections here, they pointed her at Oleg, maybe they just bumped into each other, but either way, he told her he'd find it. Find one box, in all of Samarkand."

"White cat in a snowstorm," I say. Real original. Nice going, Darya.

Farid just nods, though. "And staking the Martens' rep on it...I don't know what Oleg's thinking."

If word got to Oleg he was talking like this, it would not be good news for Farid. Thinking of that makes the guilt flare up higher. I tell myself I'm not really crossing Farid in this, just Oleg and Nina, and maybe that's even true, but it doesn't feel like it.

Why am I even doing this? Why not go to Nina like I was planning, get myself sold off? Depending on the household I end up in, it might not be so bad. Mahnaz's clique hasn't missed any meals lately; there's flesh on their bones, no dark circles under their eyes. I could even hook up with someone like Farid. Why not?

No. I know why not. Because however much I hate myself now for selling out the Martens, it's nothing next to what I'd feel if I sold out myself. I feel like I should say something, but I only manage a weak "Anything I can do?" Inane.

But Farid nods seriously. "Actually, yeah. We're hitting the next guy on the list tonight, some Kyrgyz fur-trader who fences on the side. We need a lookout. You up?"

When I was four, just before Nina took over the orphanage, the Khan threw a big party in Samarkand, I forget why. One of the attractions was a display of coloured fire from the East, and Maryam took us onto the orphanage roof to watch those sparkling flowers bloom in the night sky. Now it's like they're blooming all over again, inside my chest. A lookout job. A lookout job is what you do when they're grooming you for the thieves.

"Masoud..." I say, a little weakly. He's the one who always gets these jobs, being Nina's favourite and anointed next leader of the thieves and all.

Farid shrugs. "He's busy. This fence isn't the only one we're hitting tonight, we're busy as hell. And they tell me you want to make thief." I just barely trust myself enough to nod. He's going to back me. He's—and then I see the doubt in his eyes, and inside me the fire-flowers wilt and die.

"The reason I wanted you to meet Mahnaz," he says, "is she can get you work, maybe. She runs a crew of slaves, they go all over the city, wherever the Inalids need them. I asked her; she said she could put a word in for you." He gives me a tight smile. "Good deal, right? No climbing around in the middle of the night, anyway. No creeping over rooftops—"

"Right," I say, just to say something, just to get Farid to stop talking. I see him in bed with Mahnaz, asking her to do poor scrawny Darya a favour, get her to stop daydreaming, stop pretending she could be a thief. He's not gloating about this, like Masoud would. He's doing this because he cares about me. That hurts a thousand times worse.

He looks like he's about to say something else, but then—mercifully—he glances over his shoulder; the dice game is packing up and the Martens are heading for the alley that leads to the warehouse. "We need to get going. We can talk about it later, Darya, okay?"

"Sure," I whisper as I follow him, glad he can't see my face. The last of the fire-flowers dies inside me, leaving nothing in my heart but wet ashes.

It only occurs to me as I step into the warehouse to look at the thing I snatched in the Jewellers' Souk. I take it from one of the pockets sewn into the inside of my kameez. It's a bronze disc, inset with smaller discs that bristle with small brass hooks. It's an astrolabe, the kind the caravanbashi use to navigate by the stars. A good one is worth its weight in gold. This isn't a good one—the casting is rough, the markings are scratched carelessly into the bronze. It's a crappy knockoff made by a scam-artist; try to navigate with this and you'd point yourself at Kashgar and end up in Constantinople.

Still, it's worth more than anything I've lifted in a month, besides the Khwarezmian's purse. Yesterday I would have shoved it in Nina's face with glee; right now, I could toss it into a midden-hole instead for all I care.

Which is fine, because when Farid and I reach the warehouse's small front room, Nina's not even there. Instead, a small pile of coins and brassware, clearly the pickpockets' take for the day, sits on the low table in front of Nina's empty cushion.

"Where is she?" I ask, staring.

Farid doesn't look at me. "She's been with Oleg all day," he says. There's an edge to his voice. "Just leave your take here and let's go." I look at the astrolabe in my hand. I should be getting at least two days off for this.

"Come on, Darya," says Farid, heading into the warehouse, and that edge to his voice is even sharper. I think of his tight smile earlier. Farid is usually unflappable, but today he's wound up tight. What is going on? I hesitate, then before I can reconsider I stuff the astrolabe back in my kameez. Screw Nina, and Oleg, and Crow, and Mahnaz, and everyone else. I hurry after Farid.

At the back of the warehouse we catch up to Farouz, another pickpocket. He came up from the runners just before the kid who got the poker yesterday. He glances at me and just as quickly looks away—he might be a little turd but he's figured I'm not going to be in the pickpockets much longer, and there's no point in showing me any respect. As he turns away I see he's got a box tucked under his arm, and my heart lurches. Is this the one Crow's looking for? Is my deal with Yu Hao over, almost before it's begun?

But the writing on Farouz's box is Persian, so it probably came to Samarkand from the wrong direction entirely. Farouz knows it too, unless he's entirely stupid. He probably just goofed off the entire day, and grabbed the first likely-looking thing he could from some street stall or poorly-guarded warehouse. From the way he's holding it, I'm not sure there's even anything inside it. Any other day, if a pickpocket's day's takings amounted to an empty box he'd get the tree, no question. Big mistake of Oleg's, making such a big deal out of this.

It looks like Farouz isn't the only one who had that idea, either. There's a small pile of boxes under the dead tree's twisted branches. Not just boxes, either—I see leather wallets, even a couple of cloth sacks. Farouz places his Persian box carefully on top of the pile and retreats to the wall with the rest of the pickpockets. Someone got the poker yesterday, so we're probably safe today, but still we keep our distance from the hot coals in the brazier.

The door of the shack swings open. It's Crow, those swords at her back again. She doesn't say a word, just stalks slowly around the pile. The Martens shrink away as she passes. Oleg follows her, and when we see him more than one pickpocket flinches. We've all seen Oleg when he's not at his best—drunk and bellowing with rage like an animal, or passed out in a puddle of piss and vomit. We've never seen him like this before.

His skin is an ashy grey, and hangs in ripples from his belly. Can he have lost that much weight in a day? His eyes are so bloodshot they seem solid red, and his lips hang slack, a string of drool swinging from the bottom one like a pendulum. He hardly seems to see us as he looks around the courtyard. He coughs, sudden and explosive, and a smell tints the air, the same smell I got off his breath the day before. Like something dead, left out in the sun in high summer. Nina is at his side, guiding him into the courtyard with one wizened hand on the small of his massive back. She doesn't look at us either—just at Crow, her eyes bright with hate.

Crow doesn't say a word. With a whisper one of her big sabres is in her hand. She picks through the boxes and bags with the tip of the sword, sending them tumbling. Then just as quickly the sword is back in its scabbard on her back again, and she reaches for the brazier. I see the nails of her road-tanned hand are purplish, discoloured by bruises in the flesh beneath.

I want to yell *Hey, that's hot*, but I struggle to draw breath; Crow's presence seems to suck all the air out of the courtyard. I wince as she grips the edge of the brazier and a curl of smoke drifts up from her fingers. Nothing registers on her face at all. Then she tips the brazier over and hot coals spill out in a torrent, flaring and sparking as they hit the ground, landing all over the pile of bags and boxes.

The cloth bags go up first, bathing us in momentary warmth. The boxes take longer, black fingers of char creeping over the wood as flames lick at it. From its cage, Oleg's marten screeches as the fire takes hold.

"What are you *doing?*" shrieks Nina from behind me.

"Worthless," says Crow, without looking at her.

"We could have *sold* those, you daft bitch," Nina spits at her. "This stupid box of yours is not the only thing in Samarkand—"

Crow whirls smoothly and faces Nina, takes a couple of steps towards her. Her cold eyes never change their expression. I'm certain that sword is going to reappear, and bury itself in Nina's skull. If you'd told me a couple of days ago I'd get to watch that happen I'd have been thrilled, but right now all I feel is fear. To her credit, Nina doesn't move an inch. She even meets Crow's gaze, eye to eye; Nina's are defiant and malevolent, Crow's tired and somehow sad, but no less terrifying. Even the marten shuts up as the two face off.

"Knock it off," says Oleg wearily from behind Crow. Crow and Nina keep their eyes locked for a moment, then Crow turns away. Nina's lips quirk in a tight smile. She thinks she's won one. I want to tell her she's crazy. It's like thinking you've put one over Nina's marten by sticking your hand in its cage and then snatching it out again without it getting mauled. The marten's just waiting for the next time.

Now Oleg does look at us, and the anger in his eyes is almost reassuring after that dull stare. "Everyone who brought a box," he says. "Tree. Now."

Soon there are a dozen Martens lined up by the tree—mostly pickpockets but there are a couple of thieves and even a few of the muscle. Oleg doesn't waste any time with speeches. He goes down the line and one by one he slaps them across the face. With the first couple he holds back, just snaps his target's head around and sends him stumbling back to the wall. As he moves down the line, though, you can see him losing his temper. The third-last guy in the line is knocked to his knees, and struggles to his feet with a concussed, vacant look. The second-last guy can't get up at all, and has to crawl off drooling blood. The last—it's the little one, Farouz—just sprawls in the dirt and doesn't move. Oleg boots him in the ribs, then impatiently gestures to two other pickpockets, who drag him away.

The rest of us watch with mounting unease. This isn't right at all. Someone got the poker yesterday, so Oleg should be easing off today, that's how it works. You don't just beat the crap out of your people every day, not if you want a rep as a strong leader, instead of a weak one who needs violence to keep them in line. That, together with how awful Oleg looks, is enough to rattle us good.

Once again, Crow isn't even watching. She stares at the merrily burning pile of boxes, her eyes far away. Oleg swings around to face her. "We'll find it," he says. "The thieves—"

"Explain," says Crow, "why I shouldn't go to your competitors. These"—she kicks a burning box aside with the toe of her boot—"are not anything like what I described. I'm wasting my time here."

Oleg, like Nina, doesn't back down, but he looks scared as well as sick. Yes—*sick*, that's how he looks. Another first; Oleg has never been sick a day that I can remember, not counting hangovers. His skin shines like wax in the glow of the burning boxes, and I could be imagining it but I think there's more grey in his beard than there was yesterday.

"Fine, go ahead," he says. "But *they're* going to want *money*, you get that? How much money do you have?"

The Martens stir. Crow isn't *paying* for this? Now Crow and Oleg face each other, and I'm sure that whatever made them partners (or whatever they are) isn't going to survive this. There's going to be blood.

But again it's Crow who turns away, although it doesn't feel at all like she's backing down; just that she's tired of the whole thing. "Tomorrow," she says in her whispering voice as she disappears into the warehouse. "You have until tomorrow, to show me progress."

Oleg doesn't say anything, just heads back into his shack. It's up to Nina to dismiss us, which she does with a glare and an imperious jerk of her chin. I've never been more glad to get out of there.

Chapter Fourteen

s-salāmu 'alayka ayyuhā n-nabīyyu wa-raḥmatu llāhi wa-barakātuh..."

In the Street of the Pepper-Sellers, the last glimmers of sunlight leave the sky. Farid kneels on a dusty bit of carpet, head lowered, palms resting on his thighs. Nasr, the other thief on this job, his hair freshly gathered in three inch-long braids, stands with me, waiting for Farid to finish the *Maghrib*, the sunset prayer.

"...As-salāmu 'alaynā wa-'alā 'ibādi llāhi ṣ-ṣāliḥīn...."

My Arabic is shaky as hell, but of course I know the *tahshahhud*. *Peace be on us and on the righteous servants of God...* The Black Khans built mosques all over, and the muezzins' calls to prayer are woven into the everyday sounds of Samarkand like golden threads running through a carpet. Still, not everyone in Samarkand is a Muslim. The Khitai are Buddhist, mostly; there are Christians here, with the carved and gilded icons of their bearded god; and some still follow the old ones and their totems—sky-father, earth-mother, wolf and horse and dragon. Oleg doesn't care what we believe, as long as we make quota. Farid is the only one in the Martens who prays five times a day.

Me? When I look at the world and think about who made it, I picture a drunk giant, laying about Them with a flaming poker. Or a wizened figure hunched over the world like a counting-table, weighing everyone in it and finding them wanting. You don't flatter Someone like that, or ask Them for favours. You stay out of Their way.

Nasr has a half-dozen amulets around his neck, bought or stolen from the bazaars. He's not religious, though, just superstitious. Now the amulets jingle as he sidles closer to me. He pitches his voice low so he doesn't interrupt Farid. "What do you think of her?"

"Of who?"

"Crow, Darya, who do you think?" he says impatiently. I should have figured that out, but every time I look at Nasr I can only think of how hard it's going to be, now he's a thief. How I'm the oldest pickpocket now by at least two years. How my time is running out. "You think it's magic?"

"Huh?" I say. Farid finishes the *tahshahhud*; the prayer is winding up.

"Jalil is screwing a girl who sells amulets in the bazaar, she knows all about that stuff." Nasr can't stop touching his new braids as he chatters away. "*He* says that *she* says it sounds like the woman, Crow, she's got a spell on Oleg. Making him do what she wants."

"Huh," I say noncommittally. Nasr doesn't have a chance to develop this theory because Farid is rising, dusting off his salwar, rolling up his makeshift prayer mat.

"Let's go."

Nasr raises his voice so Farid can hear. "Spoken with the Big Man, then?" he asks mildly. "Got His permission to do crimes?"

Farid doesn't rise to the bait. "Doesn't work like that," he says evenly, stowing his rolled prayer mat just inside the squat's doorway. "Prayer is *fard*, you have to do it." He uses the Arabic word.

"Pretty sure you have to not do crimes, too, though," says Nasr, "so—"

Farid smiles his crooked smile. "Just because I do stuff I have to not do," he says, "doesn't mean I get to not do the stuff I have to."

Nasr's lips move soundlessly as he follows Farid through that sentence, then shrugs and stands himself. He gives his amulets a squeeze, then deftly wraps them in a square of cloth and ties it tight, so they don't jingle when he's working. He'd never take them off. "Let's do it."

Farid looks at me for the first time since we assembled here. "You ready? You know where it is?"

I don't look back. "Yes," I mumble.

"Darya?"

"I said *yes!*" My head whips up and I glare at him. For a second his eyes go wide, and he looks...hurt? Then the look is gone so quickly I can't be sure it was there at all.

Farid and Nasr climb the warehouse wall together. I should be running for the house of the Kyrgyz we're supposed to be ripping off, but instead I lurk at the end of the street and watch them ascend, the moonlight catching them for a moment as they reach the roof. My eyes are on Nasr, who manages the pullup without a hitch.

I should be jealous of him. I am jealous, but watching them heave their weight up the wall, I remember Red and Yu Hao, soaring miraculously out of the courtyard where they'd fought the Teuton. Before, I'd thought I'd have given anything to be as good at climbing as Farid. Now I've seen what those two can do, though... As soon as Farid and Nasr are out of sight I turn and break into a run. A slow one—the last thing I need is to blunder into an ahdath night patrol.

It's been half a day since I ate Red's Beggar's Chicken, and by rights hunger should be twisting my insides again. Instead, I barely feel it. Without thinking about it, my breath has fallen into the pattern Yu Hao taught me, as we went through his strange exercises in the yurt. Now I know this pattern, it just seems the most natural, easiest way to be; I fall into it like a cart's wooden wheel falling into a rut in dried mud, it guides me and keeps me in the current.

Soon I'm one street over from the Kyrgyz's house. I pass a ladder leaning against a wall, near a pile of bricks—someone must have had a good year, they're adding a storey to their house. I slow to a walk, creep silently to the corner and peer around.

The house and its grounds takes up one whole side of the street. It has a private garden, behind a tall plastered wall; I can see the mulberry trees poking their still-leafless branches over the top of it. Overhead arches the Straw Road, the great river of stars, already dimming as the moon rises over Samarkand. The evening dew on the trees catches the moonlight, like their branches have been dusted with silver.

I need to get closer, so I can see the house's door and windows, and raise the alarm if anyone stirs inside. I can't loiter in the street though, not with the moon lighting it up—an ahdath patrol would spot me for sure, and if the Kyrgyz has guards they'd see me too. I look down the street; twenty paces away, there's a recessed doorway opposite the house, clotted with shadow.

I can't see Farid or Nasr but I know they're there, waiting for my signal. I count *one-two-three* and dash from the corner to the doorway. I slip inside, hold my breath and count again, to ten this time, but the street remains silent, I haven't been seen.

I can see the house clearly from here. The heavy front door has elaborate polished hinges that split and curl over the wood, and reflect the moonlight like water. That's the only light coming from the house; the windows are dark and dead. No voices, no footsteps of patrolling guards.

I draw breath once more and give Farid the signal. Some crews use birdsong as a signal. They're idiots. At night? All the birds are asleep, birdsong is a dead giveaway. Our signal is a low hissing growl that hurts my throat—a cat, facing off with a rival. I let it rise to a high-pitched screech and tail off, and even before I've gone silent I hear a noise from the rooftop above me.

A soft grating sound above me, and a shower of grit prickles my scalp. I look up and see the wooden plank silhouetted against the moonlit sky, extending from the roof across the narrow lane. It wavers and I imagine Farid and Nasr with their weight on the other end, keeping it above the level of the Kyrgyz's roof. There are dozens of these makeshift bridges—planks, coiled ropes—stashed on roofs all over the city. They're shared by all the thieves in Samarkand, part of the peculiar code of honour they have. The code I want to share.

With a soft *clunk* the end of the plank comes down. For a second, nothing moves up there. Then a pair of shadows run across the plank, and in a moment they're on the Kyrgyz's roof, briefly silhouetted against the moonlit sky before they drop out of sight.

They're good, of course. They barely make a sound. But I can still hear the plank creaking slightly under their weight, grinding on the brickwork of the roof. I think again of Red and Yu Hao. They wouldn't have made that much noise. They wouldn't have needed the plank at all. Can Yu Hao really teach me to move like they do?

I draw back into the darkness of the doorway so I won't be seen, and settle in. I've stuffed all the rags from my cot into my kameez, and hug myself to further block out the cold. My eyes flick over the facade of the Kyrgyz's house—upstairs east window, upstairs west window, downstairs window, door, then back up to the upstairs east window, over and over again, looking for a light, a sound, anything that might warn me that Farid and Nasr have given themselves away. After a while it becomes automatic, and my mind begins to wander. Which is the last thing I want, because every path it wanders down seems to end in the same place: *You're screwed.*

Take tonight, for instance. It's not like curfew is a formal occasion or anything, but there's a structure to it. Turn your day's take in to Nina; assemble in the courtyard with anyone who hasn't made quota going to the tree; there's a speech from Oleg, or Nina if Oleg's too drunk; someone gets the poker if they're real unlucky; we're dismissed.

That routine has been around since before us—before anyone who was in the courtyard today was even out of the orphanage—and we've always just assumed it would be around after us as well. A routine like that, you call it a *tradition*. It makes you feel like the Martens are built on something solid, rooted deep in the earth. Tonight the earth trembled.

I don't believe, like Nasr does, that Crow has some magical hold over Oleg. I don't know what the hell Oleg thinks he's doing with her. But if Nasr is even *saying* that kind of thing out loud, it means that the Martens are losing confidence. And without that, unless Oleg gets a grip, we're going to fall apart. Other gangs will take our corners; we'll split up and join those other gangs, or start new ones; eventually Oleg and Nina will be alone, and scary or not, crazy or not, no one survives alone in Samarkand, not after they've made as many enemies as those two.

That thought might cheer me up, but what follows doesn't. What's going to happen to me, if the Martens go under? A pickpocket who's too old to be a pickpocket, and a girl along with it? Any gang I tried to join would laugh in my face, or turn around and sell me to slavers. If I come to them as a thief, maybe they'll have me—but even if Yu Hao's training works, even if I make the climb, Farid won't back me. He wants me to be a house slave.

So maybe...maybe I need to take him up on his offer. I'll let his girlfriend take me on. I'll hang out in the Street of Pepper-Sellers, giggling as thieves like Farid buy me rosewater syrup...

No. The word echoes in my head, so forceful that for a moment I think I've said it out loud.

Screw Farid. He won't back me? I'll make thief anyway. I won't make thief? Then I'll take my chances. I will *not* be a house girl for some rich old man to push around and leer at. If I do that I'll be dead anyway, dead where it counts. And I made a deal with Yu Hao...

Yu Hao.

Part of me is surprised that I'm taking my deal with him so seriously. After all, I never promised him I'd go *looking* for the box, just that I'd tell him what I hear in exchange for training. Assuming I'm even being trained. Breathing lessons, is all it's amounted to so far. I already knew how to breathe, thanks.

Maybe he doesn't even care about this box. He seems open, honest, "without folds or corners" as they say in Samarkand, but maybe he's just another do-gooder, pretending to offer me 'work' which is really just charity. In which case, screw him. Screw him...

Well, why not?

He's a caravan guard. In a week or two, a month tops, he'll be leaving Samarkand and I'll never see him again. It's not like it'd get back to the Martens—he's not going to be hanging out at the squat on

Pepper-Sellers bragging about how he scored. And he's not exactly hard to look at...

This thought is interesting enough that I almost don't hear the creak of hinges. The Kyrgyz's fancy door is swinging open. I flatten myself into the doorway. Splinters from the rough wooden door dig into my back as I watch, narrowing my eyes so they don't catch a stray moonbeam and give me away.

Someone emerges from the darkness inside the house. It's a man in a long sleeping gown, and even with the moonlight leaching the colour from everything I can see how pale he is and the unnatural red of his hair, so I'm pretty sure it's the Kyrgyz.

He moves so slowly that at first I think he might be sleepwalking—one foot carefully in front of the other like he's crossing a tightrope rather than a city street. He holds one arm across his body, cradling it with the other, and even from this side of the lane I can see there's something wrong with his hand. Carefully I draw breath to signal Farid and the others, and that's when I smell it. And a half-second later I double up and retch.

I manage to hold onto the contents of my stomach (such as they are) but I can't help letting out a harsh cough, and the Kyrgyz must hear it because he whirls to face me. He lets go of his arm, which flops at his side like all its bones are gone. Something black is spreading in patches over the sleeve of his robe, glistening in the moonlight. It drips from his limp fingers onto the ground, and I get another wave of that smell.

Every street rat in Samarkand has seen, and smelled, a dead body. The Kyrgyz smells like a corpse left in an alley for a week during high summer. And he's still alive.

But not for much longer, I think. That black stuff keeps splashing on the ground, and now it's joined by one of his fingers. Then another. The skin on that hand seems to be sloughing off. I look up, and our eyes meet, and I see the horror in his even as the black corruption creeps up over the collar of his sleeping gown and begins to soften the skin of his face. He knows what's happening to him.

He takes a half-step towards me and somehow I manage to keep a hold of myself long enough to bark like a dog, three times. The signal for Farid. He takes another half-step, then collapses in the street. His shoulder hits the ground first, and caves in with a wet *crunch* like a rotten gourd. And I thank whoever made the world that he didn't come any closer, because if he did I would have forgotten about being lookout, forgotten about ahdath patrols and Farid and Yu Hao and Red and the box and everything else, and just run screaming into the night.

We light a candle just outside the room, so as little light as possible leaks into the street. While Farid kneels before a heavy chest and goes to work on the lock, I look over the boxes on the shelves. I pick one up—it's beautiful, from the Indian kingdoms I think. Each side is inlaid with mother-of-pearl in exquisite curling patterns. It's worth more than anything I've ever lifted, but I put it back on the shelf. Right now we're here for one thing only, and as soon as someone discovers what's left of the Kyrgyz out in the lane our time will be up.

The lock finally gives way, and Farid stashes his tools, heaves the lid open and rummages inside.

"Well?" I ask.

He shakes his head. Neither of us get too close to the windows. The house is downwind of the Kyrgyz's body, and neither of us wants to be the first to say *plague*. Really, though, I've never heard of any plague that rots you to death in an hour. This is some weirdness Crow brought with her to Samarkand. Which is not to say it isn't just as deadly. And it's not just fear of the plague that's keeping my mouth shut.

Farid takes a deep breath and holds it as he sticks his head out the window, looking down the street.

"Nasr?" I ask. We sent him to tell Oleg what we saw here.

He shakes his head as he steps back. He doesn't breathe until he's on the other side of the room. "He better show up soon, though. Someone's going to notice this soon." I only shrug. "Darya?" I won't say anything. I won't. "Darya, I think we need to—"

"Why won't you back me?" I blurt. *Shit.* Still, it's out now, so I keep going. "You don't want me to be a thief. You want me out of the life. You want me to be a *serving girl.*"

Farid looks like he's just now understood something. "That's not it, Darya. That's not it at all."

"Like hell it isn't. You told your g—your friend. Mahnaz. You told her to find a *job* for me."

"Look," says Farid, and then pauses, getting his thoughts in order. He looks me in the eyes. "This is about the climb, right? You can't make the climb."

"I can make it."

"You *don't have to,* Darya," he says. "That's just it. Look at Nasr— he made the climb, so he's a thief, I guess, but he doesn't have the touch. All he really is, is a pickpocket, a small-time scammer, and that's all he'll ever be. But you—you may not have the strength, but you're a born thief, Darya." Am I blushing? "I've seen you work. I saw you in the Street of the Rope-sellers, lifting that Khwarezmian's purse."

"You've been watching me?" Thank God I didn't know at the time.

"No one cases a scene better than you. No one sees an opportunity faster. You're the best lifter out of the pickpockets and thieves put together."

I'm definitely blushing. I turn my face from the candlelight. "Masoud doesn't think so."

"Masoud is full of shit, and if he thinks I'm going to hand the thieves over to him he's got a surprise coming, whatever Nina says," says Farid, his voice hard. "Why do you think he's not made the climb yet? He's staying out of my way. He wants to just stroll in and take over once I'm gone.

"Look, Darya—if you were a house girl for the Inalids, you'd be on the inside. You could go anywhere—any time one of those rich pricks visits their clansmen's houses, their slaves go on ahead of them to help clean the place up. You could case it, lift the keys...we could steal ten *times* what we do. All we need is to get that lunatic her box so she's out of our hair."

This brings me back to earth. "Crow?" For some reason I'm whispering. "You think Nasr's right? She's cast some kind of—"

Farid shakes his head. "Nasr's about as full of shit as Masoud is." He's keeping his voice low too, although there's no way anyone could hear us. "Oleg's sick."

My stomach lurches. "Will he be okay?" Not that I give a crap about Oleg, but without him the Martens will have their backs to the wall.

"Crow is making him well. They ran Nasr about off his feet getting all the medicine she needs. She gets him well, he gets her the box, he stops pissing his rep away, the Martens get back on their feet, and you make thief."

I don't dare believe it. "If I can't make the climb—"

"Once they see how much we'll be earning, they won't care about the climb. Trust me." He takes a step closer to me. "I don't want to lose you. I want you, Darya." He says it again. "I want you."

I look up at him, and I see the look in his eyes, and my heart sinks. 'Love' has not exactly been a big part of my life, but I've spent a lot of time hanging out in bazaars while I waited to run a scam, and the street singers and storytellers absolutely will not shut up about that shit. Romantic, all-conquering love. Beggars and princesses regaling each other with poems in royal rose gardens. Fate. Destiny. Happily-ever-after.

But running all those scams in all those bazaars, I got real familiar with greed. Greed and weakness. Those two, to a scammer, are bread and butter. And Farid might call what he's feeling now 'love' but what it really is is weakness and greed, all mixed up together.

The opportunity he's offering is a good deal—a lot better than getting sold to some slave driver—but that look in his eyes tells me there are strings attached. Like the tailor in the story, he's made a dress for me in his head, and once he finds out it doesn't fit, he won't alter *it* to fit *me*, he'll try it the other way around. And if I turn him down he'll get hurt, get weird. Get angry.

I don't need this. I don't have time for this.

Footsteps smack on the bricks of the street and save me from having to think of something to say. We rush down the stairs and lean out of the doorway. Nasr is running down the street towards us. As he approaches the house he angles away from the body in the street, hugs the wall instead.

He stumbles to a stop, his chest heaving. "I..." is all he manages to say, and then, without a sound, Crow is behind him. I didn't see her in the street. Not at all.

"Where is it?" she says, in that flat whisper of hers.

Fortunately we don't have to tell her 'it' isn't here, because now Oleg is rounding the corner. He's fast when he needs to be, but now he's wheezing worse than Nasr is. As he stumbles up behind Crow I see the hectic spots of colour on his cheeks, feel the feverish heat rolling off his skin. I take a half-step back, let Farid handle this.

Oleg glances down the street, and sees the body in a spreading puddle of something thick and black. "How long has he been out here?" he splutters between wheezes. "How long...have you...been messing around?"

"He died like two hours ago," says Nasr. Oleg glares and raises a massive hand to backhand him across the face. Nasr cowers, but then Farid steps in.

"He's telling the truth. Darya saw him die." I kind of wish he'd kept me out of it. "We don't know what happened to him."

"Two hours my—" says Oleg, blustering down the street towards the Kyrgyz, and then he smells it. He doubles over like a goat butted him in the solar plexus, and heaves a great jet of vomit onto the bricks.

His knees are shaking and he falls against the wall, supporting himself with a hand. I'm glad no one from the Wolves or the Bears can see him now. He looks like a sick old man.

Crow brushes past him and walks right up to the body. The Kyrgyz's robe is gently settling, like it's wrapped around a pile of shaved ice instead of a man's body and the ice is melting. I try to picture what must be happening to the flesh underneath, then wish I hadn't. Not with that smell in my nostrils.

Now she turns and looks straight at me. Her eyes are pools of black oil in the moonlight. "It's not here," she says flatly. It's not a question, which is fortunate, because with those eyes boring into mine there's no way I could think of anything to say.

She looks at Oleg. "You failed," she says. Her voice is still utterly flat.

"Now just a minute—" begins Oleg, then he realizes that Farid, Nasr and I are watching him. "Get out," he rasps. "Back to your beds. *Go!*"

Farid doesn't take the rooftops back. He walks with me instead, and Nasr follows his lead. I stay abreast of them for half a mile or so, then I begin to lag. When I'm half a dozen paces behind them, Farid stops and looks over his shoulder at me. "You okay, Darya?"

"Bleeding," I say, "sorry." I clutch my belly. "Since yesterday. Cramps." They both blanch. Farid actually takes half a step backwards. *Boys.* "Can you give me a second? I'll catch up. Really."

Farid nods hurriedly. "Get home safe, okay?" He smiles at me, and I try to smile back. And just as soon as they've turned the next corner, my feet are pounding the bricks through the Maze, back the way we came.

I turn a final, tight corner, and unable to change direction fast enough I slam into the wall. "*Shit*," I hiss, but it's not from the pain.

It's the construction site. Not three hours ago there was a ladder here, and now it's gone. Maybe the workmen came back for it. Or, more likely, someone stole it. All that's left is the tottering pile of bricks, reaching almost all the way up the wall.

What am I doing? I don't need to climb *anything*, now. I can be a thief anyway. I don't need Yu Hao any more. I can have it all: the thieves, the Martens, Farid. But the same thing that spoke up inside me outside the Kyrgyz's house stirs again, and it says what it said then: *No.*

Because I won't be a thief, not without making the climb. I won't have earned their respect, I won't share their code. I'll be a glorified girlfriend, and whatever Farid is telling himself right now, girlfriends don't last. And I made a deal with Yu Hao.

The bricks are in more of a pile than a stack, and it clacks and clatters as I clamber up. Each step threatens to spill me back to the ground and bury me under an avalanche of baked clay. But finally I stand unsteadily on top of the bricks, looking up. There's still a few feet between my outstretched fingers and the edge of the roof. As I look up at it, all at once the hunger returns, stabbing at my insides. A wave of exhaustion blurs my vision and I have to brace myself against the wall to keep from toppling off the pile of bricks.

There's no time to think. I tense my legs and jump, and just manage to grab the lip of the roof. The easy part. Now I have to pull myself up and over the edge. Something I've never come close to doing before. But for some reason, tonight I feel like I can go for it.

My body sways and shakes, my back and arm muscles straining as I fight for every inch. For a moment I'm sure I'm not going to make it—I'm going to drop back onto the pile of bricks, which will spill me to the ground, and I'll be lucky if I get away with a broken ankle—

—and then I take a deep breath, low down in my tan-t'ien —and expel it smoothly as I force myself up just one more inch—

—and I cross some invisible leverage point and I can reach my other arm over the edge of the roof, then get one knee up onto it and roll up and over—

—and I'm falling.

For a second my guts seize up as I see myself hit the ground below. But it's only for a moment, and then I thump onto my side on the rooftop, and lie there, muscles burning. This building's roof has a low brick parapet around it, that's what I fell from. That's good; it'll hide me from anyone in the street looking up.

I suck air, feeling my muscles buzz with fatigue, and I can't help a smile from spreading across my face. I just barely made it—and it's not like I was doing it with weights, like thieves have to—but I did it. I did it.

I sit up and look across the rooftops. Far away, I can see lights burning on another roof, dozens of shadows teeming. A fight? A party? A market? The rooftops are their own world, anything could be going on over there, and the civilians who throng the streets below in the daytime would never know anything about it. Even territories are vaguer up here; thieves from different gangs are more likely to live and let live, even cooperate on some jobs. That code of honour of theirs, again. The one I want so badly.

I think of scratching a tag into the edge of the parapet, then decide against it. The warehouse district is strictly easy mode, all long, flat roofs, mostly the same height. A tag here, and only here, would only mark me as an interloper.

Between gasps for breath, I hear voices in the distance. Oleg's rumble, then a whisper on the edge of my hearing. Crow. I spring to my feet, crouching so I don't silhouette myself against the moonlit sky, and I steal across the roof, toward the voices.

There's a lane between me and the next roof over, which belongs to a little warehouse, barely a shed. Oleg and Crow's voices are coming from beyond *that* roof, from the lane with the Kyrgyz's corpse. They hover just below the edge of hearing; I need to get across this street if I want to know what they're saying, which is not great news, because I've never made a jump even close to how wide this lane is.

I look around. Behind me, at the far end of the roof I'm on, there's one of those planks the thieves stash so they can cross streets carrying loot. By the time I get it and double back here, Oleg and Crow could be done. Or...

I turn back to face the gap between me and the shed, and before I even realize I'm doing it I've backed up ten yards and taken off, sprinting light-footed across the roof towards the edge.

This is stupid. This is *so* stupid. I'm going to fall twenty feet and break my legs. Or I'll land hard, and they'll hear me. But then I inhale and fire flares in my tan-t'ien, and all of a sudden I *know* I can make it, I'm in the current and it'll bear me all the way to the other side. I speed up across the last few yards, feeling that golden heat spread through my body, into my legs, flooding them with energy—and then my toes hit a bump in the roof, and I stumble.

Only a little, but it's enough to throw me entirely out of the rhythm I've built up. And when I next look at the gap I'm sprinting toward I see how far it really is.

I'm not going to make it. I'm going to fling myself off the roof, arc out and down and smack into the ground face-first, and it's far too late to stop. My foot hits the very edge of the roof I'm on and I take a wild leap. Somehow I manage to keep quiet, hissing between my teeth although I feel like screaming.

I sail through empty space for an eternity...and I make it. Almost. My shins slam into the edge of the shed's roof. I fall, twisting, landing on my side, momentum keeping me rolling forward until I come to a stop, huddled and shaking.

"What was that?" says a soft voice from directly below me. Crow.

Once, ripping off a street stall while Nasr lured its owner away with some story or other, I reached into a chest to grab a silver bracelet just as Masoud was heaving the lid shut, and it caught me on the back of my hand. It was a few days before I was sure I could even use my fingers again. Ever since, whenever I've been in pain, I've gone back to that moment and thought, *At least this isn't as bad as that.* Now a fresh wave of pain rolls through my legs, and I think it again. And it's true. But it's close.

I bite my arm to stop myself moaning. I huddle tighter, partly to make sure no one can see me from below, but mostly to wrap myself tight around the pain. If I relax it'll blow me up like one of those Eastern fire flowers, and scatter me across the rooftops.

"Forget that," rasps Oleg's voice. "Talk to me."

Silence from Crow for a moment. Cautiously, I probe my shins with a hand. The pain makes my eyes roll back, but I don't think they're broken, which, since I must have hit the edge of the roof with my full weight, seems impossible. I lift my head and look back across the gap, which seems even wider than it did before. How did I make that?

"Hey," says Oleg, "we go again, tonight. Yes?"

This time Crow replies. "Not for another day. It'll kill you."

He hawks and spits. "I can take it."

"The thing inside you," says Crow patiently, "the thing that's killing you, its roots are right through your guts. It takes its nourishment from your own body, from your *ch'i*." I've not heard the word before. "I am giving you poison, to kill it through its roots. Any more of this poison and you die. You may die anyway."

"I—" Oleg begins, then something makes him stop talking. No one says anything for a moment, and I decide to risk moving. I roll over as quietly as I can, which brings me to edge of the shed's roof, and stretching my neck I can just see into the street below. Crow and Oleg are both looking away from the Kyrgyz's body, to the corner, where a gawky young man stands in an ahdath's uniform. The one who was pointing a sword at me yesterday, after Yu Hao and Red saved me from the Teuton.

Now Uthman appears behind him. "Mehmet here saw you hauling ass through the Maze, and I got curious. What the hell is going on, Oleg?"

"Best stay right there, Uthman," Oleg says. He spits again.

"Like hell," says Uthman, and then he shuts his mouth fast and takes a step back. Mehmet gags, and manages to go even paler than he already was.

"Told you," says Oleg. He's standing tall, chest puffed out, his voice the same powerful rumble I remember. A thousand miles from the wheezing wreck who showed up at the Kyrgyz's house. But then, he needs to be. If Uthman thinks Oleg's going down, any favours he might be doing for the Martens will stop happening.

Uthman nods at the puddle of vomit by the wall. "Learned the hard way?" Then, his voice tight, he says the thing Farid and I couldn't: "Plague?"

"Not plague," says Crow. "Poison."

Uthman exhales, loud in the quiet street. I realize I'm letting out a breath of my own. But the doubt still lingers. That *smell*. Smelling like that, you'd expect him to be flyblown and half-eaten by dogs, but we were looking in each other's eyes just a few hours ago. What kind of poison could do that? Crow crouches in front of the body, peering down at it. She doesn't seem to smell it at all.

"What happened to him?" asks Oleg.

"Remember when I told your people not to open the box?" says Crow.

"Yeah?"

"He opened the box." She prods at the dead man's chest, and her finger sinks into his flesh, dimpling the robe. A black stain spreads across the brightly coloured fabric, a fresh waft of that hellish smell rises up into the night and I nearly send a load of vomit spiraling down into the alley to join Oleg's. I press a hand over my nose and mouth and struggle with my stomach, and just barely come out on top.

"*Ku* poison," says Crow. "How my people deal with thieves.

Works by touch. He had the box in his hands, a few days ago. Got curious," says Crow. "Got greedy." She doesn't sound nauseous. Just absolutely fed-up and exhausted.

"I don't know what any of that shit means," says Uthman, "but this is not something that can happen again, Oleg. Another dihkan woke up without a head tonight and everyone's on edge."

"Assassins don't poison," says Mehmet. "They use knives—" Uthman catches his eye and he quails.

"Like anyone is going to care, when they're filling their pants with crap," says Uthman. "The Assassins are in Samarkand. Did you happen to be at the Old Mosque on Friday?"

Oleg doesn't dignify this with a reply.

"The sermon was really something. Uproot the heretics, burn them out with fire, all that. The qadi spends his time drawing up lists of Ismailians for us to arrest, and throwing their brothers in the dungeons is just going to piss those madmen off worse. The qadi's just being a prick—don't quote me on that last part, by the way—"

Oleg grunts.

"The point is, he's doubling down, so the Assassins will too, meaning this is going to get worse before it gets better. The ahdath are trying to keep a lid on it, but a *gruesome poisoning campaign* is not going to make our job easier. And you and the Martens could end up on the qadi's list very easily. You hear me?" Uthman points a thumb at the Kyrgyz's body. "Get that cleaned up. This doesn't happen again." A nod to Mehmet and the ahdath disappear around the corner.

"He has a point," rumbles Oleg. Those fists of his might have crushed skulls, but if Uthman and the ahdath decide to make life impossible for the Martens, impossible it will be.

"I don't care about any of that." Crow stands. "What are you going to do now?"

Oleg sighs. Now Uthman is gone he's stooping again, and his breath rattles in his chest. "That poor dead bastard was a middleman. Put buyers together with sellers, took a cut. Parasite. We can find out which buyers he used, hit them one at a time. Find your box." He looks at the corpse. "Get rid of it, he said—"

"Don't bother," says Crow. "By morning it will be a rag and a stain."

"And is anyone else going to—"

"I. Don't. Care." Her voice was scary before, but now it makes me feel cold all over. "Anyone who comes between me and what's mine will die like he did, or worse. That is a promise."

Mercifully, her voice fades as she and Oleg head back down the street, back to the warehouse. I sit on the roof, hugging my bruised shins. Processing what I've just heard.

Whatever's in the box is poisoned, deadly. So will Red and Yu Hao still want it? Do I tell them? It's a while before I can fully unfold myself, and longer before I can get to my feet. I can stand, although my legs tremble and I can feel the blood trickling down my ankles where I scraped them up. No more running and jumping for me tonight. Just limping home.

Once I figure out how to get down from here.

Chapter Fifteen

When I wake, the first slivers of sunlight are slipping through the cracks in the ceiling, and I don't remember any of the night before until I swing my legs over the side of my cot and twin bolts of pain shoot all the way from the soles of my feet to my bare scalp. When I stand up they rip through me again, and I can't help hissing through clenched teeth. None of the other pickpockets are awake. How much sleep did I get, after I finally made it back to the warehouse and hobbled into bed? An hour and a half? Maybe?

Wincing with each step, my legs stiff as planks, I pad over to the ladder. I climb down, slow as an old woman, and when my shin bangs against a rung I have to bite my lip to keep from hissing in pain. Once I'm out of the building I roll up my salwar and check my shins in the half-light. They're puffy with bruises, blood-dark clouds that promise a spectacular rainbow in a couple of days. I force myself through a dozen squats to limber up, and then half-jog, half-limp out into the Street of the Pepper-sellers.

The astrolabe I stole last night digs into my side with each step, but I don't mind. With the astrolabe I'll easily make quota today, maybe even get credit for tomorrow as well—assuming anyone's even collecting tonight—which means I have a day all to myself. I haven't had one of those since I was five, when I was bedridden in the orphanage with a fever that almost killed me.

I glance at the orphanage's great windowless wall as I leave the warehouse. The double doors are open, and the beggars are filing out. The kid leading them has one eye, which puts him one up on most of the others. He holds one end of a long string that loops around each beggar's wrist, so the blind ones don't wander off. They probably don't even need the string; they march the same route every single day, each one dropped off at their designated corner to start earning, each one collected again at dusk.

I missed the evening meal on account of being lookout for Farid and Nasr, and what nourishment I took from Red's chicken yesterday is long gone. Hunger cramps toll inside me like a bell, driving any other cares out of my head. Which is kind of a blessing, since I'm not at all sure I can make it to the caravanserai on my much-abused legs. I'm determined to try, but by the time I finally see China Gate looming ahead, I feel like my kneecaps are about to drop off.

I'm so focused on the pain that I almost don't hear the footsteps coming from my left. I hear them get faster, though, as whoever it is breaks into a run, coming right at me. I try to step aside, twisting my torso, but I'm not fast enough on my damaged legs to dodge them completely. Whoever it is, they wanted to knock me down, slam me into the bricks, but instead their shoulder just glances off mine, and it sends me staggering but I manage to stay upright.

I back up awkwardly, looking at the three street rats fanning out around me. Two of them I've never seen, but the third I remember, reaching for me as I squeezed between those houses to escape him.

These are Wolves.

"What do you want?" I say, just to buy some time. I can't run. I can't fight, either, not against three of them. This is deep Lion territory, so the Wolves must really be pushing for corners. The Lions have a truce with the Martens. If any were around they might even help me. But they aren't.

"No mouse-holes to run into here," says the one I remember. Although it's only just dawn there are dozens of people around the gate. A butcher wheels a barrow piled with cuts of meat past us. None of them spare us a glance. Absurdly, someone in one of the taverns across the street strikes up some music, a lively melody on a five-string tar accompanied by a wailing rebec.

"You see me running?" I shoot back, but I'm hardly thinking about what I'm saying. My brain is frantically hunting for escape routes. There aren't any.

He takes another step forward. He wants to take his time, have fun with this. There's something in his fist, something sharp. The jaunty tune carries on like none of this is happening. Is that the last thing I'm ever going to hear? Another step. I hold my ground, because I can't do anything else. He sees the fear in my eyes, and his own glitter—

"You have a talent for making friends," says a voice behind me, "looks like."

I flinch, sure it's another Wolf ready to plant a shiv in my back. I turn clumsily, lose my balance and go down, banging one knee on the ground, and the pain blurs my vision. When it clears, Red is standing between the Wolves and me. The Wolves are already backing off.

"Lucky," sneers their leader. "Lucky rat. Oh, the Teuton's looking for you. Pissed off about his sword, and he's gonna take it out of your hide." He laughs, not caring he's not going to get to stab me today. I'm not going anywhere, after all. He has all the time in the world. He glances at Red, then back to me and spits on the ground. Then they turn tail and run.

So now the Teuton wants to kill me. Perfect.

Red watches them go. Without looking at me, she extends a hand to help me up. "What was that about?" she says, still speaking Khitai and raising one perfectly-arched eyebrow. The Wolves and I were speaking Persian, which evidently Red doesn't.

I ignore her hand, struggle to my feet on my own. She shrugs, then strides off across the street towards a run-down inn. It looks terrible, one of those dumps that cluster around the city gates, for travellers too naive to realize they can get a better deal, and fewer vermin in their room, elsewhere in the city. She jerks her head—*follow me*—and disappears inside. I take a deep breath, force myself to unclench my fists, and follow her.

Once through the doorway, I descend two worn stone steps into the tavern's windowless main room, lit by a couple of oil lamps hanging from the low ceiling. The floor is damp earth. There's barely room for a couple of tables and some rickety wooden benches. At the far end is another doorway, curtained off, beyond which is presumably the kitchen and the stairs to the guest rooms.

Red sits at one of the tables, or rather slumps, landing hard, and I see how drunk she is. She's not up early, she's up late. Across the table from her is the tavern's only other patron, the Indian I saw her sparring with the other day. He's even drunker than she is, if that's possible. He's propped his head on his elbows so he can look up at Red dreamily.

Red carefully picks up a chipped jar of wine and tips it to look inside. "I have trudged through all the salt plains in Hsi-Hsia," she says, enunciating each word with the careful dignity of a drunk. "I have shaken half the sand in the Taklamakan out of my boots. The T'ien Shan just about froze my tits off, but drinking this stuff"—she shakes the jar, sloshing a gout of wine out onto the table—"this is the worst. This is the absolute low point." She raises her voice. "Is there any more?"

Movement behind the curtain, and a girl—the tavern keeper's daughter, maybe—hustles out with another jar. She sees me and gives me the exact same look the girls with Farid gave me yesterday. She flaps her wrist at me, shooing me out, but Red waves her off. "She's with me," she says, and the girl retreats behind the curtain, not before shooting me a glare—*don't steal anything*. Like there's anything to steal in this dump.

The Indian raises his head to look at Red. His brow furrows as he fishes around in his wine-soaked brain for something to say. "Apsara," he manages to say, pointing at Red with a big grin.

"That's nice," says Red, not looking at him. "Yu Hao is upstairs," she says to me. "We're rooming here now. Thought it might be easier for you. Less of a walk. Also, someone cut a hole in our roof." She snorts with laughter. She's *wasted*.

"Urvashi," murmurs the guy, his head drooping until his chin touches the sticky surface of the table.

Red pats him on the head. She looks blearily at me. "Off you go, then. Dismissed." She points at the curtain with a thumb.

Jerk.

Beyond the curtain is a narrow corridor, steam and wine-stench rolling through it from the kitchen. Off the corridor, a narrow flight of stairs leads up to the second floor, and at the top of the stairs is another curtain which I pull aside, revealing a small square room. A narrow window lets in a trickle of weak spring sunlight.

Yu is crosslegged on a straw mat, his back to the window. He's wearing the same long white robe and folded black cap he was the first time I saw him, and he holds up a book to catch the sunlight. His and Red's bedrolls are up against one wall, next to the long stringed instrument he called a ch'in. Next to that is a bundle wrapped in cloth. It steams slightly, and the aroma is mouthwatering.

I stand there for a while watching his eyes track left-to-right, left-to right. He turns a page. Eventually I say, "Your friend is hammered." Just to say something.

He doesn't move, or look up at me. "I'd guessed."

"What are you reading?"

"Something by a man named Aristarchus." He pronounces each syllable of the name carefully. "He holds that the sun is at the centre of all things, and that the planets—the bright stars—circle around it. The Earth itself is a planet, third of their number." His voice is alive with curiosity. "An interesting theory. Inasmuch as I can understand it. There were Greek primers at the library in Lin'An, but I never really—"

I've only ever talked to scholars to scam them, but I know that once they build up momentum it's like a manure cart rolling downhill. Try to follow them and you just end up wading through bullshit. So I interrupt him.

"You got that in the Street of the Book-sellers?" He nods absently, still reading. "How much?"

He turns a page. "Quite a significant portion of my wages for the journey from Tun-Huang. Which were admittedly not high."

I nod, and struggle not to say anything, and lose. "You got *screwed*."

Now he does look up, his face neutral. "Oh?"

"Yeah. Look at it. Binding's crap, cover's crap. Paper's crap—you want the kaghez, the good stuff. I bet it's not even illuminated."

"How many books have you read, Darya?" I can't tell if he's making fun of me or not.

"I've stolen a ton. And I can tell you that no one's going to buy that for more than half a dirham."

"Some might say," he says mildly, "that the words themselves, and the wisdom therein, are of value as well."

"Yeah," I say, "but the people who say that kind of thing never have any money."

His lips quirk up in a tiny smile. "No. No, I suppose they don't." He shuts the book with a *snap* and a puff of dust, and reaches behind him for the steaming bundle. He tosses it to me, and I can't help unwrapping it; roasted lamb tikku, wrapped in fresh-baked flatbread. "Eat."

I hesitate, and he adds—"And while you eat, you can share what news you have."

That he's asking for information in advance should put me on the alert that this is a scam, but instead I find it reassuring. He's really interested in the box; what I can tell him has value. I'm paying my way.

I take a big bite of the flatbread and chew, longer than I have to. As soon as I say anything, it's real—I'm betraying the Martens, crossing Oleg. For a moment I feel the heat of that poker, hear the sizzle of hot iron on human flesh. It's suddenly difficult to swallow. I draw a deep breath.

"The thieves had a job," I say, "last night..."

I've finished eating before I'm halfway through my story. I realize I'm fidgeting, wringing the flatbread's cloth wrapper, and I lean over to set it aside. My shins knock together and I grunt in pain.

Yu Hao cocks his head. "You're hurt?"

"When I jumped," I say. I pull up the legs of my salwar to show him the bruises. Can't hurt to let him know what I've gone through for this frigging box. "Missed the roof. It's nothing."

I'm going to continue but Yu Hao has already turned away to rummage in his bedroll. He produces a small plain ceramic bottle and draws the stopper. Carefully he pours out a dark, fragrant liquid onto his palms. He holds them up to show me.

"T'ieh-ta-chiu," he says. "My own formula." Then he leans over me. I don't move a muscle—except when his hands touch my legs, and I can't help hissing and drawing them back.

He ducks his head apologetically. Then his hand shoots out, lightning fast, and his finger presses hard on a point just below my knees, first one leg then the other. I suck air, expecting to yell with the pain, but there isn't any. In fact my shins are already throbbing a little less. When Yu Hao lays his hands, fragrant with t'ieh-ta-chiu (whatever that is) on them, I flinch only a little. He gently massages it into my bruised skin, and after a few moments it even starts to feel good.

"Continue, please." He doesn't look up, intent on my legs. He's washed his hair, I can smell it. It takes me a while to remember where I'm up to.

貂

"...So I make it down from the roof and I go home. And that's...that's it I guess. The Kyrgyz had the box, but he must have sold it to someone else. The thieves will follow up, hit all the guys he did business with, but that'll take them a couple of days maybe."

I clear my dry throat. Yu Hao is silent a while. Then in one flowing motion he's on his feet. "Stand."

I clench my teeth, expecting the pain to flare up when I clamber to my feet, but it stays gone. As I roll the legs of my salwar down I inspect my shins; the bruises maybe don't look quite as bad as I thought. I look at Yu Hao. "You want me to—?" I mime our hand patterns of the other day.

"Something like that. But not here." Yu Hao turns and steps onto the windowsill, and slips his body sideways through the window. It looks like he's jumping out of the building, but I've hardly had time to flinch before he reaches up at the last moment and catches the edge of the roof. One-handed, he swings himself up and out of view, light as a feather. Only a moment later he appears again, upside-down this time. "Follow, please." Somehow that cap stays on his head.

"You're kidding." He just beckons with his hand.

Gingerly I step up onto the sill. There's a bad moment when I squeeze through the window and I remember my escape from the wolves, and without quite meaning to I grab Yu Hao's hand. It's warm, and firm, and there's more calluses than I'd expect on a scholar's hand.

Then I let out an undignified squawk as Yu Hao hoists me up like I weighed nothing at all, and deposits me on the tavern's roof, my butt on the edge and my feet dangling off it. I look down; it's quite a drop. Yu Hao is already standing on the roof behind me and I scoot backwards until I can safely stand up myself.

The clouds are alight, like someone spilled a great jar of cochineal across the sky, but the sun hasn't cleared the city wall yet and

Samarkand is in shadow. I shiver as I follow Yu Hao across the roof. "So what now?"

Yu Hao responds by setting his right foot forward, the knee bent. So I do too. He does a quick circuit around me, nudging my legs with his feet to adjust my posture, then resumes his own and raises his arm. So I do too. This isn't that thigh-destroying Horse Stance, thankfully, but one more poised and graceful (on his part, anyway; I feel like I'm going to tip over). Then he leans forward a little and puts his hand against mine, so the backs of our wrists are just barely touching. His skin is much warmer than the air, and that single point of contact feels like the very centre of the world.

When he reverses his hand and pushes against my wrist with his palm, gently, firmly, until my arm is almost up against my chest, it takes me by surprise and I stiffen, try to push back. He doesn't give an inch, but he doesn't push me any further either. Instead he reverses his hand again, so once again our wrists are touching. "Now you."

I copy him, putting my hand palm-out and pushing as smoothly as I can. Next to Yu Hao's movements it seems jerky and forced. I push him harder than he pushed me, but he yields smoothly, swinging his whole body back and straightening his right leg. So when he swings forward again and pushes me like before, I do the same.

"Good," he says, "but don't push with just your hand. Put your whole self behind each movement. Behind everything you do."

"I get it," I say, and I think I actually do.

And so it goes. We're not just pushing back and forward in straight lines; instead our movements curve and flow, our hands describing a circle in the air. "Breathe," he murmurs, "remember to breathe," so I do, feeling that by-now-familiar warmth collect in my tan-t'ien and spread through me.

He changes things up. He stands the circle on its end, so our hands flow over and under each other. The upright circles become figure-eights, our wrists keeping their contact as our arms twist sinuously. Each time I fall into the new pattern without a hitch, sway back as he pushes me, then sway forward as I push back.

The rhythm becomes as natural as breathing. I can feel that strange warmth flowing through me, lighting up each bone of my spine in turn, then cresting into my chest and rushing down into my core again, circling through me just as our arms circle each other.

And it's not just me. I begin to think I can feel a similar warmth coming from Yu Hao. I can feel it where our hands touch, like I've dipped my hand into a stream and I'm feeling the flow of the current. Only this current is inside him.

When Yu Hao brings our other hands into the pattern, crossing and recrossing each other, I have to slow down, but only a little. Each new motion seems almost inevitable. At some point we've gotten very close, and a part of me feels that keenly, but mostly I'm just absorbed in what we're doing.

Then he drops into a low stance, and lunges forward—and somehow I *know* he's going to do it, and I drop too. I can't stop a silly grin from spreading across my face, but it's okay because Yu Hao's grinning too. Without warning he sidesteps, comes at me from the side strong enough to push me over, except I've already yielded and kept my balance and in the next moment I'm sidestepping myself and pushing back.

No pattern to our movements now. We sidestep, circle around each other, lunging and parrying, each trying to knock the other off balance, but anticipating each other perfectly so we just keep going. We're dancing—that's what it is, a dance, and as we dance the sun finally crests the city wall and the rooftops light up around us.

I see his next move coming a mile away; I'll push his arm back and he'll yield, drawing me in, his other arm coming up like he's going to get me in a hold. The right move is to step away, keep the pattern going, but instead I let it happen, let him fold his arm around me and draw me close. We stay there for a moment, his arm around me from behind, his chest rising and falling against my back. I lose the game, I guess, but I find it hard to care.

Then he tenses up and lets go of me, steps back, awkward and hurried. I look at him sharply; I almost care more that he's broken that beautiful flow than that he's recoiled from me. We look at each other for what seems a long time, both of us breathing hard. Then he straightens. "Enough," he says, and I don't push it.

CHAPTER SIXTEEN

When I wake up I'm lying on Yu Hao's straw mattress, and for a drowsy moment I think he's there with me, but he isn't, and the mattress would be too small for both of us anyway.

I let the drowsiness drain away and the memories surface. I'd thought it would be awkward after our dance on the rooftop ended the way it did, but then the exhaustion hit me, so hard my legs almost gave out. Not the grinding fatigue I'm used to—this was more like a luxurious weight in my limbs, a feeling like being wrapped in a warm blanket. I realized we'd been dancing for hours, and even as I stood there I'd felt my eyelids begin to flutter and droop. Yu Hao had to lower me onto the windowsill, once again as if it was no effort at all, and when I was inside my legs *did* give out and I went sprawling.

"Sleep, now," said Yu Hao, and stayed only long enough to see me lay on my side the way he showed me, and breathe the way he showed me, and then he left, and I slept.

Everything around me, every detail, is perfectly clear, the way it was on the rooftop. I can feel every knot and fibre of the mattress beneath my arm, see every hairline crack in the wall a few feet from my head. I can hear everything too, and I weave each sound into a tapestry showing me what's going on outside the room.

That scuffing sound: that's Red, in those felt riding boots of hers, climbing the stone stairs from the ground floor. A soft rustle: Yu Hao is sitting at the top of the stairs waiting for her, in his white scholar's robe. Red's tanned leather jacket creaks as she sits down one step below him, and her wine jar sloshes as she takes a gulp. *Slosh*: she offers him the jug. *Slosh, gulp*: he takes it, swigs and swallows. Red says something in that other language, liquid consonants and vowels that climb and swoop.

"Khitai," says Yu Hao. Red groans and says something else. I keep my eyes shut and don't move, just in case they check on me, even though I have no idea whether they have anything to say that's worth hearing. "Your brain would not need a rest if you hadn't soaked it in wine, Red. Khitai, please. I need practice."

"Like hell," says Red, although she says it in Khitai. "You speak it better than I do."

"Where did you learn?"

Another gulp and swallow. "We had a Chi'tan stable hand on our estate. I spoke it with him to piss my dad off. Also hooked up with him a little bit. Also to piss my dad off."

"'Filial piety'," says Yu Hao like he's quoting something, "'is the root of virtue.'" There's real disapproval in his voice.

"Funny, that's what my dad said."

"Where is your southern friend?" says Yu Hao, evidently looking for a change of subject.

"Passed-out drunk downstairs. He can get us work, by the way. There's a caravan leaving for Kashgar in a couple days."

"He seemed quite taken with you." I don't hear any jealousy in Yu Hao's voice. So Red and him probably aren't an item. Interesting.

"He's very beautiful," says Red, "but he makes love like the Eight-Precepts Pig and he in*sists* on reciting poetry to me in languages I don't speak. But I'll put up with him as far as Kashgar, if it gets us out of here."

"We only just arrived in Samarkand."

"Well we have to turn around somewhere, unless you were planning on ending up in Baghdad or something—"

"Baghdad." His voice is alive with enthusiasm. "The House of Wisdom. As great a centre of learning as Hanlin Academy, they say.

A *million* books—"

"Yu Hao," warns Red, "we are *not* going to Baghdad. We are going home."

"And turn our backs on a copy of the *Yin-yün Chen-ching*? Where anyone could get their hands on it?"

"Come on, Yu Hao. Even if that's what it is—which I doubt—these barbarians won't even know what they have."

"It's not the barbarians I'm worried about."

"Oh come *on*. 'Crow'? Seriously?" Yu Hao says nothing, and Red sighs. "Okay, fine. She sounds like a player, sure." Another pause. "You don't think she's just a player." Another. "You think she's one of *them*."

"It fits."

"They're dead, Yu Hao. Them and the Blades took each other all the way down, and good riddance to both of them. This Crow is just a chancer. Like us. Or she's from some little Wulin sect no one's ever heard of, and this box she's looking for doesn't mean anything to anyone but her. You know how it goes—it's her shih-fu's shih-fu's bamboo backscratcher or something. She'll move heaven and earth to get it, but to anyone else it's a crappy old stick."

"You really believe that?" replies Yu Hao. "You saw what Darya wrote in the yurt—"

"The kid *can't read Chinese*, Yu Hao. I bet she can't read at *all*."

'Kid'? You're not two years older than I am, you smug—but Red's speaking again.

"How's she doing, anyway?" It's her turn to change the subject, and I doubt Yu Hao is fooled but he responds evenly anyway.

"At first...well, you know. She's been starved, run ragged, probably since she could walk. The state her middle *chiao* was in, I'm surprised she *can* walk—and on top of that, to teach her ch'ing-kung... Back home, even a child would have some training, a foundation I could build on, but not out here. I thought I would teach her a little tao-yin, a little ch'ing-kung, to keep her on her feet. That was the most I could do."

I'm grinding my teeth so loudly I'm surprised they don't hear. So I'm a charity case. I knew it. I *knew* it. *You son of a bitch*, Yu Hao—

"Or so I thought," he continues, and I hold my breath and listen.

Red takes another gulp of wine. "What are you talking about now?"

"She does have a foundation, Red. And it's self-taught. She has a grasp of wu-wei, she calls it the 'current'—"

"She's a Taoist," says Red, "is what you're telling me. A Taoist barbarian street urchin."

"Not at all. Her understanding is shallow and imperfect, and in several respects completely wrong." *Thanks a lot.* "But if she were to seek the Tao, I think she would do very well. I showed her *t'ui-shou*, just now, on the roof. By the end of an hour you'd have said she'd been training for a solid week. She has potential, Red. A lot of potential."

"Potential isn't worth shit." Red's voice is flat and final. "You know that as well as I do. You could find a kid in every village from here to Angkor with that kind of talent. Talent is cheap. It doesn't mean a thing unless they work for it. Kung fu, as you like to say." There's that word again.

"She has kung fu, Red. How do you think she's survived this long? She's been through more than most people three times her age—"

"Wait a second. Do you want to stay because of the box, or because of the kid?" I'm grinding my teeth again. Silence, and Red groans. "I don't believe it. You're nobody's shih-fu, Yu Hao. And if you're right about all this, it could get real nasty, real quick—you want to drop her right in the middle of that?"

More silence, and Red hawks and spits. "Fine. Fine. At least it'll get Poetry Pig out of my hair. We stay. But just as soon as our drinking money runs out, I'm hiring on with a caravan and getting out of here. With or without you."

They don't say anything more, and although I don't hear them leave, I can tell they've gone. When I come downstairs a little while later, they're not there either.

CHAPTER SEVENTEEN

Once again, no one is at Nina's counting table. There's a pile of stolen goods there, but it's smaller than yesterday's; I guess everyone's catching on that no one's checking. I touch the astrolabe in my kameez, and hurry into the warehouse. The pile of boxes in the courtyard is smaller too. Oleg's going to be furious, but that's not what I'm most scared of right now. I'm thinking of what's inside him, the sickness Crow talked about.

That glimpse of Oleg retching in the alley returns to my mind again and again. He's sick. He's really sick, and if he goes, the Martens go. We all hate Oleg, but we couldn't survive without Oleg's rep. It's a circle of firelight, and outside all the wild animals are pacing, all the other gangs and ahdath and slavers and everyone else who wants a piece of the Martens. Fire burns—*that poker, an inch from my face*—but it keeps the beasts at bay, outside the circle. Now the fire is dying, the circle is shrinking, and the beasts are closing in. And everyone knows it. The pickpockets should be cheering, with no quota, but even the littlest of us looks uneasy. This isn't right.

"Where have you been?"

I start, then hope I didn't look too guilty. It's Masoud, of course, sidling up to me and talking out of the corner of his mouth. Beside him stands 'Uj, standing there with his arms folded over his massive chest. He's looking in my direction but his eyes don't acknowledge me at all.

"No one's seen you hustling for the past two days. I still run the pickpockets, Darya. Whatever scam this is, you need to clear it with me." I'm guessing Nina has asked him to lean on us, get us earning again.

"Where have *you* been, then?" I say, just to have a comeback, even if it's a weak one. Astonishingly, though, he flinches, and has to take a moment to think of a reply. Over 'Uj's shoulder, I see Crow and Oleg and Nina coming out of Oleg's shack.

"That's not how this works, Darya. You clear things with me, not the other way around, get it?" He glances at Crow as she stalks around the pile, then turns her back on it without saying anything. Nina clenches her bony old fists. She's clearly furious.

Masoud is on edge, and he either doesn't see them or doesn't bother to lower his voice. "So whatever you're doing, you just—" Then he isn't there any more. Oleg's grabbed him and yanked him backwards, one fist bunched in his kameez. He spins Masoud to face him and swings his huge hand back.

I'm not quite believing what's happening. Masoud is Nina's pet, and Oleg listens to Nina—her brains are the reason he's running an empire rather than brawling in an alley, and he's smart enough to know it. But not this time, apparently, because now he slaps Masoud across the face, three times, forehand, backhand, forehand again, then lets go of his kameez and dumps him on the ground.

Masoud hunches over, hands over his face, choking and snivelling. Conscious, in other words, so Oleg was just teaching him a lesson, but the suddenness of it is still shocking, and leaves me with that floaty not-all-there feeling you get when you've narrowly avoided a nasty fall, or when a horse gallops past you and misses kicking you in the face by inches.

Masoud sobs loudly. "Grandmother!" he wails, imploring Nina, but Nina looks away, not wanting to get between Oleg and the object of his rage. Everyone is standing very still. Except 'Uj, who lumbers away a couple of steps, unsubtly putting some distance between him and Masoud. Except Crow, who doesn't even glance at Masoud as she heads into the warehouse.

Insanely, this makes me feel a little bit better. This kind of sudden violence is how Oleg got where he is, and if he can still do this, then maybe his rep isn't dying after all. But then he starts coughing, so hard he has to stoop, meaty hands—not so meaty as they used to be—on his thighs, hacking and retching. It goes on for almost a full minute, while everyone shuffles their feet and stares at the sky through the crooked branches of the dead tree. He can't even dismiss us properly, just waves a hand—*piss off*—while he fights for breath. No speech, no meeting. We file out in silence.

In the dorm, everyone is too still; they're only pretending to sleep, everyone's on edge. I glance at the empty cot next to me. Maybe they took the burned kid to the orphanage to join the beggars. Maybe not.

The far end of the dorm erupts into violence. I didn't see what started it but it's 'Uj, beating down a smaller kid, who tries a couple of punches and then just huddles, hoping for it to be over. No one says anything, the only sounds are hoarse breathing and thudding blows. While everyone's looking at the fight, I roll out of my cot and slip down the ladder. I need to think.

I pad through the darkened warehouse. My legs twinge a little but otherwise don't hurt at all—whatever Yu Hao did with that bottle of goo, it seems to have worked. There's hardly any light at all, but I don't need any, I just put out my hand and touch the shelves. Cool clay, smooth and round—that's the Bukhara earthenware, I'm almost at the end of an aisle. I turn left.

We're not supposed to hang around in the warehouse itself, but most of this stuff belongs to that Bulgar merchant, not Oleg and Nina, and they don't really give a crap if we steal anything—I mean, if they find out they'll beat us until we piss blood, but only for getting caught.

I can still feel the lingering traces of whatever Yu Hao and I were doing on the rooftop, a banked fire in my belly and spine, giving off an almost feverish heat. I feel restless too, like you get with a fever, but I'm not sweaty or weak. I'm full of energy, more than I've ever felt in my life.

I put out my hand again. Cracked and corrugated leather, the spines of books. I turn left again, into another aisle. Yu Hao could read all these books, probably. He was reading Greek earlier, and not even Masoud can do that. He could tell me who wrote them, what they were about. So could Masoud, maybe, but Masoud uses knowledge like a club, to beat you down and make you feel small and stupid. Yu Hao treats it more like the music he was playing on that ch'in of his— he just loves it, the beauty of it, for its own sake. I think of his long fingers flicking over the strings. He's quiet, scholarly, what Masoud and the other Martens would call 'soft'. But there's nothing soft about Yu Hao at all. I remember his arms, all knotty muscle, catching me as I fell, and I imagine him holding me, those fingers tracing the bumps of my spine, and I shiver hard.

This isn't love. Not the storytellers' kind, and not Farid's desperate neediness either. I don't want Yu Hao to recite poetry at me or protect me from anything. I just want *him*, and as I admit this to myself I feel a rush of desire that makes my head spin, like raw hunger but shot through with something sweeter.

I think of him pulling away from me on the rooftop. We were still connected, I could still feel the currents of energy inside him, so I know: it wasn't because he didn't feel the same desire I do. It was because he did.

I'm so caught up in this idea that when sparks flare in the corner room I almost walk straight into it. Quickly I back up two steps and duck behind one of the big wooden posts that hold up the warehouse roof. I stay there, not daring to breathe, as the sparks die and the yellow glow of candlelight replaces them. I'm listening hard, but there's nothing—no. Wait. There's something just at the edge of hearing, a scratching, slithering noise. Rats? After another minute, I draw a cautious, silent breath, and lean slowly out from behind the post, just far enough for one eye to peer around it.

Once again, Crow kneels at the table, shaking out the tinder she used to light her candle. Once again she's wearing her leathers—does she ever take them off?—and her swords rest against the wall. Once again the bronze dish is on the table before her, but this time the white cloth that covered it is folded to the side. Crow's body is in the way and I can't see what's inside it..

That feverish heat flares up, goading me to get closer, to see more. Down here, though, I feel way too exposed. The shelves are inviting, with lots of hand- and footholds, but I'll make a ton of noise climbing up all that creaking wood.

The wooden post I'm hiding behind, though...in the faint candlelight I see the large notches spaced up its height, footholds cut by the carpenters who built the place. I take a deep breath, as quietly as I can. Then I crouch and spring off the ground, and manage to hook my fingers into the lowest notch. A splinter buries itself in the fleshy pad below my thumb, and I dangle there, biting my lip so I don't hiss in pain.

This is dumb. I can't do this. I'll just drop to the floor, creep away and back up the ladder, go back to bed...but the embers in my belly flare again, sparks rising up my spine, and I find the strength to swing my other arm up, grab another notch. Trying not to think too much about what I'm doing, I take up Yu Hao's breathing pattern. Almost immediately that inner warmth becomes heat, like coals in a forge brightening under the bellows. And I climb.

It's tricky—these holds were made for a grown man, much taller than I am. From each one I can just reach the next by bracing my foot against the post and then springing up. I keep breathing, fanning those embers. I have the urge to breathe faster, stoke them higher, but something tells me that I might blow them out instead; and if that happens, if I have to rely only on the strength in my muscles, I'll just be dangling here until sunup. So I breathe carefully, and I feel the heat rising up my spine until it crests and falls, and floods my chest with what feels like liquid fire. And almost before I know it I'm two thirds of the way up the post, high above the corner room's walls.

Still I keep climbing, intoxicated by how easy it is. And when I'm level with the top of the shelves and only a few feet from the roof, I reach for the next handhold, and miss.

My hands scrabble at the wood. I can feel myself toppling backwards off the post. Everything slows down as I exhale sharply, push off against the post with a foot, then again with the other foot, then once more and I'm lunging up. My palms skid over the wood, collecting one, two, three more splinters—I can feel each one by one as it punctures my skin—

My hands slide over the angled brace that supports the roof. I hook an elbow over it and hang there, swinging. Finally I manage to kick off the post, swing up and over the brace. I straddle it with my torso flat against the wood, pressing my cheek into it. I pick up another splinter, but I don't care. I look down at the post, and I can just see, in the traces of candlelight that make it this high, my footprint on the dusty wood.

The post is smooth and vertical, and I ran up it. *Ran.* For a moment I'm so amazed at what I've done that I forget what all this was for in the first place, but then I hear a sound from below and the world comes back. I breathe softly and silently. I don't know if Crow could hear me. I may or may not believe she's a witch, like Nasr does, but I'm not taking any chances. I lean out, very carefully, until I can see into the corner room. What I see convinces me that none of this is happening. I'm still in the dorm, having a dream. A bad one.

Crow still kneels before the bronze dish on the table. It's filled almost to the brim with live bugs. The candlelight slides over fat furry bodies and shining black shells—spiders, broad flat cockroaches, fleshy things with spindly legs I've never seen before. The lip of the bowl must be coated with oil, because anything that tries to crawl out just slips back into the heaving mass.

Crow's hand hovers over the dish for a moment, and then—fast, she's so *fast*—it's darted in and out, and her fingers are curled around something, making a loose cage. She turns her hand over and opens it. The biggest scorpion I've ever seen hunches in her palm. Its barbed stinger rears and quivers in the candlelight. With her other hand, Crow draws back the sleeve of her jacket, exposing her road-tanned forearm. Everything is very clear.

Then it strikes. Once, twice, three times, the stinger piercing the most delicate part of her wrist, right where her pulse makes her skin flutter. After the third strike it stays there, buried in her flesh. Her jacket creaks just a little as her whole body tenses.

I can't be sure if I'm really seeing the next part or it's just a trick of the light and my own horrified brain. From the tip of the scorpion's stinger, black lines spread down Crow's bare arm, forging through her veins to the rhythm of her heartbeat. Then Crow exhales, and for a moment steam, or smoke, seems to curl from her nostrils.

And the black lines reverse themselves, retreating along her forearm to her wrist, up and into the scorpion's barb. The scorpion jerks its tail free, shudders once, and dies. It collapses onto her palm, its legs curled underneath it. It's so quiet I can hear the tiny *crunch* as Crow casually crushes it in her fist.

Voices, raised in anger and fear, break the silence into a thousand pieces. Footsteps scuffle and squeak on the floor, and the flickering glow of a torch rises among the shelves. Crow remains still for a moment, then tosses the scorpion's corpse into the bowl of horrors. She doesn't bother covering it with the sheet, or even getting up.

The warehouse suddenly seems full of Martens, though after a moment I see there are only five, all of them muscle. Sanjar is in the lead with the torch; its flame burns bright and tall, and Sanjar's hand is shaking, and I wince, imagining what will happen if the flame kindles the goods on the shelves. Sanjar doesn't seem to notice the danger. His other arm is wrapped around something big and rectangular, wrapped in sackcloth.

Two of his friends are right behind him, on either side of a third man, marching him across the floor with their fingers digging into his forearms. A cloth bag covers the captive's head. The final two Martens are carrying an inert body, holding him by his arms and legs. It's... Azat, another of the muscle, and even from up here I can tell that he's dead. He has something on his face. They lay him down and it glitters in the torchlight—a slender length of metal, protruding from his eye.

Kazan, one of the Martens who'd been carrying their dead comrade, crosses the floor below me, heading for the back door and the courtyard. He's gone only a moment before I hear Oleg's racking cough, getting closer. By the time Oleg follows Kazan inside, still pulling on his furs, the Martens have forced their prisoner to his knees. They're not gentle with him, but I can tell they're holding back. They're afraid of him, although he looks like a bum; he wears silks but they're worn almost to rags, covered with sweat- and wine-stains. No one says anything.

As Sanjar sticks his torch in a bracket on the wall, Oleg strides up to the prisoner and, without any theatrics, pulls the bag off his head. If I'd hoped for some revelation from seeing his face, I'm disappointed. He's from the East, like Yu Hao and Red and Crow herself, but other than that he's just a guy. In fact, he looks more like a bum than ever, sweaty from the bag and red-faced with drink.

"He had this on him," says Sanjar, and casts something at Oleg's feet. It's a sword, of a type I haven't seen before—not as big as the Teuton's or as broad as Crow's sabres; it's slender and straight, clearly meant to be used one-handed. It hits the floor with a clatter.

"*Pick it up.*" It's Crow, and her voice is an animal snarl. She strides from the corner room, her swords at her back, her eyes bright in the torchlight. "*Pick. It. Up.*" She doesn't reach for her sword. She doesn't have to. The cold fury in her voice is enough. Sanjar drops to his knees, his face ashen, and scrabbles for the sword, which he offers to Crow. She snatches it from him, and instantly she seems to forget he's even there. She holds the slender blade up, turning it in the light.

Kazan is saying something to Oleg: "—was staying at the Three Peaches, the whorehouse? The Kyrgyz hung out there, that's why we checked. The whores said he took a room there a few days ago, and then yesterday for no reason he flips out and kills their pimp. The girls run, and he just stays there, drinking. The pimp was *still there* when we found him, dead on the floor."

He rambles on. "We bust into his room, he's drunk off his ass, but when we go to get him he just"—Kazan flicks his hand, like he's throwing something—"and then Azat is frigging *dead*." His voice is close to breaking. "That thing, it went straight into Azat's eye, right into his *brain*—"

"Shut up," says Oleg. He's watching Crow and the prisoner.

The prisoner looks up at Crow. Like her, he seems to have forgotten that Oleg and the Martens are even there. "*Ni shih shui?*"

Crow is still examining the sword; she doesn't answer or even look at him. Instead she steps aside slightly, so the prisoner can look past her into the corner room, where the bugs scuttle and writhe in their bronze dish. All the redness drains out of the captive's face. He says, "*Wu tu ch'uan.*" He looks back at Crow. He says, "*Pai-hsieh.*" His throat is tight with terror and the words come out as a hoarse bark.

Crow looks at him for the first time. She speaks in Khitai: "I'm sick of half-barbarian *hua-pei* grunting. I don't intend to speak it, or listen to it, ever again."

The man takes a deep breath, and finds some reserve of drunken courage. As he exhales his spine straightens and a haughty expression settles on his face. "You must be delighted, White Scorpion. Another Celestial Blade for you to butcher."

Crow's gaze is back on the sword. "Did they make the novices scrub the kitchen floors on Pai-Hu Mountain? When you finished, as the sun came up, and you couldn't feel your hands any more, and you put all your brushes and pails away, and then realized you missed a spot? Were you 'delighted'?" She turns away. "You should have kept running, Blade." She swipes the sword through the air a few times, testing its weight and balance.

The captive's eyes flare. "Don't you—" he almost shouts, but his voice cracks and he has to clear his throat, and when he continues his voice is lower, but full of venom. "Your hands are stained with innocents' blood, Scorpion. They defile that sword."

"Stained?" A hiss that might be a laugh. "Soaked. To the elbow." Once again her voice is soft and dead. "So who are you, then, whose hands are so pure?"

He half-rises, lifting his chin with pride. "I am—" and one of the Martens strikes him on the shoulder, driving him down again.

"Let him go," says Crow. "Get out. All of you, out." She points at Oleg with the captive's sword. "Except you." The sword now points at Sanjar and his sackcloth bundle. "And you."

No one needs Oleg to speak. It looks like everyone knows what the score is, now, in the Martens. Where the orders are coming from. Oleg included, because although he doesn't look happy he stays where he is.

Once they've left—even the dead one, carried by the same two friends who brought him in—everything is very quiet. Even though I'm breathing as shallowly as I can, I still sound to myself like a blacksmith's bellows. And if they hear me, there's nowhere to run.

"You were saying?" says Crow, finally, to the captive. "Who are you?"

Any pride he's shown has flickered out. He looks at the floor. "Does it matter?"

"I have chased you and what you stole across half the world. Call me curious."

"I am Yang Jing, of Pai-Hu Mountain Temple—"

"There is no Pai-Hu Mountain Temple," says Crow wearily. "Not anymore."

"Because you murdered us!"

"Yes, we murdered you. All of you. We counted. So I repeat—who are you? A novice? Or not even that? Kitchen hand? Stable boy? Cleaner of temple latrines?" The captive, Yang Jing, hawks and spits noisily on the floor in defiance—but it feels hollow. Crow has scored a hit.

She sighs bitterly. "I was hoping, after all this time, coming all this way, that if I had to kill again, it would at least be someone worth killing. But I dare say you had your own hopes as well. We are both disappointed." She crosses the floor slowly, until they are only a stride apart, and stands there, looking down at him. "While your temple burned, amid the killing and the looting, you got your hands on a sword you hadn't earned." She crouches, her eyes level with his, and points the sword at his chest. He goes very still. "But that's not all you got your hands on, was it?"

His eyes flick to hers, suddenly terrified, and back again. "Yes," says Crow. "Now we come to it. Where is it?" He doesn't say a word. A dozen emotions cross his face—anger, bitterness, sullenness, all of them shot through with dread.

Exasperation animates Crow's voice. "The box belongs to us. To the Scorpions. This has never been in dispute. I want our property back. Is this...*unreasonable*? Should I have had to ride two thousand miles to this latrine of a city, take it apart with my bare hands, to find what all along *belonged to me*?" Her bitterness grows with each word. "I can make you talk. You know that. Why prolong this? Why not save yourself the agony?"

That sets something off in Yang Jing. "Everyone at Pai-Hu Mountain, did you save them any agony? I was there, I saw what happened. To the women, the children—"

I don't see her move but suddenly Crow is on her feet, and shouting. She's ranting something in a language I don't know, not the same one she was using with the captive. Her hoarse voice raps out syllable after syllable, spittle flecking her lips. A minute ago, her losing control like this would have been impossible, unthinkable. What blood was left in Yang Jing's face drains away under Crow's barrage of words.

She draws a hitching breath, and *shrieks*, in Khitai again. "*Where is it?*" There are cracks in her voice, and as she continues they widen and the bright light of madness pours through. "*Where is it? Where is it, where is it, WHERE IS IT—*"

"*I sold it!*" Yang Jing almost yells it, and I think he does so less from fear of whatever torture Crow is holding over him than just to stop that terrible mad screaming.

It works, because the flood of Crow's words stops instantly, like a torch going out when it's plunged in water. I realise I have my hands pressed over my ears, and ease them off. Below me, Oleg looks like he'd rather be anywhere but here. Which is understandable. He's just seen that the woman he hopes will save his life is utterly insane.

The silence that falls is somehow even more terrible than the screaming, and just to fill it, Yang Jing continues: "I sold it to the first person who'd buy it. It had been a long journey. I needed wine. A man, they called him the Kyrgyz, arranged the purchase. You can find him at—"

"I found him," says Crow.

Yang doesn't need to ask how. "I *told* him not to open the box. So...I sold it to that prick of a pimp. When I had some wine in me and I could think straight, I realized I'd gotten a tenth part of a tenth part of what it was worth. So I went back and murdered him, but by then he'd sold it himself. I was drinking my way through his wine cellar when your people found me."

"Where is it?" asks Crow again. Her voice is back to a whisper, but filled with dreadful intensity.

He shrugs, some of the drunken insolence coming back. He nods at Sanjar and his bundle. Crow drops the sword with a clatter, strides over to Sanjar and pulls it out of his hands. "Out," she says, and he obliges. She strips the sackcloth off with shaking hands. There's no box underneath it, though, just a battered leather-bound book.

"This will never end." Crow is looking up, and my heart seizes in my chest, but she's not looking at me. She's not looking at anything. That madness I heard in her voice...I can see it in her eyes now. The madness of exhaustion, of despair. Her knuckles are white as she grips the book. "This will never, ever end. This is my punishment, to hunt the *Yin-Yün Chen-Ching* across the earth forever." She speaks with flat certainty.

Yang shrugs again. "Every time he bought something, sold something, he wrote it all down in that. What he sold, who to and how much. It'll be in there."

Crow looks down at him sharply. She presses the book into Oleg's hands. He flips through some pages in the torchlight—I didn't know he could read—and finally he nods. "It's here. Just a few days ago. Whoever he sold it to, probably they still have it." He tosses the book into the corner room, onto the table.

Crow's back sags then, just a little, as though an immense weight has come off her shoulders. Then her spine is straight again, and she turns to the captive, who is on his feet and holding the sword she dropped, his arm straight and the point of the blade pointed at her throat.

"Crow?" Oleg says.

"The *chien*," Crow says, nodding at the sword. Her voice is once again cold and dead but somehow lighter, like any minute she's going to smile. I do not want to see Crow's smile. "The 'gentleman of weapons'. And no school of swordsmanship purer than the Falling Blossom Style of the Celestial Blades." She looks at him, speaks almost conversationally. "I missed the fight, did you know that? Such as it was. I was in the kitchens."

"*You evil whore*—" Yang Jing bursts out, then stops himself, terror on his face even though there's a sword in his hand.

"Were I a whore," says Crow, "I would have a full purse, at least, to show for all this. No." Her voice is shot through with bitterness. "I did what I did for *love*." Now one of her own sabres is in her hand. The other remains sheathed at her back.

"I wanted someone worth killing," she says. "But you will have to do." She raises her blade. Yang draws himself up to stand almost on tiptoe, his sword arm cocked behind his head with the blade pointed at Crow and his other arm extended in front of him, first two fingers raised in a formal fighting pose.

"What are you *doing*—" Oleg manages to say, but in that time Yang has closed the distance between himself and Crow. Crow meets the edge of his sword with her own, and the fight begins.

The first time Crow and Yang Jing cross swords, Crow's sabre sweeping aside his chien's stabbing thrust, I realize I've made a mistake. The second time, Yang parrying Crow's strike at his neck and drawing sparks from their blades, I know I've made a *huge* mistake. The third time their swords meet, I know I'm dead.

I'd known Crow was dangerous, of course. From the very first time I saw her, stalking the courtyard like a lioness, I'd been as hesitant to cross her as I was to cross Oleg and Nina. I knew helping Yu Hao and Red to snatch this mystery box from under her nose could be deadly... but at the same time, I'd seen Red and Yu Hao drop the Teuton, and do it with style. I'd thought that I could go to them, if I was in trouble. That they could protect me.

But Yang Jing is already on the defensive, stepping back as Crow's blade cuts at him high and low. He moves like Red and Yu Hao move, like he weighs nothing, like he's walking on air, but Crow is on another level entirely. She doesn't float, she doesn't seem to move at all; she's just *there*, wherever she needs to be to block Yang's attack or counter with one of her own. Like the scorpion on her palm just now, its tail moving too fast to see.

Yang Jing knows it, too. He tries to make the fight three-dimensional, to soar up onto the shelves, but each time Crow is there to stop him. Her sabre chops down at him, forcing him back to the ground. She kicks at Yang's legs, her foot flicking out in a blur that makes him leap back instead of up to save his kneecap.

I can see it all. And I can see Crow is toying with her opponent, leaving him illusory escape routes that vanish when he tries to take advantage of them. Like a cat with a half-dead mouse, and like a cat she doesn't even seem to be enjoying it. No more mad shrieking, she's as dead-eyed as always.

No way even Red and Yu Hao can stand up to her. I'd thought Red fighting the Teuton was fast? I had *no idea* what fast was. Even Yang, a drunk in stained silks, is better than them, and only barely holding his own here. Their blades flicker too fast to see, steel clashing on steel over and over again so fast my ears can't separate one strike from the next.

I couldn't follow most of what those two were talking about, but I got some of it. The Blades and the Scorpions—they're crews, gangs, like the Martens and the Wolves. Yang was a Blade, and he stole this box from the Scorpions. That's what this is all about. Red and Yu Hao don't even act like they have a crew. They can't protect me, not if Crow decides to come for me. I'm done.

Now Crow's sabre slices at Yang's knees and he manages to leap over it, and finally he can soar into the air. He lands atop a shelf, light as a feather, balancing on a stack of porcelain cups without knocking over a one. Crow leaps after him, cutting through the air like a cracked whip.

Then what I'd been praying wouldn't happen happens. Yang, crouching on top of the shelf, catches my eye. His face goes blank with surprise, and he opens his mouth to say something, to give me away. Then Crow erupts from between the shelves and her sabre whips around in a long arc that passes through his shoulder joint and takes his left arm off.

He falls, still light as a feather, landing with barely a sound even as bright blood pumps from severed arteries. Crow lands in front of him. Her blade is bright too—it passed through him so quickly it didn't catch a drop of blood.

Yang stands, swaying on his feet a little, and I wait for him to drop. Then his nostrils flare and I see him falling into a breathing pattern—different from the one Yu Hao taught me, more complex. And to my astonishment, the pulse of blood from his arm slows to a trickle, and stops. And he raises his chien again. Crow watches him, and nods with approval, and then she butchers him.

He barely gets his sword up before Crow smashes it aside. Then her sabre whickers through his flesh once, twice, three times, each time followed by a gout of blood. He crumples without a sound.

Crow looks down at him. Blood mists her face. Blood runs down her arms, rains from her sabre and patters on the floor. He looks up at her, his silks dark with more blood, sitting in a pool of it that spreads out all around him. And she turns and walks away.

He sags with relief. Whatever he'd feared Crow would do to him, bleeding out on the warehouse floor is mercy by comparison—

Crow changes her mind. She turns, looms over him, and he holds up a hand to placate her but she's already reaching down and grabbing a fistful of silk, hauling him up. He splutters as she drags him, feet twisting on the floor, leaving shining streaks in the torchlight. Then he sees where she's taking him, and despite how much blood he's lost, he finds it in himself to scream.

When she drags him into the corner room, his slick hands scrabbling ineffectually at her fingers, and pushes him face-first into the bronze dish full of bugs, I very nearly scream myself. They swarm through his hair, biting and stinging, and at first he tries to lift his head but then his whole body goes slack, paralysed. He's still shrieking, but his shrieks become muffled as the bugs flood into his mouth and then, finally, *finally*, they fade.

Everything is silent, for the longest time. I hold onto the wooden brace like it's going to buck like a bull and throw me off. Maybe it will. If *that* just happened, then anything could happen, there are no limits to the world, it's a boulder careening down a mountainside and no one can stop it.

"When?" asks Crow. A spider is crawling up her arm and she absently brushes it off.

"I know—" Oleg's voice is tight and he stops to clear his throat. "I know this man, that he sold the box to. A son of Inal. This will be difficult." Crow says nothing. "Big house, many guards. Gardens all around, so no getting in over the rooftops. Difficult."

"I will go myself," says Crow quietly. "I will kill the guards, I will kill everything else that breathes, and then I will tear the house apart brick from brick until I find what I am looking for."

He shakes his head. "The first scream will bring every ahdath in the city down on you. The Assassins are in Samarkand, no one's taking any chances. But," he continues hurriedly, "that's the good news. All the Inalids, they're leaving town, before they get their heads cut off. Going to Bukhara, in three days. Leaving their stuff here—Assassins don't care about their stuff.

"After that, no guards, nothing, easy picking for the thieves. Wait three days—give me the rest of my medicine—and we can get your box. And you can leave."

She remains silent, and finally he takes the silence for assent, and he nods and steps out of the torchlight. Crow stands there, head bowed, then follows him, dragging her feet like someone bone-tired. Faintly I hear Oleg barking at one of the Martens waiting outside, telling him to get someone to clean up the warehouse. Then, finally, silence falls.

I have to move, before whoever's cleaning up what's left of Yang Jing arrives. But it's forever before I can finally ease my hands from the brace they're wrapped around. Then what Oleg said finally penetrates my brain.

Three days, then Crow will have her box. I have three more days with Yu Hao, at most. No way he can teach me what I need to know in that time. But that's okay. Because I'm done.

Chapter Eighteen

I'm done," I say.

"You're late," says Yu Hao. I've only just entered his room upstairs in the tavern, but he's already at the window in the sleeveless tunic he was wearing at the caravanserai, one foot up on the sill. Now he leans out, reaches up to grab the edge of the roof.

"Actually I'm not," I say, "because I'm—" He's already swinging himself out and up.

The hell with this. The hell with him. I should turn and walk right out of here. Instead I step up onto the windowsill and lean carefully out so I can look up. He's grinning down at me. "Lots to do," he says, reaching down to take my hand.

"No, I—okay, fine." His calloused hand tightens on mine and I watch the muscles in his forearm bunch under his smooth skin as he lifts me up without any apparent effort.

My head clears the edge of the roof and a shadow whips across my face and makes me blink. I squint against the sunlight and see it's Red with her spear, standing on the roof of the building next door. The sun has just cleared the city wall and it silhouettes her long lithe body as she whips the spear around herself and spins it over her head, snapping it down so it's braced under her arm.

The briefest pause and then she's moving again, stepping across the roof with footwork as intricate as a dance's. Except dances don't usually include lightning-quick spear-thrusts and slashing sweeps like

Red's does. Her moves are harder, more emphatic, than Yu Hao's fluid circles, and I can easily imagine that steel point punching into someone's chest and bursting right out of their back. The horsetail tassel tied behind the blade is whipping around like it's in a hurricane as she dispatches a horde of unseen enemies. My eyes are getting used to the harsh sunlight, and I see she's grinning.

Now she drops into the splits, whirling the wooden shaft above her head, then effortlessly pulls her whole body up onto the tip of one foot as she sweeps the spear in a circle around herself, her beaded hair fanning out in a whirl of colour. Finally she comes to rest, chest rising and falling and that grin spread all the way across her sweaty face.

"Are you done?" I say. She shrugs, wiping sweat from her forehead, and without even a runup she's drifting through the air to the roof we're on, unhooking a gourd-shaped bottle from her belt and taking a swig in midair. I'm not in the mood for any of this. So I just say: "I can't do this anymore."

"Our agreement—" begins Yu Hao.

"It's off." It's all of a sudden very hard to speak. "Deal's off. Sorry."

Red shrugs, but Yu Hao keeps pressing. "There's nothing more about the box? You've learned nothing more?"

My throat is too tight for words. The disappointment in Yu Hao's eyes, the dismissal in Red's, make me clench my fists almost hard enough to draw blood. But I'm done with this. I'm not going to be cut to pieces or have my face eaten by bugs.

Yu Hao sighs. "Well, we—"

"They found it!" I blurt out. And like that the words are pouring out of me, I couldn't stop talking if I tried. "The box. They found it. They're going after it in just a few days."

"Where is it?" asks Yu Hao, a hard edge to his voice. He takes a step forward; Red puts a hand on his shoulder to draw him back.

I shake my head. "I don't know. There's a book, in the warehouse, but...I can't get it. I can't." My throat constricts. "She killed him," I whisper.

Red looks at me, and her voice isn't gentle but for once it isn't mocking either. "Killed who?" she says, and then the tears do come, but I keep talking.

Somewhere along the line Red takes a cloth-wrapped bundle out of her jacket and spreads it out on the roof between us—cured suktu sausage, yufka flatbread, even lauzinaj, crushed and greasy but still so sweet it makes my head spin.

I eat it. I'm still giving them information, after all, so I can tell myself I haven't dropped my end of the deal yet. Although even if I didn't have that excuse I'm not sure I could refuse. Getting used to a full stomach has been frighteningly easy, and suddenly I realize I haven't felt real hunger for days now. It's like my whole life I've been crawling on my belly, my horizon no further than my next meal, and since that morning at the caravanserai I've been able to stand up and see what's around me for the first time.

And that's what I'm really seeing as I talk, not Red or Yu Hao or Samarkand. I'm seeing my future, stretched out like an endless street, doors lining either side. And all my life, those doors have been slamming shut, one by one. I can't stay a pickpocket—Nina closes that door. I can't make thief—Masoud slams that one. Be even halfway a thief, a housemaid spying for Farid? Farid himself is behind that door, although he probably thinks he's holding it open for me even as he swings it shut. *Slam, slam, slam.* And it turns out that street does have an end, and it's a blank wall, and soon there's only one door left, my deal with Yu Hao, but behind that final door is Crow, face dripping blood, swinging it closed as she watches me with dead eyes.

I trail off. I want to be off this roof more than anything, so I stand up, and I've been sitting for so long that I have to pause for a moment while the blood starts pumping through my legs again. There's nothing more to say. I turn and look down off the rooftop at Yu Hao's window. The ground looks very far away, but no way I can bear asking them to help me down. No one's said anything for a while. They're looking at me, I can tell, I can feel their gaze prickling between my shoulder blades as I consider how to get down without breaking my neck.

Knowing it's a mistake, I look back at them. Yu Hao is still kneeling on the roof, lost in thought. Red is watching me, and the cool look in her eyes makes me say "What?" although I know it's a bad idea.

"Nothing," she says. "I think you're playing it smart, for what it's worth." But the cool look remains, belying the easy tone of her voice. I glance at Yu Hao, and he shrugs slightly. That shrug hurts more than Red's disdain, but it's not nearly enough to change my mind. I have nothing more to say. I'm done here. I turn my back on them and lean forward to study the drop to the windowsill.

I'm done here. I'm— I straighten and turn to face them again. "What have we even been *doing?*" I say to Yu Hao. "You were going to teach me to fly. How much flying have we done? Jack—"

"You did say," says Yu Hao mildly, "that you would follow my—"

"And you said you'd teach me!" I burst out. "All I've done with you is eat, breathe and dance. I *know* how to eat and breathe and I don't care about dancing *what are you smiling about?*" This last to Red, who's trying and failing to repress a grin.

"'Dancing'?" she says to Yu Hao, who shrugs.

"T'ui shou," he says, and Red's grin becomes a laugh.

"This I have to see," she says. Two strides of Red's long legs bring her across the roof to me. I look up at her and she holds up her hands, fist pressed to palm, saluting me like she did the Teuton. Then she drops into an easy stance, arms up and palms open.

"C'mon then," she says. "Dance with me."

I draw breath to tell her to get out of my face, but her hand is already moving, arcing around in an open-palm slap. I surprise myself by swinging my torso back and dodging it, mostly; her fingertips graze my nose. I clutch it and stare up at her through watering eyes. "*Ow!* You crazy—" I turn to Yu Hao. "Tell her to stop it!"

"Red—" Yu Hao begins, but she's driving a punch, fist held vertical, at my stomach.

This time I'm ready, or I think I am, and I dodge sideways, but it turns out the punch is a feint, which I just have time to realize before her foot lashes out and the tip of her felt riding boot strikes my bruised shin. I howl and stagger backwards almost to the edge of the roof, tears starting in my eyes.

"'Dancing', she calls it," says Red as she bears down on me. "What a waste of time." She's not trying to take me down—how would I still be standing, if she was? She's just a mean drunk who's out to humiliate me, and I'm damned if I'll let her. I close my eyes tight for a moment, squeezing the tears out of them, and when I open them again I'm breathing slow and deep, falling naturally into Yu Hao's pattern. Yu Hao himself stands to the side, watching us with his hands folded behind his back, not making a move to help me. Damn him too, then.

Red lashes out with the heel of her palm, but this time I sway aside and she hits nothing but air. She follows it up with a kick to my midsection, which only barely grazes my hip as I take an easy step sideways. My heels are not even a foot away from the edge, and from there it's two storeys straight down to sun-baked brick, but I can't make myself care.

Because I'm in the current now, like never before, and just like with Yu Hao, it's like we'd planned every move and practised it endlessly before this moment. I can't feel it inside Red the way I could with Yu Hao, when our hands were touching—except I kind of *can*, I can feel each surge of energy that lets me know when she's going to move and how.

"That's enough," says Yu Hao, standing beside us.

"Not quite," says Red, and her hand blurs as she jabs at my chest, too fast for me to dodge. And before I know I've done it, my arm has swept up and deflected the blow with my forearm, and just as quickly whipped out in a punch that thuds into her shoulder. I look at my hand in surprise. Red nods.

"Yep," she says, "thought so," and then the bitch pushes me off the roof.

CHAPTER NINETEEN

unches me off the roof, actually, more like. She drives both her hands forward in a double palm strike that launches me backwards into empty air. My stomach twists up as I fall, and there's an awful moment that lasts an eternity as I wait for my legs or my skull to shatter against the ground below—

—And then I'm skidding backwards along the ground—no, not the ground. I've landed on the rooftop across the street, looking at Red and Yu Hao across fifteen feet of empty air. As I stumble to a halt, I see with perfect clarity the twin scuff marks on the dusty brick where I landed, a good three feet from this roof's edge. I'd thought I was falling, but I was wrong.

I was flying.

"Was that necessary?" asks Yu Hao mildly. Although he's on the other side of the street I can hear him. It feels like I can hear everything, see everything. "We didn't know she was ready."

Red gives him a casual shrug. "Saved us some time either way."

"You *ASSHOLE!*" I practically scream it. I'm shaking like a leaf in a hurricane. "What did you do that for?"

Without even gathering her strength, Red leaps, and once again I watch her *float* over the alley. She lands a few feet in front of me, her boots scuffing the tracks my own feet made. Did I, could I, have soared like that?

Right now I don't care, because *she pushed me off a goddamn roof* and now she's going to pay for it. Almost before she lands I lunge at her, my fist swinging out in a clumsy haymaker. She sees it coming, of course, and I hit nothing but air as she neatly sidesteps. She looks bored.

That does it. I lash out with my foot this time, and again without exerting herself at all she soars away, arms out, spear in one hand, her beaded hair fluttering in the wind. Did I look like that, so graceful? She lands on the next roof over, the one kitty-corner with the tavern roof where Yu Hao still stands, his arms folded, watching us. I barely notice him. I'm leaping after Red, because I'm not done with her yet.

My first couple of leaps are clumsy—I land hard, stumble, nearly run myself off a roof on the second one. By the third I'm lighter on my feet, not as graceful as Red, but still...I'm flying.

Well, not flying, but close enough—there's no way muscle-power could carry me this far, even if I had any. I'm cheating, getting away with something, and although part of me is focused on catching Red, another part—one that's growing by the second—is revelling in it.

The next roof Red lands on is covered by a small forest of slender poles. A cat's cradle of washing lines stretches between them, clothes and sheets flapping in the wind. Her foot touches down on the top of a pole, and it doesn't even bend when she launches herself off it again. I'm not bold enough to try that (yet) so I run in leaping strides along the edge of the roof before soaring after her. By the next roof I'm smiling, and as we both land on the one after that I can't keep the biggest grin of my life breaking across my face. Red's grinning too, I can see her, and as she reaches the end of the final roof before the broad Boulevard of Roses and takes to the air I'm so full of joy I don't even think about stopping.

We hang in the air for an endless few seconds, then we're across the boulevard and traversing part of the Maze, now soaring up a storey, now floating down one, over the mismatched roofs. A shadow falls over us, and I look up at the Mausoleum, an immense oblong at least four storeys tall, roof flared out over delicate patterns of brickwork. At first I think Red is going to veer left or right, make me chase her around it, but that's not what she has in mind at all. She glides across the last street, and her boot touches the Mausoleum's wall, raising a puff of dust…and then she's running up the vertical wall itself, in long loping strides.

I almost hesitate then, but to hesitate would be to lose this feeling, and I'd rather fall. My sole lands with the lightest touch on the sun-warmed brick, and then I'm running after her.

I'm so in love with the sheer audacity of it that I slow down just a little, savouring the sensation. Then my bare foot slips on the wall with a squeak, and I feel the tug of gravity, just enough to remind me the earth is still there below me, and a spurt of fear sends me sprinting up until I crest the wall and land on the roof and crouch there, staring at the bricks between my feet, reassuring myself for a moment that I'm not going to fall.

I look up. I'd thought I'd had a good view of the city from the tavern roof, but right now I'm higher than anything in Samarkand but the Old Mosque's minaret, and I can see my whole world—the bazaars and the mosques and the Maze, the boulevards radiating out to the gates, the city wall around it all, and beyond, all the way to the horizon, the hills and half-tilled fields, the orchards dusted with the first green of spring and the sparkling canals. I stare.

"Not bad," says Red casually. She stands at my side, looking at it all with me. I look up at her and she looks down at me, and then we're both laughing like fools.

CHAPTER TWENTY

T hen I kick her in the shin. "Ouch," she says mildly.

"You threw me off a roof."

She lifts her leg to rub it, leaning on her spear. "The alternative was watching you take a run-up and stop at the edge a hundred times before you had the guts to jump. Dull."

She might have a point. If she'd just told me to jump like that, I never would have believed I could. I just *did* it, and I'm still not sure I believe it.

"You were sure I wouldn't fall?" I say, maybe a little bit mollified.

"Ninety-nine per cent." She thinks about it. "Ninety-five."

"You jerk." She really, really, is one. But I'm not going to let it kill my buzz.

We fall silent for a while, looking out across the city. I can't quite see Monk's Gate in the west—the dome of the Old Mosque is in the way—but there's a cloud of dust rising over there, the wind tugging at it. One of the great Silk Road caravans, either arriving or departing.

The plaza in front of the Mausoleum boils with activity, even this early in the morning; the food-sellers, carrying their mobile kitchens on their backs or those of their donkeys, are claiming the choicest spots, the ones that can expect the most traffic. I see a head of sandy hair, a head taller than the rest of the crowd. The Teuton. At the other end of the plaza, a splash of vivid colour, so far below us it looks like a child's toy. It's the Khwarezmian, the horse-merchant we ripped off. That was just a few days ago, although it feels like forever. But there's no way they'll see us up here. They wouldn't even think to look, because who could do what we've just done?

The silence stretches out until it's bowstring-taut. I'm not used to hanging around girls, to tell the truth. (Nina doesn't count.) The only ones I see are serving girls like Farid's squeeze, Mahnaz, and old women running stalls in the bazaar. Mahnaz's kind don't have any time for a pickpocket—they all think that serving a rich man makes you as good as one—and the women in the stalls all assume I'd steal their stuff as soon as their backs were turned. Which I would. So just being here with Red, I'm off the map. But there's one question I need to ask, and I turn to her. "How?"

She grins. "Ch'ing-kung." She gropes for a translation. "'Lightness-skill'? Chinese and Khitai, neither of them are my language, so—"

"But how—"

"*Ch'i*," says Yu Hao behind us.

Red rolls her eyes. "Here we go."

Yu Hao, his black lacquered ch'in slung across his back again, strolls across the roof to stand beside us. I didn't see him at all during our flight across the rooftops. How did he get here so fast? I should be used to this kind of thing, with these two, but I'm not sure I ever will be.

"Ch'i," he repeats. "One of the three…energies?…of the body." He considers. "That's not quite the right word, but it will have to do. Ch'i is…" He considers again, then points into the distance. Over the city walls, there's a bright glimmer where the morning sun strikes water behind a stand of trees. "You see that?"

I look at it. "The canal?"

"'Canal', yes. Water circulates through the canals. It waters crops, you can travel on it… Ch'i is like that. Somewhat. Not really."

"I don't know if this is helping, Yu Hao—"

He ignores Red and carries on. "It circulates through the body, runs the…bodily processes. With ch'ing-kung, we regulate our ch'i to make the body lighter." He looks at me. "But you knew some of this already. Getting onto our yurt, that first night…"

I shrug. "I just…did it, I guess."

"Exactly," says Red. "You just do it. You don't need to know anything about ch'i condensation, or foundation establishment, or nascent souls, or—"

"It exists whether or not you believe in it, Red—"

I have the idea that they've been around (and around and around) this argument before, and so do they, because they both break it off without another word. "Anyway," says Red, turning to me, "whether you knew you were doing it or not, you've practiced. Hard. You have," and she leans forward slightly and enunciates in a not-particularly-kind impression of Yu Hao, "kung fu."

"Right," I say. "So what's kung fu?"

She has to think about it. "Skill. Skill from practice, from hard work."

Yu Hao chimes in. "Ability. Not only in the forms of an art, but in its essence. One may have kung fu in calligraphy, in painting, in cooking—"

"Or in hitting people," finishes Red, grinning. "You would know," says Yu Hao.

She ostentatiously examines the fingernails of one shapely hand. "I may have a little kung fu in that area. Among other things."

"What 'things'?" asks Yu Hao, amused. "Drinking? Sleeping with other caravan guards? Not gambling, I remember you at that dice table in Kashgar."

Red raises an eyebrow, and then her fist blurs out, but Yu Hao's already floating backwards out of the way. He lands on the top of the mausoleum's dome, balancing there on the sole of one foot, arms still folded in his sleeves. Red laughs out loud, and then she's leaping after him, her whole body spinning around, scything her foot out at Yu Hao's shin-level. He springs off the spire, somersaulting through the air before landing gracefully, facing Red.

"What was that?" he asks mildly.

She raises her hands, shaking them out of her jacket's sleeves in an exaggerated fighting stance. "Flower-scattering Tornado Kick. Like it?"

He sniffs, unslinging his ch'in from his back and laying it carefully on the roof before finally raising his own hands. "Where did you learn it?"

"Something called the 'Spring Blossom Manual'. Picked it up in Lin'an."

"Doubtless you purchased it from some disgraced doctor with a medicine show, who swore up and down it contained the deepest secrets of wu shu."

"Doubtless," agrees Red, "but try this on for size—Ghost-Shadow Foot!" And she's leaping into the air, her boots kicking out twice, three, four times at Yu Hao's head before she lands again. He dodges the first two, deflects the others with the heels of his palms, and then he's backing across the roof with her following.

"You practice Flying Long Fist," he says. "Works well, if you can keep others at arm's length...but up close—" and he's up in her face with his arm wrapped around hers, her elbow trapped and almost bending backwards. She raises an eyebrow.

He shrugs, not letting up. "*Hsüeh Lu-Ssu.*"

"Snowy Egret style? Never heard of it."

"Evidently you've never been to my hometown. Big Hong the blacksmith could tie your arms in knots. I told you your kung fu was weak, up close."

She throws her head back and her rich, throaty laugh booms across the mausoleum roof. "Oh," she says, "that is *it*," and it's on.

Like when Red fought the Teuton, I'm watching a whirlwind of blocks and blows. That time, I couldn't follow them at all. But now, to my surprise, I can pick out each individual movement—Red charges across the Mausoleum's roof and leaps, one foot lashing out at Yu Hao's head; he sweeps his arms around, locking her ankle between them, and twists like he means to wrench her foot off; she breaks free, her body whipping around itself parallel with the ground…

It's not just that I can follow each beat of the fight. I can see the unity of everything they do, that all of it is an expression of one essential flow. *Ch'i.* I mouth the word. And once again, I'm struck by the grace of it, the artistry. It's breathtaking. They care about being…

Beautiful. That's the word. It's beautiful. They're messing around, I know, showing off, but it was beautiful when they went up against the Teuton too. Before that day, I'd have told you that if you fought like that, the first real fighter you met would leave you gutted and bleeding out, but then I saw these two leave Samarkand's most brutal killer sprawled in the dust.

Beauty, art, all that stuff…before, it all seemed too fragile for this world. Too easily broken to risk caring about. But now, once again, Red and Yu Hao show me how beauty and power can coexist, can even be the same thing.

And I get an idea.

CHAPTER TWENTY-ONE

Who are you two?"

We're sitting on the edge of the mausoleum roof, looking out over Samarkand. The mausoleum's dome shelters us from the ever-present wind, and it's surprisingly warm. Yu Hao's ch'in is balanced on his knees and his fingers idly pluck the strings, the notes sharp and strange in the cold clear air. Red winces occasionally but lets him play, for which I'm thankful. It sounds fine to me. It sounds beautiful.

"*Piao-shih*," replies Red, dangling her long legs off the edge of the roof. She's taken her boots off and stretches out her pale and surprisingly delicate feet in the sun. "Caravan guards. The money's not great, but you get to see the world."

"You know what I mean," I say. "Where did you learn all that? Ghost-shadow Kicks and Egret Styles and, and *flying*? And who's Crow? And what's in this stupid box?" My voice rises. Since last night I've been too scared to feel anything else, but our flight across the city have blown the fear away (almost), and now what I mostly feel is pissed off at being kept in the dark. "What is going *on?*"

Yu Hao draws a breath, lets it out in a long sigh as his fingers brush the ch'in's strings. "Right. Very well."

"Hey," says Red, a warning in the tone of her voice, "I don't know if we should be—"

He raises a hand gently. "She's risked a lot, Red, to help us out."

"Not for free, she hasn't." She shrugs. "I mean, it's no skin off my ass. But knowing could be dangerous for her." She looks at me, and her eyes are as serious as I've ever seen them. "You okay with that?"

There's no way I'm going to say no at this point. How much more danger could I possibly be in anyway? So I just nod, impatient for them to get on with it. Red raises her hands in surrender and nods at Yu Hao. "You take it. You're the scholar."

He considers. "To begin: Red and I are wanderers of *chiang-hu*. The 'rivers and lakes'."

"Is that in China?"

"It is many places. I am from 'China' as you call it, Red is from the Jusen lands to its north, but we are also of chiang-hu, and so is this 'Crow' from the sound of things. And so"—and he points at me— "are you."

"I've never seen a lake in my life," I object, and it's Red who replies.

"Look here." She points at the edge of the roof, where someone's scratched a line of symbols, Turkic runes, into the roof between us. "What's that?"

I look at the tag. I can't read, of course, but the style—every gang has its own—and the crude drawing of a bear's head beside them tell me more than the runes would even if I understood them.

"It's a...I guess it's a memorial," I say. "When a thief dies, their gang tags his name somewhere up high, somewhere it's not going to get chipped off. The Bears did this one." Climbing all the way to the top of the Mausoleum must have taken some guts. I tap the brickwork next to the bear's head, where someone's scratched the crude outline of a water jug. "It's for Jalil, he was the one who stole that golden ewer from a mansion on the west side a couple of years ago, everyone was talking about it. The Wolves dropped him off a roof onto his head last summer."

"Right," says Red. "Now, if you brought one of *those* people up here"—she points at the crowd below with a bare and elegant toe—

"one of the landlords, or traders, or ladies-in-waiting, what would they see?"

I shrug. "Just a tag. They probably wouldn't see it at all." I think I'm beginning to get it.

Red's nodding. "They see a vandalized wall, but you're looking at a monument. And it works the other way too. Like with this place," and she thumps the Mausoleum wall with her heel. "They see the tomb of some king or khan or something, some big-shot hero, but do you even know his name? No, thought not. You have your own heroes. You and them might as well be in different worlds.

"And that other world, the one for bandits and thieves, dancing girls and street-rats and adventurers, that's chiang-hu."

"Chiang-hu," continues Yu Hao, "is not so much one world as several, overlapping ones." A lecturing tone has crept into his voice— he's a scholar, all right. Red rolls her eyes and I stifle a laugh. "Bandits, for example, have the *lü-lin*, the 'greenwood'. Beggars have their world, courtesans another." His fingers blur over the strings, producing a fast ripple of notes like running water. "And for the fighters, there is the 'martial grove'. The *Wulin*."

"Crow," I prompt before he's off on another tangent. "And the box."

Yu Hao nods. "Almost certainly she belongs to the Wulin. Based on what you saw last night, she is a member of the *Pai-Hsieh-P'ai*, the White Scorpion Sect."

I remember Crow playing with her pet scorpion and shudder. "And you?"

Red is shaking her head. "We're a couple of caravan guards, Darya, like I said. We've picked up some stuff here and there, we can handle ourselves, but we're not really Wulin." Yu Hao says nothing.

"And the box?"

"It's difficult to believe," says Yu Hao, "but the box may contain a copy of the *Yin-yün Chen-ching*, the…" He turns the translation over in his mind. "'Yin-Harmony Manual', I would say. The Scorpions' most secret techniques."

"But who *are* they?"

He draws a deep breath. "Well…"

I don't get all of Yu Hao's explanation, and it doesn't help that Red keeps chiming in to offer her own opinion, usually the opposite of his—leading at one point to an argument in Chinese lasting a full minute before Yu Hao gets back to it—but I'm pretty sure I get the important parts.

For a start, Crow's White Scorpions and that other gang, the Celestial Blades, are crews, like I thought. The Wulin is full of them, and they have all kinds of names—Sects, Societies, Clans, Schools—but from what Red and Yu Hao are saying, they're crews, like beggar gangs in Samarkand. They're all different sizes; one might have only a single master (the word they use is *shih-fu*) and a handful of disciples, while another might have hundreds of followers, with the strength to take on armies. Each crew has its own traditions, its own fighting styles known only to its initiates—stances, moves, ch'i techniques. Just like in Samarkand, the landscape of the Wulin is constantly changing, with alliances made and broken, crews on their way up or down. Unlike in Samarkand, though, they aren't constantly at each other's' throats. They're interested in perfecting their skills and testing them against each other, not money or territory; it's a contest of strength, not a fight to the death.

It sounds great. A little too great. In the orphanage, they told us the pickpockets had a code too, but I saw how much that was worth when Masoud left me to the Wolves. Then they said the same thing about the thieves, that if you made it in, you were in, and you got as much respect as any other thief. But all it took is Farid getting weird about me to ruin that too. Is the Wulin any different?

Yu Hao talks about the Wulin code, about their principles—compassion, justice, courage, loyalty. How they come down like a ton of bricks on a crew who dishonours them. Like the White Scorpion Sect. The Scorpions are—

("Were," says Red.

("Or so we'd prefer to think," says Yu Hao.

("Seriously?" says Red.

("Just tell the story," I say.)

The Scorpions' home was in the jungles of the far South-East. Their speciality was cultivating their ch'i, not with the kind of exercises Yu Hao has been teaching me, but through alchemy. They experimented with strange medicines, disrupting and reshaping their ch'i flow. Peasants and travellers in the lands around the Scorpions' stronghold would disappear, become research subjects for the Sect, and turn up dead, or…disfigured. (He doesn't go into details.) And eventually, the Scorpions hit on a cocktail of poisons that boosted their abilities almost into the superhuman. I think again of Crow facing off against Yang Jing, so appallingly fast. *Wu-tu ch'uan*, Yu Hao calls it: Five Venom Fist.

All this outraged the more orthodox crews in the Wulin. One of the most powerful, the Celestial Blade Society, considered the Scorpions an abomination and moved to wipe them out.

("That's what pissed them off?" I ask. "Not the disappearing-peasants thing? Just the ch'i stuff?"

("What you have to understand about the Blades," says Red, "is that first and foremost they were *assholes*."

("They were certainly…set in their ways," admits Yu Hao. "Normally, when a question of, let's say 'discipline', arises in the Wulin, the societies meet and elect a *Meng-Chu*, a leader, who will direct the campaign. The Celestial Blade Society chose instead to act alone—"

("—Because they were *assholes* and nobody liked them," finishes Red, "and they got what was coming to them." He gives her a look and she raises her hands. "Carry on.")

The Blades attacked without warning, storming the Scorpions' fortress and killing everyone they could find—not only the Scorpions themselves, but their disciples, novices, even the servants. Some of them children. Not a high point in the history of the Wulin, says Yu Hao, but like Red said, the Blades ended up getting theirs.

Because if the Celestial Blades hadn't been so proud they acted alone, they might have been able to destroy the Scorpions cleanly and completely. Instead, some managed to slip away, and those survivors had their revenge. They infiltrated the Blades' own servants, and at a banquet to celebrate the Blades' victory, they struck. Most of the Blades died by poison that night, and the rest by the sword. And villages for twenty miles around could see the flames as the Blades' great temple on Pai-Hu Mountain burned.

"And whatever Scorpions were left went up with it," says Red, "because that was two years ago and no one's heard a thing from them since." She unhooks the gourd-bottle from her belt and drinks, then offers it to Yu Hao, who shakes his head.

"Self-deception is not an admirable trait, Red."

"Neither is paranoia, Yu Hao. Okay, this 'Crow' called herself a Scorpion—or anyway that's what Darya thinks she heard, no offense, Darya—"

"None taken," I say through clenched teeth.

"But any chancer could be dressing up like a Scorpion right now, borrowing their rep to scare people. You are *reaching*—"

"Even before we left Tun-Huang, there'd been crackdowns on martial societies all over China. And from what news has come to us on the road, it's getting worse. The government has limited influence in chiang-hu, but it can make life difficult for the Wulin nonetheless. And it's coordinated, Red. Whoever is behind it, they're in Lin'an. Perhaps they have the ear of the Emperor himself."

Red holds up a hand. "Wait a second—"

"If matters continue as they have, all of chiang-hu will be in disarray, ripe for takeover. And if whoever is behind all this obtains the Yin-Harmony Manual, it *will* continue. The White Scorpions' ch'i techniques are immensely strong—properly used, almost invincible. To know what the Scorpions did of infiltration, assassination, poisons that enslave the mind...they could crush all opposition, become the Wulin superpower that the Blades only imagined they were. And with the Wulin *and* the Emperor under their thumb, who could then threaten them? They would rule unopposed for a thousand years."

"Wait, wait, wait. So, what, we're just going to burn the thing?"

"There are other sects in the Wulin. Responsible sects. If their sages were to study the Manual they might find a flaw, something that could be exploited."

"All those sects are *broke*."

"Selling it is exactly what this Yang Jing, tried to do," Yu Hao points out. "He ran halfway across the Earth to do it, too. The Scorpions still found him."

"It sounds like he'd never been off of Pai-Hu Mountain before," says Red, "plus he was a drunk. I know people who know people from here to Kuang-chou. We get our hands on this thing, I can move it easy, as long as we don't get too greedy."

"And who, exactly, would we be moving it to? The Scorpions themselves, or someone even worse? If your horizon extended beyond the bottom of a bottle, Red"—she stiffens, but Yu Hao just keeps going—"you might consider that your precious self-interest would be better served by making sure the Manual ends up in a responsible pair of hands, or, yes, none at all—"

"No." Red cuts him off, her voice flint-hard and obsidian-sharp. "Yu Hao, you need to come back to earth for a second. We're not Wulin, we're not *wu-hsia*, and we're not getting mixed up in this. I'm Jusen, in case you've forgotten. Every Han in China would happily cut my head off. And you're just a failed scholar, wandering chiang-hu." When Red says 'failed', Yu Hao looks away.

Red turns to me, face as hard as her voice, and points at him. More than anything in the world I want her to stop talking, right now.

"Yu Hao went to Lin'an to sit the imperial examinations. Very big deal, pass them and you're set for life, cushy government job and all that. His little village in the South just about went broke paying for his books and his tutors. He washed out. He couldn't show his face back home again, had nowhere to go but chiang-hu. So you can see how he might think he has something to *prove* here." She tilts her bottle back, drinks deep.

Yu Hao's looking out over Samarkand, but I can tell he's not seeing it. Then he glances at me and I can see the pain in his eyes. I look away, not fast enough, and stare at the crowds milling below us. I hate Red all over again, but then she turns back to Yu Hao and there's real compassion in her voice.

"I'm sorry for that. We have been through a lot of crap together, I love you like a brother and if you want to go for the box, I've got your back. But Darya needs all the facts here. We are strictly small-time and *if you're right* then this Crow is at least a novice in the Scorpions— although not a *chen-niao*, we have that going for us at least. But if she comes for Darya," she adds, echoing my own thoughts, "she will go right through us."

Silence, and finally I ask "What's a chen-niao?" just to fill it. It's Yu Hao who replies.

"The highest rank within the Scorpions. It is the name of a rare bird, a venomous one." He still isn't looking at me, but that lecturing tone is back in his voice and he sounds a little better. "All women. All with white hair—a side-effect of the poison corrupting their ch'i."

"I heard they can spit venom, like, ten feet," puts in Red. "And they have acid for blood. Maybe a little bit of an exaggeration, but I do *not* want to go up against one of those bitches."

All this is a lot to take in. I focus on that last part. "So we can be fighters, in China? Women, I mean? We have it that good?"

"We have it about as good as anywhere else," says Red, "for

exactly what that's worth. Sometimes not so good." A muscle tightens along the delicate line of her jaw, and for some reason she bunches her bare toes, hard, the little bones crackling.

A line pops into my head, from some book or other that Masoud likes to quote. *'The best is if daughters are not born at all, or else do not survive'*. And all of a sudden I'm full of cold fury.

"But in chiang-hu? If you can handle yourself? You get as much respect as anyone. And you can handle yourself, Darya." She looks at me. "You have kung fu."

The idea that's been germinating in my head suddenly sprouts, and blooms. The last few days I've watched door after door slam shut, cutting off my futures, but now another one's opened. And it's the city gate.

"I come too," I say. "I get you the box, I come too."

"You get us the box," observes Red, "you learn ch'ing-kung, was the deal. Which you did. And still no box. So I'd say you've come out ahead already, and now you want to *change* the deal?"

"Nice try," I say, "but no way. The deal was, you train me, I give you *information*. I've done that. Now I'm saying"—my voice sticks a little; I'm taking a leap here—"I'm saying I can get you the box. And in return, you take me to China. That's the new deal. You sell the box—"

"We haven't decided we're going to sell it," says Yu Hao, and Red says, "Later for that." She looks at me. "You just told us you couldn't get the box. They found it, you said."

"I might have a couple of ideas about that," I say, and I do, although I'm not too keen on what it'll involve. "I can find out where it is, get it first."

"If you tell us where it is, Darya—" says Yu Hao.

"Not a chance. Oleg was right—an Inalid mansion is not somewhere you just stroll into and start poking around. Either the guards will kill you or the ahdath will. Besides, how much thieving have you guys done?"

They look at each other.

"Yeah, thought so. So listen to a professional. When you sell it"—
Yu Hao wants to object but I don't let him—"I want my cut, and
you're not going to be coming all the way back here to give it to me,
are you? So I'm coming back with you. That's the deal."

There it is. I've said it. I try to look confident, fold my arms so
they can't see my hands trembling.

"Darya," says Yu Hao gently, "it's just not possible. We can't pay
your way, not on our wages. We wouldn't get any money for the Yin-
Harmony Manual until we got to China, and a caravanbashi won't
take an IOU."

I taste bitter ashes, but then Red says. "Wait a second." She looks
at me. "That first day in the tavern. Those little thugs you were talking
to—what language was that?"

"Just Persian. Everyone here speaks it, just about."

"And how many other languages do you speak? Not well, just
enough to get by in."

I shrug and start counting them off. When I run out of fingers
and have to start over, Red says, "Never mind." She turns to Yu Hao.
"Poetry Pig—my Indian friend I mean—was telling me they're looking
for a translator on the next caravan out East. Make it a package deal,
two guards and Darya...I reckon they'd go for it."

I narrow my eyes. "Why are you helping me?"

She looks at me with surprise. "Because you're interesting," she
says. "I've been bored out of my mind, this whole journey. All over
the world it's the same old shit...but a barbarian doing ch'ing-kung?
That's something new. I kind of want to show you off, back home."
She grins. I'm not sure I'm not being talked down to, but I'll take what
I can get. I need this to work.

"And what then? How are you going to get back?" asks Yu Hao.

"I'm not going back." It takes a surprising effort to get the words
out. Samarkand is all I've ever known. "If I do this...I'm crossing
everyone I know. I won't last five minutes here." I'm not thinking of

Oleg right now, or Masoud, or Crow. I'm thinking of Farid. The kind of feelings he has for me can turn bad in an instant. I have no idea what he'd do to me, if they did.

"So?" I say. "We have a deal?"

Red and Yu Hao look at each other. Red's on board, I can tell; she may or may not find me 'interesting', but she's definitely interested in the kind of money she thinks she can make out of this. Yu Hao hesitates. I don't think he wants to put me in harm's way…but he also wants this Yin-Harmony Manual, and finally, slowly, he nods.

"Time to talk to Poetry Pig, then, I guess." Red sighs, and she and Yu Hao look at me. "So what now?"

"Wait at the tavern," I say. "This'll take a day or so to put together. Just be ready to move fast." Red grins at that. Yu Hao doesn't, but he doesn't object.

Chapter Twenty-Two

After they've left I stay there for a while, looking over the city, thinking about…well, trying not to think about anything. And failing.

The idea of leaving Samarkand just doesn't seem real, that's the problem. I go through all I've heard about the Silk Road, names from half-remembered traders' stories marching through my head. The green Ferghana valley, where the best horses in the world roam. The T'ien Shan, the Mountains of Heaven. The Taklamakan desert where the sands wail like lost souls. And beyond them, China, unimaginably vast… I think again of Red's tales of chiang-hu and Wulin. If it's true…I wouldn't have to hide anything there. I could be a warrior. I could be a woman.

But I can't make myself believe in any of it. Maryam told us stories in the orphanage, fairy tales like Aldar-Kose and his magic coat, or the girl who cried a lake, or Oskus-Ool and his nine red horses. China, chiang-hu, the Wulin—they all feel more like those fairy tales than anything to do with the world I live in. And now, like one of the fools in those old stories, I've sold out Samarkand and everyone I know for a promise of magic that doesn't, can't, exist.

But thinking about what happens if this fails isn't why I'm panicking. Because what happens if it *works?* All my life I've made choices in a split second, done whatever I needed to do to keep me alive for the next five minutes, and the next five minutes after that.

But if I make it, if this works—the future's wide open after that, not a walled street but a vast open plain. I'll have a choice, a real choice of what to do. And I can't imagine living like that. I don't know how to choose.

A sudden chill make me turn and look behind me, to the west. While I was lost in thought, the sun sank behind the dome of the Mausoleum and the building's long shadow is creeping over Samarkand.

I need to get moving, get to the warehouse. I need to set things in motion.

When I finally stand up to go, I half-believe that I won't be able to do it again, that there's not even any such thing as ch'ing-kung, that I've dreamed it all and I'm still dreaming. But as soon as I draw a breath, feel that warmth circulating through my stomach and spine, and leap from the Mausoleum's roof, I soar as easily as I did earlier.

As I cross the rooftops, I hunt for that crazy joy I felt chasing Red, but instead I just feel...exposed. The back of my neck prickles as I imagine someone below glancing up and seeing me, and what they'd think. With ch'ing-kung I can climb anywhere, steal anything...but a reputation as a great thief is one thing. A reputation as a witch is something else. Not that it'll matter. If I'm anywhere in Samarkand this time next week, it'll be at the bottom of a midden-hole with my throat cut.

I leap from a two-storey to a one-storey building and then down into an empty courtyard. I land a little hard and stagger, but it's hardly the pair of broken ankles that a leap like that would have earned me a week ago. No one's there to see.

The Street of Pepper-sellers is deserted. The muscle are out on their corners; the thieves are asleep in the squat. Or maybe they're all just out goofing off, since no one seems to care about quotas any more. My chest tightens—it really is happening, the Martens are falling apart.

The astrolabe shifts a little in the inside pocket of my kameez. I'd clean forgotten about it. A week ago it would have felt like an unimaginable treasure. I can't even imagine that feeling now.

I lean around the corner and cast a quick eye over the warehouse. No one there either. I take a cautious step towards the darkened front door, and then I stop dead in my tracks with the back of my neck prickling, as the worst sound I've ever heard rings out from behind the building. At first I think it's an animal, some sick dog or fox that's wandered into the Maze looking for a place to die. But then I hear it again, moaning and retching, and I realize it's a man.

Part of me just wants to run. I ignore it, although I couldn't say why. The howl, or groan, rises up again, and this time it's joined by an unearthly screech—Nina's marten. That voice is Oleg's.

I hug the wall as I pad down the alley. The dead tree's branches hang over the wall. They point at me like twisted and accusing fingers, ghastly even in the sunlight.

"You're killing him." My heart just about explodes. Nina's voice, less than two feet away from me on the other side of the wall. "Do you hear me?" Her voice is climbing hysterically. I've never heard Nina lose it; when she punished us in the orphanage, bent back our fingers, she stayed ice cold. Even when they broke. I hold my breath. Blood pounds in my head, so loud she *must* be able to hear it.

"If I stop he'll die anyway." Crow's terrible dead whisper.

"He's bleeding! Oh, look at how he's bleeding. Oh, Oleg…" Oleg cries out again. This must be Crow's cure.

I remember a night in the loft, soon after I got there; a pickpocket had gotten in a fight, I can't even remember his name now, and shattered three of his teeth. The pain of the exposed nerves had turned him into an animal, roaring and lashing out at anyone who came near. We all had to pile on him to stop him moving, so Nina could reach into his mouth with pliers and gouge out the shattered stumps. That's how Oleg sounds. I can't imagine what's wrong with him that's worse than what I'm hearing now.

"Are you listening to me?" I can't tell if the panic in Nina's voice is on Oleg's behalf or her own. I can see why she'd be losing it—if Oleg dies, then Nina's going to join him before he's halfway cold. It'll just be a tossup whether it's another gang or one of her own Martens who gets to her first.

Oleg draws a shuddering breath and screams, a bubbling liquid sound, rising up through the branches of the tree into the cold air. Crow ignores him. "He still has some blood left in him. And I still don't have the box."

"To hell with you!" Nina's furious, her accent growing so thick I can barely understand her. "Oleg and I, we came here with nothing. Nothing! Not even a knife, Oleg had to strangle the first man he killed, with his hands! And we built an empire! Now you put that empire on the scale, weigh it against your stupid box? How *dare* you, you *suka*, you *blyat'*—" She fires off another couple of curses in Rus. "To hell with your box and whatever's inside it—"

Something cuts her off, sharp and clean. She just stops talking.

"Is there anything else?" says Crow's voice. No big speeches in her. A high whine from Nina, like a tiny animal in pain, echoed by another screech from the marten. "I see," says Crow, and the whine trails off. Nina draws breath, and, appallingly, begins to sob. "Where were we?" Crow asks from further away. Oleg moans.

I back away. I can't believe I'm going to do this, with Oleg and Nina and Crow so close. But if I hesitate I'll lose my nerve altogether. I have to move fast.

The sun is low but still bright, and when I first step into the warehouse it's like going blind. I stand against the wall beside the door, letting my pupils dilate. Spindly giants loom out of the darkness, resolve themselves into towering rows of shelves.

When I can see well enough, I sidle along the wall towards the corner room. No candlelight this time, but that doesn't mean anything. I can't hear Oleg's cries any more, and I tell myself that's just the walls of the warehouse swallowing the sound, that they're not done yet, that Crow even now isn't stepping silently towards me, her sabre drawn…

I'm listening so intently that it barely registers when the texture under my bare feet changes. It's only when I lift one off the floor that I realise how sticky it is. Whatever it is holds onto my sole for a second, then lets go with a faint ripping noise that's as loud, in the almost-perfect silence of the warehouse, as the world ending.

I hold my breath and will my heart to beat softer. I'm pretty sure I know what I've stepped in. Looks like they didn't clean up all the blood that Yang Jing left on the warehouse floor.

It doesn't matter. I have to keep going. I need to tell myself that a few times before I can move. Two steps, three, and I still haven't cleared the puddle of half-dried blood. I've stepped in blood before, of course, and worse, but never so much of it. I'm appalled to feel my gorge rising. I press a hand over my mouth and slowly the urge to vomit passes.

I can hear something now, a dry rasping, a clicking and shuffling, and I'm very much afraid that I know what it is. Then I'm standing between piled rolls of wool, looking into the small corner room. My eyes have adapted to the gloom as much as they're going to, and I can pick out the low table, and the bronze dish on it. There's no cloth covering the vermin inside. In the darkness I can't make out the individual bugs; it looks like the dish is half-full of black liquid, boiling away.

I can see the book, too. It's on the table, where Oleg threw it last night. One corner is up on the lip of the dish. I can't be sure in the darkness, but there might be something crawling slowly across the cover.

If I think about what I'm going to do, I'm finished, so I just do it. I pull my sleeve up over my hand, then sweep that arm over the cover of the book, while with my other hand I yank the book back across the table. For a moment, my sleeve makes contact with something fat and furry, or I think it does. Then it's gone, and I stagger backwards with the book in a white-knuckled one-handed grip.

My heart feels like it's going to batter its way out of my chest. My skin buzzes and tingles where I touched whatever it was through my sleeve, but I don't think I've been bitten or stung, and after a couple of seconds I'm able to draw an unsteady breath.

Outside the corner room again, I lay the book on the floor in a patch of sunlight slanting through a hole in the wall, and flip through. The pages flicker past, right to left, and there's just enough light to tell which ones have writing on them. I don't know which one has the buyer of the box on it, but I figure it must be one of the last ones, since the owner of this book was dead not long after. When I reach the final page with writing, I rip it out—loudly, but I'm past caring; I need to be *out of here*—and then rip the previous half-dozen pages out as well, just in case. I roll them up, stick them in my kameez, and leave the book where I found it. I'm not going near that dish of nightmares again.

As I stride through the shelves, back towards the warehouse door, I allow myself a small, tense smile. I emerge into the front room with Nina's counting-table, the bright doorway right there in front of me. A silhouette steps into it, huge, cutting out half the light. A smaller one steps in front of it.

"Darya," it says.

Masoud.

He steps into the front room, behind him 'Uj stands in the doorway, unmoving.

"Where have you been, Darya?" Masoud asks. His voice is thick. His face is a mess from when Oleg slapped him down—cheeks puffy and mottled with bruises, one eye swollen almost closed.

"Loft," I say. "Forgot something." I ease back, trying to make it seem as much as possible like I'm not moving at all, until the counting-table is between me and Masoud. He glares at me across it. 'Uj's bright eyes track me across the room from within his lumpy face, but he remains in the doorway. There's no way past him.

"Don't mess around," Masoud spits.

"I have no idea what you're talking about, Masoud," I say. I try to keep my voice casual with an edge of insolence, but it's getting hard to breathe. With 'Uj in the doorway the only way to flee is back into the warehouse, and beyond that the courtyard, and Oleg. Nina. Crow.

"Where have you been during the day?" he says, his eyes not leaving mine for a second. "When we're supposed to be hustling. Don't tell me you've been making quota."

Ever since I struck my deal with Yu Hao, I thought this might come up, and I have an answer ready. One that happens to be true, technically. "Looking for this mystery box. You know, like Oleg told us to?" I say it slowly and patiently, like I'm talking to a child or an idiot, but each word is harder than the one before. I can't seem to draw a full breath, like I'm back in that tiny alley, the walls pressing on my chest. "Like most of the pickpockets have been doing."

"*Found* anything?"

I roll my eyes. "I didn't find squat. Or I'd have handed it over already. Did *you?*"

"Enough, Darya," says Masoud. "You've been hanging out with a couple of strangers. For a few days now. Strangers who look like Crow."

I'm damn sure no Martens saw me with Red and Yu Hao, let alone Masoud himself, but somehow, he knows. His voice is full of cold certainty, bluffing won't get me anywhere.

So I face into the storm. "No kidding," I say. "They're traders, came in on an eastern caravan a while ago. Like Oleg said the box did? So I'm playing guide, showing them around town, seeing if I can get a lead off them." I turn my defence into an attack. "Are you following me, Masoud? Instead of, you know, doing something useful, like looking for the box yourself? Oleg might want to know about that…"

I stop, because his glare hasn't wavered. He's not having any of it. "It doesn't look like you're fishing for a lead. It looks like *you're* telling *them* stuff." He is flexing his hands, bunching them into fists and squeezing, working up his nerve. Behind him 'Uj holds up his own hand, cracks each knuckle in turn, *pop-pop-pop.*

I know where he's going with this. I'm not the only person Masoud has pushed around, knowing he's got Nina, and therefore Oleg, behind him. There are a lot of pickpockets, runners, even muscle that he's humiliated, and they'd be happy to take it out of his hide. He knows that things are falling apart, and if Oleg—and therefore Nina—goes, all his victims are going to get their chance.

So he needs to make them fear him in his own right, and he can only do that with his fists. Picking a scapegoat—me—he can call a traitor would be a start. But beating me bloody won't be nearly enough. He needs to do something a little more drastic. Like drag my half-dead body into the courtyard at tonight's curfew.

So right now I should be sweat-slick and terrified. Except, for some reason, I'm not. Part of it is that ever since I saw these two I've been breathing in Yu Hao's pattern, feeling that familiar warmth kindle in my lower belly. Part of it is curiosity about where he's getting this information from. Whenever I've gone to meet Red and Yu Hao, I've steered clear of anywhere *near* Marten territory. In fact, the tavern they're rooming in is closer to the…

A few things start rattling around in my head, but before I can snap them into place, Masoud reaches across the table, finger extended. "What—are—you—*doing?*" He pokes me in the chest, hard, and all three of us hear the paper inside my kameez crackle.

Not a single thought goes through my head. I just whip up my hand, and before Masoud even has time to widen his eyes, I've closed it on his arm, my fingers digging into the skin. I've only seen Yu Hao do this once, but my ch'i is surging and each move seems to follow inevitably from the last.

By the time Masoud has begun to think about pulling his arm back, I've got it arm extended across the counting table and I'm putting enough pressure on his elbow I can feel the joint grinding. His face goes red, then white. I put on a little more pressure and he whines, a high thin sound like steam escaping a kettle. I back off a little. Just a little.

The rush almost overwhelms me. I did it because it was the only thing I could do, didn't even think about it, but...this is what being stronger feels like. Making other people afraid. This is power. No wonder Masoud's spent his whole life scrabbling after it.

"Disappear," I snarl at 'Uj. 'Uj doesn't move, just watches everything with that same contemplative look on his face. So I let go of Masoud's arm at the same time as I bring my leg up and kick him as hard as I can in the chest. My movements are clumsy, rushed—I can only imagine what Yu Hao would say—but with ch'i behind it, the kick sends Masoud almost flying backwards, into 'Uj. He'll knock 'Uj off his feet, and when the two of them go down, I'll hurdle the counting-table and them in one leap, and I'm free—

'Uj doesn't budge. He sweeps one heavy arm out and knocks Masoud aside. Then he folds his arms and just looks at me with those bright little eyes. Masoud rebounds off the wall and sprawls on the floor.

Now I'm sweating, I can feel it tickling my back between my shoulder blades. I've seen 'Uj fight. If he gets any kind of a grip on me, I'm done. He'll choke me out in about ten seconds. Or just twist my head off. Ch'i or not, kung fu or not, I can't take him.

Beside him Masoud struggles to his feet, his lip curled in a furious sneer. "I was going to make it quick, Darya," he spits. "Now you've—"

The tickling on my back intensifies. Then it's on my shoulder blade, and rising. When it crests my shoulder, and 'Uj's eyes flick downwards and his face goes pale, I realize it's not sweat. Without thinking, I reach up and flick my bare hand across my shoulder, and a plump black spider the size of my fist goes flying across the room and hits 'Uj in the chest.

It plops to the floor, but 'Uj is already yelling, one short hoarse shout after another, pure panic in his eyes. He stumbles backwards, his eyes fixed on the spider, and when it scuttles towards him he breaks completely and runs, lumbering awkwardly out of the doorway and out of sight. Masoud stares after him in disbelief.

"No wonder he wouldn't sleep on the floor," I say. "Scared of bugs. Go figure." I raise my hands in a fighting stance, copied from one of Red's on the mausoleum roof.

I'm not sure Masoud has ever has so many things not go his way in a row. He's beginning to get the idea that he's not the centre of Creation, and the rush I feel at the new doubt in his eyes is intoxicating. But he draws himself up, and one slippered foot comes down on the spider, bursting it like a zit. He raises his own fists. "Come on, then."

So I do.

貂

I don't think Red would find much to admire in my fighting style, let alone Yu Hao. I don't have anything in the way of technique. All I have is breath and ch'i, on top of the reflexes I was born with. But against Masoud I might as well be fighting one of the orphanage's blind beggars.

He's been in more fights than I have, but in the end he's always relied on his tongue, not his fists, to get him ahead, and it shows. He comes at me like he's struggling through syrup, taking wild stiff-armed swings. Brawling. And I'm in the current and I can see how his body is fighting itself, muscle working against muscle, going in a dozen directions at once. Not moving with a unified purpose. Not like me.

I just dodge his first couple of blows, ducking and sidestepping, and he hits nothing but air, knocking himself off balance each time. The third time he does that I strike him on the shoulder with the heel of my palm, not even hard, but enough to tip him over and through the doorway, where he sprawls in the dust outside.

I follow him, blinking in the sunlight. I let him struggle to his feet once more, keeping my distance while my eyes adjust, then when he charges at me I flick my foot out at his shin, barely raising my knee, and down he goes again with a howl of pain.

As I wait for him to get his feet under him, I glance back at the warehouse door and see a dull red footprint, half in shadow. My footprint. I remember stepping in the blood just now, and very clearly I see Crow again, toying with Yang Jing like a cat. So when Masoud takes another wild swing at me, I don't do anything fancy. I just turn the blow aside with my hand while the other makes a fist that catches him under the chin, and puts him down for good.

He groans and rolls onto his side, spits a wad of bloody phlegm onto the ground. I stand over him, my whole body singing with that feeling of *power*...and then another image flashes through my brain— Masoud cowering just like this after Oleg beat him. And I wonder if this feeling is what Oleg feels, if it's why he does what he does. And for a moment I can't blame him.

I hear Masoud in my head, saying *go sell yourself to a whorehouse*, and I draw my leg back and kick him in the ribs, and I don't feel anything but fierce cruel joy. He doesn't even try to get up, just wraps his arms around himself and draws his legs up, huddling like an animal. I step forward to hurt him again, and a hand lands on my shoulder. I whip around, fists raised.

It's Farid. "'Uj just ran past me," he says, "howling like all the *shayatin* in the abyss were after him." He looks down at Masoud, who's snuffling to clear his bloody nose. "What is going *on?*"

"Ask her what she's got in her shirt," Masoud says through his puffy lips.

Farid looks at my kameez and I look down at it too. The roll of paper is poking out of the bottom. Before I can think of anything to say Farid's plucked it out. I'm too stunned by how fast things have unraveled to stop him. The crackle of the paper as Farid unrolls it is very loud. He holds them up, squints with the effort of reading, then his eyes widen as he realizes. "This is—" he says.

I try to get ahead of him. "It's where the box is. I took it from the warehouse."

He looks at me, furious. "What the hell were you doing? Now I'm going to have to—how could you, Darya?" It's not taking the pages he's mad at me for. It's the betrayal. I've wrecked that perfect image of me he had in his head. He's trembling with anger. I have to think fast.

"I was taking it to you," I say. Masoud scoffs, although it comes out more like a sob. I look at him and he flinches. That rush of power again.

Farid shakes his head, still looking at the pages in his hand, eyes dark with pain. "How am I supposed to believe that?"

"You better," I say. "Listen: what good are those to me? I can't read them. Even if I could, okay, I know where the box is—so what? It's not like I could take it, *you* can't even take it for a couple of days, not till the Inalids leave."

He looks up sharply. "So—"

"*So*, I think I *can* take it. With your help."

Masoud is on his feet again. He spits more blood on the ground between his feet. "What's in it for him?"

I don't bother to look at him. It's a fair question, anyway. I take a deep breath. "The Martens are done. Am I right? Even if Oleg bounces back, our rep is all busted up. We can't survive that."

It's the first time I've said that out loud. I even dodged around the topic when I was talking to Red and Yu Hao. I didn't want to give it power by saying it, make it real. But it is real. Oleg's sickness, the curfew ritual falling apart, losing our corners to the Wolves, Nina losing her hold on the pickpockets…we're done.

"Our rep is busted up, but what we can do is grab the biggest piece we can, use it for leverage so another gang will take us. So how much rep you think we'd get by bringing Crow's box to her early? Showing we don't need Oleg at all?" It sounds shaky as hell even to me, but I'm all in now.

Farid looks doubtful. "Oleg will kill us if he finds out. Sick or not. I don't know, Darya—"

"I'm in," says Masoud.

"Piss off," I say instantly.

"Fine," says Masoud, "then I'm going straight to Nina and telling her everything you just said."

"No you're—oh, screw this," and I advance on him with my fist raised. As he backs off, Farid lays a hand on my shoulder.

"Easy, Darya."

Masoud keeps backing up. "What are you going to do? Kill me? Even if you do, 'Uj saw you. He'd still talk."

"'Uj couldn't string three words together if you gave him a week," I say.

He clears his throat. "You really want to take that chance?" He speaks calmly, reasonably. Using words like a crowbar, forcing things open so he can crawl inside. "And anyway, whatever you've got in mind, no way it's a solo job, right?"

I'm already looking at Farid, who shakes his head. "I told you the other day, we're busy as hell. No way I can sneak off without someone wondering what's up."

"Nasr—"

"He's just as busy as I am, and anyway, you think he'd keep his mouth shut?"

My brain is buzzing, looking for ways out of this. There aren't any.

"Shit," I hiss under my breath. Then I turn to Masoud. "You don't say a word. 'Uj doesn't say a word. And when we're done, we're *done*. I don't want to see you again."

He shrugs. "So what's the job?" Farid nods, looking at me expectantly.

I know what the next step is, but saying the words turns out to be the hardest thing I've had to do all day. I take a deep breath and turn to Farid. "We need to see Mahnaz."

Chapter Twenty-Three

The dress goes right down to the floor, and the hem keeps sneaking under my feet so I have to take little shuffling baby-steps if I don't want to trip. The headscarf is tight under my chin and makes my stubbly scalp itch, until I have to keep flexing my fingers to stop myself just ripping it off and scratching my head bloody. All the other girls here are dressed the same, but they're used to it. They're taller than me, and there are too many of us to fit comfortably in the small kitchen and I'm getting elbow-jabbed to death.

"Girls," someone says, and it takes me a moment to remember I'm supposed to *be* a girl today. I'm the last to turn to face the speaker, and I step on the dress again and narrowly avoid going flat on my face.

She stands in the doorway. Long thin face, sharp nose and chin making it look like the blade of a hatchet. The leader of our cleaning crew. Mahnaz must have used her name at some point, when she was introducing me, but I've clean forgotten it and I'm too scared of this next part to remember names anyway, so she'll just have to be Hatchet to me. Hatchet jerks her head impatiently. "Cart's here. Get moving."

As I shuffle out, the things hidden in the hem of the dress bang against my ankle with each step, hard enough to make my eyes water. The girls and I file out of the kitchen into an alley where a cart hitched to a bored donkey waits for us. I try to imagine myself as a house slave, doing this every day. The life I came so close to giving myself up to. I can't do it.

Seeing Mahnaz was about as excruciating as I'd thought it would be, although in a different way than I expected. Farid took us up to one of the sprawling fancy mansions up by the Citadel. The servants' door was at the back. The girl who opened it when Farid knocked didn't even say anything, just gave him a raised eyebrow and a knowing grin and went to get Mahnaz. How often did he come there, anyway?

"You better step back," Farid said. He was stiff with me, still processing my betrayal of the Martens and the thieves, even though he was complicit in it now himself. "She's going to take some convincing. We always figured we'd try this scam on one of the smaller Inalid houses first. Not the main clan's mansion."

"So she's not going to go for it?" I said, as Masoud smirked.

"She'll go for it, but I'm going to need to sweet-talk her a little. So you and Masoud just back up, okay?"

So Masoud and I backed up. We waited by a pile of kitchen garbage, vegetable peelings and offal just beginning to crawl with maggots, while we watched Mahnaz throw herself at Farid and the two of them make out. Then talk in low tones. Then argue. Then make out again. The whole thing seemed to take about a year and a half. I didn't look at Masoud, and he didn't say anything. If he had I would have kicked him onto the garbage pile and pounded on his face until my hand fell off, plan or no plan.

Finally Farid turned and nodded to us. Mahnaz didn't look happy, especially once she'd looked me over, but all she said was "Okay." She looked at Farid and Masoud. "You ready?"

Farid nodded. "It'll be the rope trick, I reckon. The tools are in the squat—you know where they are, Masoud?"

"Sure," said Masoud.

"Great. Get them and head for the mansion's west wall. West?" He looked at Mahnaz and she nodded professionally.

"West. Mostly guest rooms, no one will be there after dark."

Farid nodded back. "There you go, then. I have to go, Nina's got a job for us. Wants to pretend everything's the same as always, I guess." He looked at Masoud, then at me. "Good luck." Then he was gone, and so was Masoud. I was alone with Mahnaz.

She looked at me for a long time, then sniffed. "I thought you weren't much," she says almost conversationally, "when I saw you that time in Pepper-Sellers. I thought after that I might've been mistaken. But no. You really are…not much." She sniffed again. "Not much to set Farid's head spinning like that." Was Mahnaz jealous? I should have thought of that, but like I said before, this isn't my area.

"Regardless of how fast his head's spinning, though, he still sees straight enough to find his way into my bed about every night." She smirked. That hurt more than it should have, although I should have known. Whatever Farid thought he was feeling, a guy's still a guy.

"Do we have a problem?" I asked cautiously.

She snorted. "If I stopped to squabble with every little bundle of rags like you, I'd never get anything done. And there's good money in this, if you don't screw it up."

That would have to be good enough. And I had plenty to worry about without starting anything with Mahnaz. "Thank you," I said to her. It turned out to be easy to say.

She shrugged. "No risk to me. You get caught, you're just some girl I hired off the street. All on you. I'm not even going to be there."

I blinked. "You're not?"

There's barely enough room in the cart for us all to find a seat. Hatchet doesn't seem much interested in small talk, just stares straight ahead from the front of the cart as the donkey plods through the wide streets of the Citadel district, but some of the girls are chattering away. Kitchen gossip. I'm too wound up to pay any attention. Fortunately, the two I'm squeezed between don't even look at me, much less start a conversation. I guess as the new girl I'm getting the silent treatment, which works for me. I'd braced myself for stares, whispers, glares, but there aren't any, and I realize—I look just like them, and for all they know, I am. With the loose dress hiding my scrawny figure, my shaved head covered up by the headscarf, I even feel like them. Certainly not like myself. It feels weird.

I've never been in a cart before. I don't want to draw attention to myself by gawking, but I can't help stealing glimpses at the street passing by as the donkey trudges along. Everyone seems to know who the cart belongs to, and quickly step aside to give us room. We're in the crowd but at the same time apart from it; we pass a little kid begging, not one of the Martens', and Hatchet rummages in her dress and tosses a few coins down at her, which she scrambles to recover. The girl to my right sniffs with contempt. Is this what we look like— we beggars, pickpockets and thieves—to outsiders?

Then the cart is rattling past one of the tall brick walls that surround each of Samarkand's private gardens. Between the wall and the neighbouring buildings is a narrow alley, and as we pass I see Masoud lurking there, next to a barrow bearing a long wooden box. I push all those thoughts out of my mind as the donkey stops before a wooden gate.

"You—ground floor, sweeping. You, you and you—ground floor, dust, cover the furniture. You and you—packing. Crates are by the kitchen entrance. Plenty of straw for the porcelain."

Hatchet counts us off as we clamber stiff-legged off the cart. This is another unpleasant surprise. If she tells me to muck out the stables or scrub the latrines, how am I going to look for the box?

But when it's my turn, Hatchet gives me a curt "Stairs and hallways, scrub 'em down." Free passage through the house, in other words. I'm sure she's in on this with Mahnaz, but I'm just as sure I'm still on my own here.

As soon as we're through the gate and I see the layout of the grounds, my heart sinks. I'd been halfway hoping I could cut Masoud clean out of this whole deal. He figures that once I've cased the house and found the box, I'll still need him to come back after dark and steal it. Only he doesn't know about ch'ing-kung. If I can leap the distance from the wall to the mansion, I don't need the thieves' rope trick, and I don't need Masoud.

Except one look at this place wrecks any hope of that. The grounds are huge, almost like I'm outside the city walls, and the mansion sits square in the middle of them, in a vast cleared area fringed with trees. Even with ch'ing-kung, I'd have to touch down at least three times before I got from the wall to the house.

Which wouldn't matter so much, if the grounds were deserted and dark. But from the gate I can see at least a dozen guards, either walking patrol routes or standing and surveying the gardens and mansion. Every one of them has a bow. And worse, torches have been driven into the earth every few yards, their ends freshly wrapped in cloth and pitch. I know that as soon as the sun goes down they'll all be blazing with light. The Inalids aren't taking any chances with Assassins on their last night in Samarkand.

As soon as I touched the ground, I'd be all lit up in the middle of those guards. I might make it to the house, but not without collecting a few arrows on the way. So it looks like I'm stuck with Masoud for the time being.

The guards look us over as we file up the gravel path to the mansion. Fortunately I'm concentrating so hard on not tripping over my dress that I don't have time to look guilty. I hope. I wonder if any of these guards *is* an Assassin. They say it's the one you least expect who plants the dagger in you—

"Who are these?" A skeletal grey-haired man, probably one of the kitchen slaves, stands in front of the mansion, bony arms folded.

Hatchet shrugs. "You wanted maids to pack the place up. These are them."

He looks us over. "You know them? You can vouch for them?"

Hatchet snorts. "Ha. I just bring 'em in and tell 'em what to do."

"They look like thieving little slags to me." Is he looking at me? I feel like all the blood in my body has rushed to my face. Should I run? Then he shrugs. "They'll be patted down when they leave, so tell 'em not to filch any spoons, right? In you go." I feel his gaze on me as we file past, into the gloom of the mansion. Not going to lose any sleep if *that* guy gets his head cut off.

Sweep and scrub, Hatchet said. So I do, working my way up the entrance hall's massive staircase. I have to stoop awkwardly over the stairs with the scrubbing brush, and by the time I reach the top my hands are raw and something's gnawing at the bottom of my spine, right between my hips. I look down the stairs to make sure no one's watching, and I see I didn't even do that good a job. I think of all those times I nearly gave up on being a Marten, nearly went to Nina and asked her to sell me off. I imagine scrubbing stairs all day, every day.

I'm wasting time. I toss the brush aside and look down the upstairs hallway. There's no one else around; most of the maids were assigned to the ground floor. I'd worried some of the actual Inalids, or their servants, would be around, but they all seem to be sticking to one wing. The door to that wing is shut tight, and there are four guards on it. If the box is in there with them, I'm screwed.

Nevertheless, there's a spring in my step as I head down the hallway. It's not the same as being a proper thief, but it's the closest I've been yet, and it's enough to make me smile.

The smile disappears as I drop into the current. I know now that what I'm feeling is just a heightened awareness of the ch'i moving through my body, harmonizing with the greater rhythm of the world outside myself, but that doesn't make it any less exhilarating.

The first door I open leads to a guest chamber, the second is a linen cupboard. I can tell almost at a glance that neither of them have the box. The flow makes every detail crystal-clear.

The third room, bigger than the others, is clearly a storeroom for the Inalids' art collection. Rolled rugs are stacked in a pyramid in the corner and trinkets of brass and bronze, gold and silver and glass crowd the shelves that run along the walls. A double handful of this stuff would put me so far over quota I wouldn't have to work for a *year*—but however this goes, I know my pickpocket days are done, and if I don't find Crow's manual, I won't even live to fence anything.

The shutters are half-closed, but the sliver of light they allow into the room is enough to see by. I quarter and search the room. The moments drip away one by one, and I have to stop myself from skimming over the shelves instead of looking properly.

Even so, I almost miss it. I've reached the end of the shelf it's on before what I've just seen sinks into my brain. I back up, and I'm looking at the box.

My breath catches in my throat. It's just like Crow said, black and so beautifully lacquered that even in the dim room it seems to glow with an inner light that seems somehow unwholesome, like the shiny leaf of a poisonous plant. There's a bird on it, just like Crow said, the lines picked out in scintillating mother-of-pearl. Beneath the drawing are those three characters, carved into the box's lid in exquisite detail.

I reach out a trembling hand, and then hesitate. The outside of the box is supposed to be safe to touch, but I remember the Kyrgyz all too well. I step over to the window and ease the shutter open. A piece of luck: the window faces the grounds' western wall, which Masoud, if everything's going to plan, will be climbing right now. We'll be able to run the rope right to this window.

The rope trick is a specialty of the Martens' thieves, but I'm not sure they've used it over a distance like this before. It seems like a mile from here to the wall. And Masoud, of course, for all his bluster, isn't a thief. I doubt he's ever done this before. But he's all I have.

Sewn into the lining of the dress's skirt are a couple of cloth patches. I rip the first of them away and a small hand-mirror drops into my palm. Standing at the shutter, I angle it to bounce the lowering sun's rays back at the wall, two short pulses of light. I wait a minute, then do it again.

Two maids hurry past in the hallway outside. I resist the almost-overwhelming urge to look away, and keep scanning the wall. The maids' voices fade and vanish.

I flash the mirror again. Again. Nothing from the wall. Masoud screwed up, or else he never meant to hold up his end of the deal at all. What am I going to do now? The despair is the first thing that hits me, and right on its heels comes anger that eclipses even the rage I felt when he left me in that alley with the Wolves at my heels. I should have killed him in the warehouse. I should have—

Two flashes, then a pause, then a third. Coming from the top of the wall, near a just-budding peach tree. I don't have time for relief. I respond with three quick flashes from the mirror, and quickly draw back behind the window frame. The silence stretches out. I glance back at the doorway, and glance back just as the crossbow bolt strikes the shutter's handle in a shower of sparks.

It was supposed to bury itself in the shutter; Masoud has bad aim, or the special bolt didn't fly right, or we were just unlucky. Whichever it was, the bolt ricochets and tumbles away from the window.

I reach out and grab for it and I nearly overbalance and go out the window myself. I dig my toes into the wall below the window frame and manage to pull myself back. It's only once I'm back in the room that I realize I caught the bolt.

There's a loop in the tail of the iron shaft, with the slimmest of silken threads threaded through it. . The thread extends out towards the wall, where Masoud has both the ends. Or I hope he does. I don't tug on it to check, I could break the thread. I rip away the second patch under my dress and retrieve a tiny hammer.

None of the guards below are looking up at me, but I still feel horribly exposed as I lean out and pound the bolt into the bottom of the window frame, careful not to entangle the hammer with the fragile silk. From down there it looks like I'm just cleaning the shutters or something. I hope.

Once it's done I retreat into the room so fast I nearly bash my head against the window frame. My heart is pumping like it's going to burst. I drop the hammer behind the stack of rugs and take a moment to adjust my headscarf and smooth my dress—and then I whirl as the door swings open behind me.

"Are you done?" says Hatchet. I can't make my voice work, so I nod. She sniffs, scanning the shelves, and jerks her head. "We're leaving."

By the gate, the maids wait in a patient line while the skinny old guy from before pats us all down, making sure we haven't lifted anything. The scumbag's hands linger over the girls with fuller figures. They don't linger over mine, which I suppose I should be thankful for. His breath isn't as bad as Oleg's but it's bad enough.

"Scrawny little thing," he grunts. "Bony, like a bag of pig knuckles. Sure you're not a boy?" Mad laughter boils up inside me but I manage to keep a lid on it, and he waves me on as the next girl steps up.

"Where were you?" In the narrow gap, not even an alley, between the Inalids' wall and that of their neighbours, I advance on Masoud and he backs up, hands up to placate me.

"Darya—"

"You don't leave me hanging, Masoud. You don't do that ever again."

"I had to—"

"*Ever.*"

It's cold—the lane is too narrow, the walls too tall, for the sun to ever reach inside, but Masoud's shiver has nothing to do with the chill. He's really scared of me...and there's that rush again.

"I had to wait, okay?" he whines. "They were changing the guard at the front gate, they were walking right by here, I had to hide, okay?"

Even though it's a decent excuse, I have the urge to push him around some more, watch him squirm. Instead I just say, "Let's get on with it."

I tell myself I'm dropping it because I'm not like Masoud; I don't want to push him around just for the pleasure of it, like he did to me. That's what I tell myself, but I don't know if I believe it. What it really is, is that I can't wait to do this. A real thief job, like I've always dreamed about.

Masoud just nods, relieved, and presses his back against the smooth plaster wall of the Inalid compound. Then he lifts one foot, then the other, and braces them against the wall of the building opposite. By shuffling his feet up the wall, squirming his body up with them, he ascends the narrow gap inch by inch.

I keep my eyes open for Inalid guards and ahdath patrols, clenching my fists impatiently. One breath to fill my tan-t'ien, one standing leap and I'd be at the top of the wall in a moment...but there's no way I'm letting Masoud know I can do something like that. We may be stealing the box together but I don't trust him even a little bit, and the more secrets I have, the more of an edge they give me.

Finally Masoud reaches the top of the wall, twisting himself around until he can throw an arm over it and haul himself up. He crouches on the top, keeping low to minimize his silhouette against the sky. He runs his hand carefully over the top of the wall, then looks down and beckons impatiently to me. I let out a breath I didn't know I'd been holding. The silken strand is still there, tied off on an iron spike Masoud hammered into the top of the wall. My ordeal in the mansion wasn't pointless.

The crossbow is long gone—back at the squat, or stashed in one of the thieves' hiding places where we can retrieve it later—but he's left a coil of slender cord in the shadow of the wall, and now I find its end and throw it up to Masoud.

Carefully, he unties the silk from the spike, not letting it fall and disappear in the evening half-light. Carefully, he ties one of the loose ends to the end of the cord. Carefully—oh, so carefully—he starts pulling on the thread's other end, drawing the silk through the loop at the end of the crossbow bolt I hammered into the window frame, all those dozens of yards away.

As he pulls I feed the cord up to him, length after length, careful not to get it tangled. We keep it taut. Not too taut, or the thread will snap, and we're screwed. Not too slack, or as it inches toward the window it'll sag, dip into the torchlight, and the guards will see what's going on, and we're screwed.

A tickle on my cheek, like the faintest breeze—the end of the thread, brushing my face as it descends. Masoud stops pulling. He gives the slightest tug on the thread. I know what's happened—the end of the cord has reached the eyelet of the crossbow bolt, and it's caught. He tugs again, and then again, ever so softly. Once again I can't draw breath—

—And then the cord is moving again. I relax, but not too much. If anything was going to go wrong with the rope trick, it would have gone wrong already. That means I really have to *do* this.

Masoud pulls on the thread faster. Then he's pulling on the end of the cord. He snaps the thread and tosses it aside—a moment ago it was our lifeline, and now it's trash. He ties the cord to the spike on the wall. Now there's a doubled length of slender braided silk stretching from wall to window, in the darkness above the mansion's torchlit grounds.

Once again resisting the urge to just leap, I chimney up the gap between the wall and the neighbouring building just like Masoud did. From the top I can just see the cord, a black squiggle barely visible in the last fading embers of sunset. Now it bows as Masoud puts his weight on it, arms out for balance. I want to follow him right away, but the cord won't take both of us.

Masoud reaches the window. The mansion's plaster walls reflect the torches and light him up for a moment, and I brace myself for a shout from below. It doesn't come, and he swings himself inside. I fill my tan-t'ien with a breath and step onto the cord myself. With ch'ing-kung I'm light as a feather, and it barely tightens beneath my feet as I practically stroll across it. I reach out as I pass the peach tree and brush the end of one budding branch with my palm, keeping my balance perfectly. I feel exultant…and disappointed. Is this all there is to it? I've fought my whole life for this, and now I can do what I can do, it feels like I was thinking small.

I reach the window only moments after Masoud, and step lightly inside. He's got his back to me\ and he's not moving, and a moment later I see why. It's the bony household slave, the one who was feeling up the girls when we left the mansion. The knife in his hand glimmers in the torchlight from outside, pointed at Masoud's chest.

I don't think, I just move. I cross the room in no time at all, and my fist sinks into the slave's solar plexus. Even as he's folding double, I bring my knee up into his balls. As he drops, I grab a fistful of his shirt and swing him around so he lands on the rolled rugs in the corner with a thud and not on the floor with a crash. Then I drop on top of him with my forearm across his throat, and in a moment he's limp, choked out.

I stand up, only shaking a little from the rush. Masoud's eyes are saucer-wide. It's the kind of look I used to dream of getting from the other Martens; now I find I don't care. I step silently over to the shelves, listening all the while. Why hadn't the slave woken the household with a shout when he saw Masoud? Probably because he wasn't meant to be in the room at all. I glance down, and sure enough there's an open sack on the floor, half full. It seems we weren't the only ones stealing stuff tonight.

The box, though, is still sitting on the shelf where I left it. Even in the dim torchlight, the lacquer has an unearthly glow, crimson flickering deep under the surface. Now I can grab it and run. With ch'ing-kung, Masoud would never be able to stop me. Hand it over to Red and Yu Hao, and go with them to China. Roam chiang-hu, join the Wulin—

But I don't. Out of nowhere, one memory has pushed everything else out of my head: Oleg's poker, glowing and hissing an inch from my eyeball. Reminding me how small I am, how everything's bigger than me and can crush me underfoot without even noticing I'm there.

I can't do this. I was an idiot to ever think I could try. I cough gently, and Masoud shakes himself out of his trance. He kneels in front of the box, like he's going to open it. I hadn't considered this, and for a moment I think I'm going to let him do it, consign him to the same fate as the Kyrgyz. Before I can decide either way, I see the cloth bag in his hands. Expertly he flips the mouth of the bag over the box without touching it, then with a shake of his wrists the box slides neatly inside. Evidently word of what happened to the Kyrgyz got back to him, and he took it to heart.

He pulls the drawstring tight and knots it, then slings the bag over his shoulder, the woven strap across his chest. I don't know how I feel, watching him do it. I'm not sure I've even broken my word to Yu Hao and Red. I said I'd try to get the box—well, I did try, and I failed. Now I'll tell them Crow has the box, and they can go up against her. *And get butchered.* It still feels like a betrayal.

We pad back to the window and the rope stretching to the wall. None of the guards seem to have seen it—I can hear one of them now, clattering along below us, and give thanks to Allah and Tengri, as does every thief in Samarkand, that most people would rather look at the ground between their feet than up at the stars.

I step aside to let Masoud get a foot on the windowsill—*loot goes first*, that's the thieves' code. He steadies himself and steps out onto the rope. I watch him edge along it, glancing back at the bony slave every other moment, expecting to see him awake and lunging at me.

Soon I can no longer restrain my impatience, and when Masoud is two-thirds of the way across I step out after him.

Once again, with ch'ing-kung it's easy; even using my ch'i only a little, I almost catch up to him before he reaches the wall. So I'm nearly there, level with the bare branches of the peach tree, when Masoud steps onto the wall and draws the slave's knife from where he's stashed it in his kameez. His eyes meet mine, wide with surprise, and hold them for what seems like a very long time, before he cuts the rope.

CHAPTER TWENTY-FOUR

As the cord goes slack under me I push off with my feet, gaining just enough momentum to leap to the peach tree. I land, light as a soap bubble, at the very tip of a slender branch. It should be bowing almost to the grand, but instead it just bobs gently as I stand there, like my weight was no more than a bird's.

A shout. The guards have seen the cord coiling on the ground between the torches.

Masoud's still staring at me, his mouth hanging open. He'd expected to see me on the ground with my brains leaking out, or nursing a broken leg, the guards closing in. Now he's seen not only that I'm alive, but what I can do.

My gaze bores into his eyes, letting that new knowledge sink in, before a guard's arrow whistles through the air between us and breaks the spell.

I spring from the branch, take a skipping half-step on the wall and float to the ground just in time to see Masoud's shadow darting down a narrow alley and into the Maze. I remember the Wolves chasing us the day all this started, him leaving me in that dead-end, and I'm after him.

Bloodlust rises, scattering my ch'i. I don't have nearly enough self-control to use ch'ing-kung as I pound after Masoud. It wouldn't help me anyway, not in a chase through the Maze at night. The last sunlight has drained from the sky and the moon's not yet risen, and it's almost pitch black. The only light comes from the stars of the Straw Road over our heads, and the occasional flashes of torchlight coming down the side streets as they flash past.

We're more a danger to ourselves here than each other; at this speed, one wrong turn and you'll break your leg, or smack into a wall at full speed and drive your nose into your brain. I'm too caught up in the fury to worry about any of that. My foot connects with a loose brick and I go stumbling forward, out of control, for ten feet before I regain my balance. My face just grazes the corner of a house that, had I been an inch closer, would have crushed my cheekbone. I keep running, hot on Masoud's trail. His footsteps echo crazily off the walls and make it almost impossible to tell where he is and which way he's going.

Finally, though, I hurdle the cover of a midden-hole and turn a corner, and I see he's run himself into a dead end. He skids to a halt and tries to double back, but as soon as he turns I cannon into him at full speed, knocking us both off our feet and sending us rolling along the ground in a tangle of limbs.

When we come to a halt, Masoud happens to be on top, and he takes advantage of it by driving his fist down into my face. I manage to jerk aside in time for the blow to smack into my ear instead, making my head ring. He's straddling my chest, pinning my arms with his knees, and when his hands grip my throat I twist my neck and sink my teeth into his wrist. He howls and tries to pull back, and I ride the momentum up and over, slamming him down onto the ground, and then I'm just hitting him and hitting him.

Anything I knew about kung fu, about ch'ing-kung and No-Shadow Kicks and Snowy Egret style, flies right out of my head. I'm just bellowing and pounding on him with my knuckles; I'm probably doing more damage to my hands than I am to his face but I don't even feel it.

Finally he manages to flail out with a fist that connects with my temple and sends me sprawling. It's like plunging underwater. My vision blurs, everything slows to a crawl, and I struggle up and scoot on my butt away from Masoud until my back presses against the alley wall, trying to give myself a minute, but he's not coming after me. Painfully he heaves himself up and leans back against the opposite wall, fresh bruises flowering on his already banged-up face.

We're both fighting for breath, sucking air, but I manage to draw enough to say, "You." He looks at me. It's too dark to read his face. "You," I say again, then I have to cough up a thick wad of spit and blood. "You sold us out. To the Wolves." I can't believe I didn't see it before. He looks at the ground.

"I didn't get away. That day in the alley. Dropped right into a pack of them. Ali was going to cut my *tongue out*, Darya—"

"What are they giving you for the box, Masoud? What were the Martens worth to you?" I throw the words at him as hard as I did my fists earlier, trying to hurt him just as much.

"Besides my tongue?" He shakes his head. "You think Ali ever *gave* anyone anything?"

That stops me. I scramble for words. "Then…why?" He barks, and for a second I think it's a yell of anger, that he's going to attack again, and my hands fly up, but he's only laughing.

"'Why?'" he pants. "'Why?' You of all people…Oleg, Darya. It's *Oleg.*"

Then I get it. My mind throws up the image of Masoud in the courtyard, the tears streaming after Oleg slapped him down. "Crow doesn't get her box, so she doesn't fix Oleg," I say slowly. "You want him to die."

Another hoarse bark. "You don't?"

"And you told Ali he was sick. That's why the Wolves have been coming at us so hard." I spit. "Even if the Martens are finished, Masoud…selling us out to the Wolves—"

"What does it matter who—"

"*Not the Wolves.* Ali's ten times worse than Oleg ever was—"

"Screw the Wolves," he says, his voice harsh. "I don't care about the Wolves. I don't care what they do with the box either, they can sell it to Crow, or somebody else, or burn it for all I care. I just want to see Oleg go down."

"And then what? What crew's going to let you in, with everyone knowing you're a scumbag backstabber?"

"You're the only one who knows. And you weren't supposed to be a problem, after tonight." He shrugs.

I've always thought of Masoud as just a climber, working his way up the ladder with flattery and treachery. Not even a person, more like a wicked serpent in a story. The idea that he would give up his place on the ladder for revenge—revenge that won't help his prospects in the slightest—makes me see him for the first time as human. Too late to help him though.

I heave myself to my feet, and so does Masoud. "You sold me out, Masoud."

"Give me a break," he says bitterly. "What happened back there, Darya? You *flew*, I saw it. You cut some kind of a deal to learn that, didn't you? And you did it a while ago. I think you sold *us* out *first*—"

One last victory for Masoud, running rings around me with words again. He better enjoy it, because I've got a comeback for him. My head is clear enough for me to focus on my breath, and I feel my ch'i flow as I drop into an imitation of one of Yu Hao's fighting stances. "You're not walking out of here," I say.

"True, as far as it goes," says a voice, "but it doesn't go quite far enough." Firelight climbs the walls as they come around the corner. Wolves, holding torches, with Ali at their head. "He's *not* walking out of here," says Ali, "but neither are you."

Two Wolves grab Masoud, pulling the bag off his arm and throwing it to Ali. Two more twist my arms behind me; I struggle until it hurts too much, then stop. Ali's standing beside a covered midden-hole. He picks the knot of the drawstring open and looks in the bag. He grunts in satisfaction.

"I was taking it to you," says Masoud. His voice cracks. "I was—"

Ali doesn't even look at him, just kicks the cover off the midden-hole and nods to the Wolves holding Masoud and me. "Throw them in." He gives us a thin smile.

They frog-march us to the midden-hole. Masoud is still talking, panic rising in his voice. "Wait—just *wait*—"

The fetid stench rises around us from the darkness below. Fear and revulsion give me strength, and I yank my arms back, hard. The pain makes me cry out, but the Wolves holding me loosen their grip for a moment. I wrench an arm free and bring my elbow up into one Wolf's throat. He gags and I twist away from him to face the other Wolf, pivoting from my waist and putting my whole torso into it as I strike him in the chest with the heel of my palm. I manage to put some ch'i behind the blow, and the impact sends him stumbling back.

Ali grunts with irritation and draws a knife from his belt. I just need a moment to collect myself, draw breath and spring up and over the alley wall, but Ali doesn't take even a moment before that knife's at my throat. I close my eyes. A tear trickles down the side of my nose. The point of the knife begins to dimple my skin.

Then a bored, deep voice says, "What's all this then?"

I open my eyes and see Captain Uthman and three other ahdath, their curved swords drawn. One of them is the green recruit. Mehmet, that's his name.

Ali tries to make a break for it. The knifepoint leaves my throat, leaving a tiny bubble of blood—it tickles—and he rushes at Mehmet. Mehmet's nerve fails him and he lowers his sword, but Uthman steps smoothly in front of him and stops Ali with a punch to the face. Bone crunches, and he drops without a sound. Some of the other Wolves were looking like they were going to run too, but now they freeze.

Uthman glares at me. "What did I tell you? Stealing stuff, getting everyone all riled up?" He grunts as he squats beside Ali's prone body, pulls the bag with the box off his arm and holds it up for another ahdath, the one with the scar and moustache, to take.

Maybe I can convince him it's mine. "Thanks," I say, "I—" and I don't say anything else, because now Uthman grabs a fistful of Ali's hair and lifts his head while his other hand pulls a dagger from his belt. He draws the tip casually across Ali's throat. Blood gushes, steaming in the cold air, and Uthman stands and kicks the body into the midden-hole.

Tough but fair. One of the good ones. You'd almost think he cared. Until you see what a street rat's life is worth to him. Mehmet gags, covers it with a cough. Even Moustache raises an eyebrow. "Was that necessary?" he says mildly.

"Kid was a nutcase," says Uthman, "give him a few years and he'd be a real headache. I don't need another headache."

"Listen—" begins Masoud.

A short and humourless laugh from Uthman. He ignores Masoud, looks at me. "What did I say, housecat? What did I tell you about sneaking around rich men's property? Now I've got a houseful of *very* rich men screaming blue murder about tightropes and strangled slaves and Assassins." He shrugs. "Looks like I've got scapegoats now, though." He looks at me and Masoud and the Wolves. "You're going to the qadi."

CHAPTER TWENTY-FIVE

I barely get a look at my cell, just enough to see it's about as big as my cot in the warehouse loft, before the door slams and cuts off the light. Without sight, all I can do is trail my hand along the wall, feeling the rough stone under my fingertips, the trickles of moisture running down and collecting in puddles on the floor.

I find the least wet corner and curl up there. I'm reeling with fatigue, and I cradle my throbbing ear with my throbbing hand and even manage an hour of uneasy sleep. Or a day—it's impossible to tell in the silence and the dark. When an ahdath I don't recognize yanks the door open, the gloomy light outside feels like staring right at the sun, shocks me so much I cry out.

He drives me through endless stone corridors. Somewhere along the line I notice two of the Wolves from last night stumbling along beside me, the three of us on the same side just for a moment.

They shove us into a narrow room facing a pair of tall, ornately carved wooden doors. The other Wolves are there with their own ahdath guards. I see Masoud for just a moment, at the other end of the room, and then the ahdath who let me out of my cell asks "That all of them?" and another grunts an affirmative. "Send 'em in, then." Two of the ahdath push the double doors open.

The room we troop into is the most luxurious I've seen in my life. Chandeliers hang from the ceiling high above, holding too many candles to count. Finely-woven rugs overlap on the floor, so plush they almost swallow my feet. The plaster walls are a flawless white, covered with paintings from floor to ceiling—huntsmen and dancers with calligraphy curling around them, so ornate I doubt I could read it even if I could read.

There are people here, a bunch of nervous-looking well-dressed men who form a loose queue pointed at the far end of the room. They don't spare us a glance as the ahdath herd us forward, just murmur with their neighbours.

Crossing the room takes us an age, but it's still not long enough for me. Because at the far end, sitting on a raised platform, is an old man with a bristling white beard and a tulip-shaped turban sitting on his head. He's surrounded by ahdath, and I see Uthman among them, with rookie Mehmet and the gravel-voiced corporal. Two men stand on the rug in front of him.

The old man is saying something, and between his wheezy old voice and the flowery Persian he's using I can't follow it right away. Then it clicks—the two men in front of him are dihkans in some dispute over land, and he's passing judgement.

This is the qadi. The high magistrate of all Samarkand. Pickpockets don't ever get judged by the qadi, we're not worth his time. Not unless somebody's trying to make a point.

In this case, the point is Uthman's. The Inalids must have really been panicking last night. They thought we were Assassins, and Uthman's dragging us out in front of Samarkand's rich and powerful to show everyone we were just common burglars. Failed burglars—I see Uthman's holding Masoud's bag, the one with the box inside. The qadi will pass judgement and Uthman won't waste time in carrying it out. I'm going to be dead by dusk.

Wait, my brain insists, *wait wait wait. Death? You didn't kill anybody. You're only on the hook for thieving*. Great, so I'll be missing a hand instead. Even if I don't "accidentally" bleed out, you can't hustle without a hand. You can't even beg, someone sees your stump and boom, there goes any sympathy they have.

Uthman could pin it on the Wolves. Ali's not around to say any different. You could be here just for show, a chance for the qadi to show clemency maybe— I'm too afraid to know whether this line of thought makes sense or it's just a lame, desperate hope, but I'll take what I can get.

Then we're up. The qadi dismisses the two dihkans with a gesture and the ahdath push us in front of the dais. A couple of kicks to the backs of our legs drop us to our knees, and rough hands on the backs of our heads push them down into a bow. By rolling my eyes almost all the way up, I can just see the qadi wave a wizened hand. "Begin."

Uthman steps forward and clears his throat. He's still holding the bag with the box in it. "Last night," he begins, "on or about the—"

"*Thief!*" I know that voice. It bellows from the back of the diwan. The ahdath holding my head down relaxes his grip as he turns, letting me look too.

It's the big Khwarezmian, the one we ripped off in the bazaar about a thousand years ago. He's pushing his way to the front of the line, making his way through the crowd by virtue of sheer mass. His face is scarlet with anger as he points a sausage finger at me. "That one!" he's yelling. "The dark one! He stole my purse!"

I hear a half-hysterical giggle, and I'm pretty sure it's me. So much for walking out of here with both my hands. I turn to see how the qadi's reacting to all this, but there's something wrong with the way the old man is sitting on his dais. I can't see his face.

Then it clicks. His face, along with the rest of his head, is lying on the rug beside the dais, turban still perfectly wound. And standing behind the headless body, his sword extended at the end of its swing, is the rookie, Mehmet.

Chapter Twenty-Six

For just a moment, everything is perfectly still. Then bright blood shoots up from the qadi's neck in a gory fountain. The sight of the blood seems to unfreeze Uthman, whose jaw had just started to drop in surprise. He drops the cloth bag and his hand flies to the hilt of his sword.

Mehmet, his face calm, focused, his eyes intent—no trace of the watery unsure look they had up to now—brings his sword back around in a tight arc that ends with the blade buried in Uthman's chest. Uthman makes a small surprised sound—*Huh. Would you look at that*—and his legs go from under him.

Then all hell breaks loose. The crowd stampede for the door, screaming and trampling each other in their rush to get away. The other ahdath pile on Mehmet with a yell. Mehmet is yelling something too, something in Arabic I don't catch, and pulling a knife from his tunic, and before he disappears under the militiamen his foot shoots out and hooks the bag with the box inside, sending it flying off the dais.

My eyes track it as it skids across the floor, because I have no idea what else to do, and I see it come to a halt against the edge of one of the qadi's rugs....where a fat hand scoops it up and stuffs it into the folds of an elaborate silk robe, whose owner turns and makes his way smoothly towards the by-now unclogged exit. The Khwarezmian.

Leaving the courthouse without permission is against the law, I suppose, but I think we've left the world of laws and rules way behind at this point. The ahdath are too busy with Mehmet to even notice me running like hell. The Wolves are running with me, none of us looking at each other. I don't see Masoud.

Everyone's escaped through a set of double doors at the back of the room. The floor is scattered with things the crowd dropped in their haste to get the hell out—hats, purses, rolls of papers. Finally I emerge blinking into the sunlight into the Square of the Money-changers.

The square is deserted, which is fair enough; if I was standing here and everyone came bursting out of the courthouse screaming about how an Assassin just cut the qadi's head off, I'd want to clear out as well. I look around, just in time to see the tail of a silken robe flickering as it disappears through an archway.

I cross the square at a dead run, feet slapping on the bricks, loud in the otherwise silent square. Through the archway is a narrow lane, the buildings on either side extending so far out they almost meet in the middle, creating a kind of tunnel. I take a moment to let my eyes adjust to the darkness. It's only then I hear the footsteps coming up behind me. A hand shoves me hard, pushing me into the lane.

Sandy hair. Peeling skin. Breath that stinks of booze. And pale eyes, like blue cloth left out in the sun. "You owe me a sword," says the Teuton. I stare up at him. "The one your friend broke was a Langschwert from Solingen. Made for me by the best blacksmith in Bergischesland."

He's talking gibberish. How drunk is he? I'm horrified to hear myself laugh. His hand shoots out and grabs my throat. He lifts me off the ground with no effort at all. "So unless you have another one," says the Teuton, and a rusty knife is in his other hand, "I will take it out of your *hide—*"

Behind him, the Khwarezmian's face emerges smooth and silent from the darkness. My eyes leave the Teuton's to look at him. The Teuton notices this and half-turns himself, just as the merchant raises his hand, which contains a long narrow blade more like a meat skewer than a dagger, and drives it into his temple.

I look back at the Teuton. The tip of the Khwarezmian's blade protrudes a quarter-inch from the other side of his head, a tiny droplet of blood on the tip. The big man's eyes cross and his hand tightens its grip unbearably, until I'm sure my neck will snap…and then it relaxes and I slide down the wall, landing on the ground on my butt. Black fireworks burst behind my eyes and I hear, not see, the Teuton's body crash to the ground.

I take a breath that scorches my throat and my vision clears a little, enough to see the Khwarezmian kneeling by the Teuton's corpse and retrieving his blade. It grates on bone, and the sound makes me shudder. Then he stands, with a grace he's not shown a hint of until now. It reminds me of the way Yu Hao moves, of someone entirely in command of his own body, no wasted motion at all. He looks down at me. I'm pretty sure I haven't peed myself, which is a minor miracle at this point.

"I think I owed you that," he says. "You have proved yourself quite useful, little girl." He rubs the side of his nose, where the yellow-green remnant of a black eye still lingers. "Although not without creating your share of inconvenience."

He's wearing the silks of the merchant in the Street of the Rope-sellers that day, but this is a completely different man. His eyes are alive with keen intelligence and he holds himself with perfect stillness.

"Assassin," I manage to croak, looking up at him.

"A *da'i*, specifically," he says. "I train the faithful."

"Mehmet."

He nods. "That was not his name, but yes. That oppressor, that so-called qadi, was doomed the moment Mehmet was named his executioner. My assignment to Samarkand was practically routine." He holds up the cloth bag. "But then we heard about this."

"That's nothing," I croak. "Just...just something we ripped off some merchant."

"Like me, you mean?" There's even a hint of amusement in the Khwarezmian's...the Assassin's voice. "And this is just some dihkan's land grant? Not, for example, a copy of the *Yin-yün Chen-Ching?*" His voice is suddenly musical with the swooping tones of Yu Hao's language. I look up at him, my eyes blurring with tears.

"We are the *Assassins*, little girl," he says. "We make it our business to know these things. Many here are of our faith—the keeper of the tavern where your friends lodge, for one. He understood enough of their talk to know what this is." He shakes the bag. "You have my thanks. We have had an interest in the techniques of the Wulin for some time."

He turns to go. "Tonight I will take this scroll to Alamut, where it will be studied. Insofar as its contents are compatible with our faith, they will be used against our oppressors. If they are not, it will be burned."

Then he disappears into the darkness.

CHAPTER TWENTY-SEVEN

Yu Hao and Red find me sitting on the rim of the fountain in the square, scooping up handfuls of water and letting them fall through my fingers.

"Darya?" says Yu Hao.

"How did you know I was here?" I say.

"We didn't," says Red, "we just heard all the running and the screaming and wanted to know what was up." I don't react, so she adds, "What's up?"

"You have to get out of here," I say. "You have to go back to China or wherever. It's not safe for you here. It's—it's—Oh my God, I ripped off an *Assassin*." I start to shake.

Yu Hao holds out a hand, and I seize it like I'm falling. "Perhaps," he says gently, "you should start from the beginning."

"So they have a rep, is what you're telling me. These Assassins." Red scoops a handful of yellow rice from the bowl in front of her and sucks it off her fingers. "Everyone's scared of them."

"You could say that." We're sitting outside a tavern in an otherwise empty lane. The owner set down the food and wine Red paid for and then disappeared inside and shut the door. We only see a few people, either hurrying along the street or standing in small knots, talking in hushed and urgent tones. The news of what happened in the courthouse will be halfway to Bukhara by now.

The ahdath will go berserk after this. They're going to straight-up murder any street rat who looks at them funny. The margin of safety we operated on, thin to start with, is completely gone now. I try to make myself care about that, and fail. All the way from the square, it didn't feel like my feet touched the ground once, and it had nothing to do with ch'ing-kung. Nothing seems real.

It takes a lot more than the brutal murder of one of the highest officials in Samarkand to close this city down, though, and we had no trouble finding a tavern that was open for business, which is how we got the lamb and rice Red is eating. Mine sits untouched on the table. She chews for a while then turns to Yu Hao, sitting beside us with his hands clasped behind his back. " *'Lei sheng ta, yü tien hsiao?'*"

"You mind telling me what that means?" I ask, some of the numbness replaced by irritation.

"'The thunder is loud, the rain drops are small,'" Yu Hao translates. "She is asking if...you would say...their bark is worse than their bite?"

"'Bark'?" I stare at Red. "These are the *Assassins* I'm talking about. Were you listening to a word I said?" I see a troop of ahdath across the street, hands gripping their sword-hilts nervously, and I become aware my voice has been climbing. I shut up. If they're not looking for me now, they will be once they review the court records, looking for whoever was in the room when the qadi got murdered.

"They do have a reputation, Red," says Yu Hao. "They are people it might be better, all else being equal, to avoid."

"As opposed to the chen-niao, you mean?" says Red around a mouthful of lamb.

Yu Hao sighs. "Precisely. All else is not equal."

I stare at him with dawning horror. "You want to go after him."

"They have the Yin-Harmony Manual, Darya. If it were merely lost in Samarkand, that would be one thing. But to have the deepest

Wulin secrets fall into the hands of barbarians, who not only know what it is but would be able to apply it…" He falls silent, and when he speaks again, he chooses his words carefully. "I have an…obligation… to stop it."

"Do you now?" says Red, looking at him.

Yu looks at her. "No obligation on your part, Red."

"I got your back, you know that," Red says easily. "And this could work for us. We know where the box is going to be tonight—with that herd of Ferghana horses out by the caravanserai. If it's just this Assassin we have to deal with, then fine. If Crow finds out about this fake horse-trader and goes for him…we stand back, let them go at each other, tire each other out, and then we go in and take on whatever's left. One arrow, two vultures. And either way, they don't know we're coming, so we can surprise 'em."

"You're both insane," I say wonderingly. "Well, you can count me out."

"Darya—" says Yu Hao.

"No," I say. "No. Forget this. I'm done. For real this time."

"Darya—" says Red.

"I'm done. I've had enough." I'm still backing up. "Before all this started, all I had to worry about was Oleg, Nina, and starving to death. Now there's Oleg, Nina, Masoud, the Wolves—who probably blame me for Ali getting dumped in a shithole—plus also Crow and the White Scorpion Sect and now the Assassins, *plus* every ahdath in the city—because I was ten feet away from the *qadi of Samarkand* getting his *head cut off*—"

Yu Hao leans forward, intent. "All the more reason to leave, Darya. To come with us."

I start laughing, I just can't help it. "The two of you aren't going anywhere but the Heathen's Cemetery, if you're taking on Crow and that Assassin together. And anyway—who says the box is even yours to take? All I've got is the story you spun me on the Mausoleum. Who says you're any better than Crow is?"

"Then come with us and find out," says Yu Hao. "See for yourself."

"I *can't*." The hate in my voice stops Yu Hao cold, but it's not him I hate. "I don't deserve to." Suddenly I'm more tired than I've ever been.

"You have kung fu, Darya," murmurs Red. "You owe it to yourself to realize your potential, and you can't do that here. And you kept up your end of our deal. You went above and beyond—"

"But I didn't. Don't you see? I had it. The box. I could have run with it, I could have done it so easily—" My voice catches and I have to clear my throat, and when I resume it's almost in a whisper. "I should have taken it. But I didn't."

I don't wait to see how they take that, and anyway my eyes are full of tears. I turn and run. I collide with a couple of pedestrians, bang my hip on the corner of a stall, but I keep running, and thank God, thank God, they don't try to follow me.

CHAPTER TWENTY-EIGHT

I keep running for as long as I can take it, but eventually I have to stumble to a halt, my head swimming. I lean against a wall, desperately sucking air into my burning lungs. I can't feel the current, or ch'i, or anything. The way my stomach and my mind are churning, I doubt I ever will again. I realize I'll have to think of somewhere to go, and it seems like so much effort I just want to curl into a ball right there on the ground and not move ever again.

Then I think of Farid. Word might have got back to the warehouse about the Inalids, about how two Martens tried to rip them off way ahead of time. Masoud might have made it back there already, pinned the whole thing on Farid and me to save his own skin. I'm a dead girl walking right now, so I'm not too worried about what happens to me. But, regardless of what he thinks of me, Farid's had my back this whole time. I can do some good there.

Then I can lie down. Give up. Beg on a corner, maybe, while I wait for the ahdath to get me, or Crow or the Wolves, or whoever the hell wants me.

The Street of the Pepper-Sellers is deserted, the squat silent and dark. There's usually *someone* there, and the emptiness of the place creeps me out enough that I try a "Hello?" Nothing. I walk up to the squat's dark doorway and try again—"Farid? Anyone there?" A dim wedge of sunlight extends from the doorway a few yards into the squat, and beyond that is darkness so absolute it seems to swallow all sound. There's no reply.

Are those footsteps, coming from the direction of the warehouse? I listen hard, but there's nothing. I need to move, before I lose all nerve and stay rooted here forever. Still, I hesitate on the threshold. It's not just fear, although there's plenty of that—it seems like any one of the dozens of people who now want me dead could be hiding in that darkness. It's not like only thieves and muscle can set foot in the squat. Pickpockets and even runners come and go all the time, on errands and to see old friends.

But I've never tried. I wanted to make damn sure no one mistook me for the only kind of girl who comes here—the arm candy, the casual hookups. I wanted to get here on my own. Earn it. None of that matters any more, of course, but I still pause for a moment. But warning Farid is still the only thing I can think of to do, and I step inside.

It smells musty, worse than the loft even. My feet kick aside a couple of old bones, trash from a weeks-old meal. Soft skittering from the corner as a rat investigates them for any slivers of meat. Is this really where I've been killing myself all these years to get to?

In the distance, a lozenge of half-light marks a window covered with a cloth, sunlight trickling through the coarse weave. Not enough to light the floor between there and here. So there's no warning before I step on something that yields sickeningly under my feet.

I recoil, back up a couple of steps, and crouch there in the darkness for what seems a long time. I whip my head around, looking at the doorways behind and in front of me, but there's nothing silhouetted in them, no movement at all.

Finally my eyes become used enough to the darkness to see a vague outline on the floor, and I can tell it's a body. It's sprawled by the rear door of the squat, limbs splayed out in that careless way that only the dead have. Its hand—that's what I stepped on—is stretched out almost imploringly, and now my pupils have dilated enough to see it's Sanjar. There's no blood that I can see, no wound. Nothing to say he didn't just drop where he stood, like a puppet with its strings cut, for no reason at all.

I'm about to turn, run, but then I feel a tiny pain in my neck, no more than a louse-bite but it sends fire streaming through my veins and the floor swings up into my face and when it hits I don't even feel it.

CHAPTER TWENTY-NINE

The world burns. Flames lick at the corners of my vision but when I twist my head to see them there's nothing there, only the brick walls of the courtyard and the dead tree's roots splitting the earth, but there must be a fire because everything's sagging and melting from the heat.

I'm hanging from the tree, impaled on its dead branches. I look down at the bloody twigs protruding from my arms and legs, my chest and stomach. The rough bark scrapes against my lungs when I breathe.

I blink and the wounds blur and disappear. Instead I'm tied to the tree with ropes, iron-hard knots binding my arms to the branches, two more tight coils holding my torso and knees fast against the trunk. I must have been thrashing in my sleep, because my kameez is in tatters around my wrists and the skin underneath is raw and burning. Then the ropes fade and once again the branches are piercing my flesh. Ropes. Branches. I don't know which is real, or if either of them are.

The branches' jagged shadows are like cracks in the ground that reach into every corner of the courtyard. The sun is low behind me, then; either I've been here all night, or it's decided to set in the east today. I can't tell which is more likely. The shadows boil with insectile shapes and I look away. By painfully twisting my neck I can see my fingers. They have a blue tinge that doesn't look good. Ice crackles in my clothes as I try to move. It hurts too much and I stop. What time is it? What day is it?

Oleg and Nina are lying in the corner of the courtyard. I stare at them for almost a minute before I realize what I'm seeing. Oleg slumps on the ground, little more than a skeleton in befouled furs, skin sagging like half-melted wax. Nina is curled on top of him, face down. A knife lies a foot from her outstretched hand. The marten sits in its cage, looking at me attentively, quiet for once.

I'm sure they're dead, if they're even there at all. Then Oleg slowly raises his head. He looks at me, but I can't tell if his glassy eyes see me or not. He opens his mouth, and a thick black centipede crawls out. The thin rattle from my parched throat might be a scream. I do it again, then whimper, a high keening whine that sets my own teeth on edge.

"Good morning," says a voice. I flinch, and those branches running through my flesh move, and whether they're real or not they *hurt* and I cry out. "Easy." Crow emerges from the warehouse. She's not wearing her jacket for once, just a sleeveless silk vest, but she's not shivering. I don't even see any gooseflesh on her skinny road-tanned arms.

As she walks past Oleg she reaches out and smoothly picks up the centipede, holding it just behind its head. It's as thick as her thumb and its tail thrashes, slapping against her bare forearm as it tries to sink its jaws into her, but it can't break her grip. Oleg's head lolls.

I struggle against the ropes as she approaches me. She puts her free hand on my shoulder, holds me steady. "Easy," she says again. "Wouldn't want your heart to burst. Not before we're done." I watch the centipede writhe in her hand. When I stop moving, she sits down on the curve of one of the dead tree's roots. A small, skinny wooden box and a wooden bowl are laid out beside her. Did she bring them out with her? I can't remember.

"You probably feel a little strange," she says, not looking at me. "That was me. Just something to make you talk. A little more subtle than a hot poker." That makes me think of—

"Oleg," I croak.

She glances at the corner where Oleg and Nina lie. "Yes. When I heard you'd lost the box, you and your friend…I might have lost my temper."

Masoud, I think, and at the same time I hear myself say it, although I didn't mean to. Is he dead? She sees the question in my eyes and shakes her head. "Your colleague didn't come here. Paid a beggar to deliver the message. Clever. Anyway." She nods at Oleg. "I told him our deal was off. He didn't like that."

Oleg shudders. I flinch. She sees me looking. "No, he's not dead. I just gave him something to keep him still." She holds up the squirming centipede. "My friends need live flesh."

Before I can react, she continues. "The medicine wasn't working anyway. No point in continuing. Of course," and she nods at Nina, "*she* didn't see it that way. Came at me with a knife." With her free hand she pinches the centipede's head with thumb and forefinger and twists it off. "She was quick, for a dried-up old bitch. Not quick enough, of course. But quick." She holds the centipede's still-quivering body over the wooden bowl at her feet, wrings the fat body out like you would a washcloth. Black ichor and pale guts patter on the curved wood.

So I'm not dreaming Oleg and Nina's bodies, unless this whole thing is a dream. I can't fit it in my head. It's like the Old Mosque vanishing, or the city wall, or the sky. I'd say that it wasn't the end I'd imagined for those two, but that's not it—I never imagined they *would* have an end, not deep in my soul. Not even with Oleg's sickness and the Wolves picking us off. He and Nina were immutable, immovable. I'm shaking. I'm pretty sure I'm going into shock. But there's one more thing I have to know. "Farid."

Crow casts the centipede's broken body aside. The bowl is half-full of steaming innards. "I don't know who that is. But I didn't kill anyone but those two, and the one in the other building. I'm almost done with killing, I think."

She passes a hand wearily through her hair and something gleams in the light of the sunrise. The skin behind her ear is discoloured, a patch of flawless white. No: it's the rest of her. That's not a road tan, she's stained her skin somehow—

"Chen-niao." Once again the word tumbles from my lips as soon as I think it, Crow's poison doing its work.

Crow nods. "We'll start there."

So I talk. I talk as the sunrise floods the clouds with colour until they glow like inflamed flesh. The colours pulse and roil as the poison eats my mind, and I talk. At first I try to stop myself. But when Crow asks a question I can't help but think of the answer, and as soon as I think it I hear it pouring out of my mouth in a rambling flood, and after a while I just let it happen.

She asks about the da'i who took the box, about the Assassins and Alamut, and I tell her what little I know. She asks about Yu Hao and Red. About that first day with the Teuton, before I even met Crow. About the caravanserai and the deal I made, about ch'i and ch'ing-kung and kung fu. About their names and where they said they come from and what they taught me and how they fight.

Somewhere along the line she upends the narrow wooden box, long wooden darts with iron points tumbling out onto the earth at her feet. She picks up each one and rolls it in the bowl of centipede guts, then puts it back in the box in a steady, unchanging rhythm I find utterly hypnotic.

I talk. I no longer even remember how to try to stop myself. I tell her things I didn't even know I remembered, but which come spilling out of my mouth all the same. The words hang in the air, I can see them curling and spreading like ink in water, darkening the courtyard until I can barely see. And I talk.

I'm alone with Oleg and Nina. Oleg's stopped moving, mercifully. It's later, the shadows are shorter. I can still see those toxic sunrise colours, though, thrilling through the sky. Everything is quivering and pulsing, nothing stays still. Whatever's inside me, it isn't wearing off. It's getting worse.

My throat is on fire and my lips are cracked and bleeding. The only sound is my ragged breathing. Was Crow ever there at all? As I think her name she appears, walking around the tree from behind me. She's rubbing a wet rag through her hair. When she takes it away, her hair, and face, are shining white.

She rubs the rag along her arm, and the stain she used on her skin to fake the tan of a Silk Road traveller comes off in a broad swath, leaving more of that unnatural white. It doesn't look like living skin at all. Not like she's dead, though; more like she was never alive, like she's a statue of made of snow, or mutton-fat jade. Her hair and skin seem to glimmer with their own light, the cold light of faraway stars, although that's probably the poison talking.

I stare slack-jawed. I can feel the tears making channels in the grime on my cheeks. In my current state—and there's enough of my mind left to know how deeply wrong it is—it feels like she's the most beautiful thing I've ever seen.

She tosses the rag away and takes her jacket from the branch she's hung it on, and shrugs it on. Her sabres lean against the trunk of the tree and she straps them to her back. She's gearing up to go to war, but her movements are relaxed, unhurried. From the very first time I saw her, Crow's been wound up tight, tension barely held in check. Like a fist clenched around a stone it's going to throw, white-knuckled and trembling. Now, though, the stone is in flight, committed to its arc and to where it's going to hit, and there's no changing its path now. She's someone who knows exactly what she's doing next. She looks almost at peace.

I try to speak but my lips won't move. When she holds a wooden cup of water to them I don't even hesitate, just suck it up greedily. I don't know where she got the cup from. I think I lost a few minutes there. She tips the cup to allow the last drops to trickle into my mouth, then lets it fall to the ground. Her beautiful lifeless face is suddenly very close to mine.

"Your friends lied to you, you know," she says. Her breath is sweet. "You want a code, a way to live with honour. Something to fight for, greater than yourself. But there isn't one."

She steps back and one of her sabres is in her hand. "There isn't any more *honour*—" She brings it down in a sweeping, angry stroke. "—Or *nobility*—" Another stroke. I try to cry out. "—Or *compassion* in the whole Wulin than in you little barbarians squabbling over a beggar's corner." The sabre sweeps up my body in a third stroke. I feel it nick my chin. All at once, the ropes holding me to the tree go slack and I slide down the trunk to the earth, landing in a boneless heap.

She stands over me. "All lies. All just the trickery of foul old men, to make you do their bidding." I manage to turn my head to look up at her. Her sabre is once again at her back. "And sooner or later you'll do things that stain your soul *black*, for 'honour'. Better you die before you find that out.

"So I'm doing you a favour, although it probably doesn't look that way. Even if I let you live, the drug will burn out your mind. You'd be a mad beggar on a street corner for the rest of your life—"

"Quit pissing around, then," I rasp. "Do it."

She considers, then nods. A flicker of motion and a tiny steel dart, little more than a length of wire, is in her hand. Another flicker and she's thrown it at me, turning to leave as she does it. She only flicks it with her thumb and forefinger, almost casually, but there's ch'i behind it and it feels like being punched in the heart. My vision greys out.

"I'm done," I hear Crow say as she strides out of the courthouse. "Done with killing children. Killing anyone. Apart from this Assassin. And your two friends. And anyone else who gets between me and the *Yin-yün Chen-ching*." As she passes the marten's cage she reaches out and flicks the latch, letting the door swing open. She walks into the darkness of the warehouse, and leaves me only her voice. "And then, perhaps myself. And *then* I'm done."

The marten flows out of its cage, up and over the wall and it's gone. I force myself to look down and I see the dart sticking out of me, out of my heart, and that's the last thing I see at all.

CHAPTER THIRTY

When I come around, the dart is lying beside me, its steel head blunted. There's a hole in my kameez right over my heart, and through it I see the dull gleam of bronze. The astrolabe. So it looks like I'm not going to die from Crow's poison after all. I'm going to lie here in agony with my mind gone, pissing myself and drooling, and then die of thirst instead.

My hand is lying awkwardly on one of the tree's exposed branches, but I can't move it. I can't move anything. It's a struggle to breathe—sometimes I forget how and strangle for a moment before I can heave my chest and suck air again.

Nina raises her head from Oleg's chest. Her eyes are pure black, and leak black tears that drip from her chin. "Foolish girl," she says. "Ungrateful little cow. After all we did for you."

Screw you, I scream, or I think I do. The hate makes the poison run through my blood faster, but it clears my head a little and I seize on that.

The courtyard is falling apart, shards of brick and earth and sky whirling away into nothingness. My mind is coming apart too, it's cracking and the poison is forcing the cracks open like the roots of the tree have done to the dirt of the courtyard. Parts of it are already crumbling into that void. I'm losing pieces of myself and there's nothing I can do to stop it.

I'm way past making a conscious effort to do anything. About all I have left is reflex, so I fall back on that. And the one reflex I've had drilled into me constantly this whole past week is—breathe. So I breathe. In through my nose. Out through my mouth, smooth and deep, each time filling my tan-t'ien, my reservoir of ch'i. And my ch'i begins to stir.

It feels sluggish, polluted by the poison raging through my veins, but I keep breathing, forcing it to move. It makes the pain worse, so much worse, but I clench my teeth and fight through it. I breathe faster, harder, building up my energy but deliberately holding it back, damming it up. With my brains scrambled like this I'm unable to put a plan into words even to myself, but I have a strong feeling that this is a very bad idea.

I hear Yu Hao's voice, very clearly. Talking about the White Scorpions. Talking about the dangers of tampering with ch'i, how it twists the mind, warps the body…But I keep breathing, although every breath fans the fire inside me, although after every exhale I just want to give up and never breathe again.

The rhythm of my body, whatever keeps my heart and lungs and guts pulsing in time, is gone. My heart skips, then skips again. Heat rises inside me, at first like a fever and then like I've swallowed a burning coal, and it might be my imagination but I feel a cold trickle against my skin as the ice in my clothes melts away. The trickle turns warm, then hot, and now I see steam rising from me, or else it's just my vision blurring again.

The pain snarls and thrashes inside me and I snarl and thrash with it. Even to my own ears, I sound like an animal. I see it very clearly: I'm going to die. My whole body is going to incinerate itself in one furious white glare—and, with a scream that shreds my throat, I let the dam break. Agony roars through me, burning up all before it and leaving nothing but emptiness behind. It's over in a moment, but that moment

takes

an

eternity.

When I come around, I'm shaking and my limbs are as weak as a newborn lamb's—but my eyes, and my mind, are clear. The drug is gone. Sobbing with effort, I heave myself up so I can sit against the tree. There's a scorch mark on one of the exposed roots, the exact shape of my hand. I can see the lines of my palm burned into the dead wood.

Right now I just want to drag myself into the warehouse, curl up under a shelf and sleep for about six days straight. But I can't. Crow was asking about the Assassin, so he hasn't left Samarkand yet. Red and Yu Hao will be going after him tonight, then—and so will Crow. And I've told Crow all about them, their plans, how they fight, everything. From the light in the sky, it's less than an hour to sunset. I have to warn them.

I draw a breath to fill my tan-t'ien. The breath turns into a gasp of pain. Something's wrong—whatever I did to burn the drug out of my blood, it's messed me up somehow. So ch'ing-kung is out. No big deal. All I have to do is cross the whole of Samarkand, faster than I've ever done it before, when it feels like there's no way I can even stand up.

Kung fu. Mastery through discipline. Skill through hard work. Red's voice in my head. I groan, trying to drown the annoying bitch out. *You have kung fu, Darya. You have kung fu. So get up. Get up.* So, just to shut her up, I do.

My run through the Maze lasts forever. There's no way I'll remember all this, I tell myself. At least, I hope there isn't. I take a step, then fall. Up again, another two tottering steps, and I go down on my knees again. The warehouse doorway is no closer. I get up. Left foot in front of the right, dragging in the dirt. Right in front of the left. Every few steps the thought comes into my mind: this is it. I have to stop. It was a good run, but now it's over. I don't argue with the thought or try to beat it back, but somehow, every time, I keep on moving. Then the world spins around me and I have to stop and throw up, steaming black bile splattering on the bricks, but then I'm moving again.

I can't run, can't manage anything more than a limping half-jog, but now I've purged my veins of whatever Crow put in there, my mind is crystal clear. I remember every time I've ever run through the Maze, all those memories coalescing into a single gleaming map of Samarkand revolving in my head. I take shortcuts I never knew I knew, I duck through the crowds like the streets were empty. And then, incredibly, I see China Gate looming up in front of me. I just need to—

My legs turn to water. I fall, skidding on the bricks., and just barely muster the strength to roll over on my back and look up at the Gate. Almost. I almost made it. But almost isn't good enough.

Darya? Red says in my head.

"Go away," I mumble, and darkness claims me.

CHAPTER THIRTY-ONE

I'm in the tavern's upstairs room, lying on Yu Hao's straw mattress. Someone's bundled me in two layers of fleece; I should be sweating my ass off but instead I'm freezing cold. Yu Hao is kneeling by my side, leaning over me, his face coming into focus a few inches from mine; his hand takes my chin. A lock of his long hair tickles my nose. For a moment I think he's going to kiss me, and even with the pain and the dizziness my heart seizes up for a moment. But no. He appears to be peering into my mouth. I try to ask him why but all that comes out is a wordless sigh.

"Shh," he says absently, and I shh. I like this dream, even if I feel like an entire troop of Khitai cavalry have paraded over me, and I'm in no hurry to wake up. He takes my hand in his, rests three fingers across my wrist. I can feel my pulse fluttering against them. They feel deliciously warm against my frozen skin.

"Well?" says Red's voice, from very far away.

"Poison," says Yu's voice, "but—" It also seems to be coming from miles away, although his hand is still right there on mine.

"But what?" Red again. *Piss off, Red.*

"But it's gone. Somehow. I can see where it's been, but it's just not there any more."

"So she's going to be fine?"

"She's very far from fine, Red. Her ch'i flow is…deranged. Her *tsang* and *fu* are shutting down one by one." His voice is tight with frustration.

"Then stop it." Red's voice is tight too.

"I can't stop it if I don't know what caused it, Red." He sounds angry and desperate, which is not sexy at all. I'll have to do something about that.

"Ch'i," I murmur.

His head turns as quick as a bird's, his eyes lock on mine. "Darya?"

"Built it up." I say. My lips and tongue are numb and I slur the words badly, but he seems to understand. I slowly raise my hand, flutter it over my abdomen. "Tan-t'ien. Then…" I sweep my hand over my chest, trying to show how I let the energy rage through my body, but my strength goes before it gets halfway there, and it falls onto my breastbone. Yu looks at me, comprehension dawning on his face. Then he rips the fleece away from my chest.

Now this is interesting. I manage to raise my head to see what he's going to do next, which turns out to be driving the knuckle of his forefinger into my chest, just below my ribcage. I yelp with pain, but his hands keep roaming over my torso and arms, prodding and twisting in specific places. Finally he presses down on my collarbone—

And just like that, I feel my ch'i snap back into its proper pathways, warmth flooding into me. I flop back onto the mattress, drawing deep and unrestricted breaths. Yu Hao leans over me again and peers into my eyes. He opens his mouth to speak, but I take advantage of my new freedom of movement to wrap a lazy arm around his neck, pull him down to me and kiss him.

Red snorts. I feel her gently pull my arm away, letting Yu Hao sit up. He blinks and opens and closes his mouth a couple of times but nothing comes out. "Why did you do that?" I protest mildly to Red. "Why—" Then my brain catches up with me and I sit bolt upright.

"Oh, shit," I say.

Chapter Thirty-Two

I'm coming with you."

"Like hell," says Red. We're on the tavern's roof watching the sun dip to the horizon. She's sitting cross-legged with her spear's double-edged blade in her lap, running a whetstone over it. Yu Hao and I sit on opposite sides of the spear's shaft, and now I turn to him, although we don't quite meet each other's eyes. He has his ch'in in his lap, and absently plucks a string as he tightens and loosens it.

"I can fight. Seriously." Now he does looks at me and the surge of teeth-grinding embarrassment is enough to make me consider backing down, but this is too important.

"Darya," he says, "I'm not sure you understand by how slim a margin you've just escaped death. The ch'i technique you used was... extraordinary...but it did at least as much damage to you as the poison. Your *wei-ch'i* is utterly depleted."

"I don't know what that—"

"It means," says Red, not looking up from her spear-blade, "a strong breeze could finish you off. Stay here, Darya. You've done enough."

"I told Crow everything. I sold you out."

"You couldn't have helped but talk," Yu Hao replies. "And you've told us about her, too."

"Nothing you can use. She made me remember *everything*. I—"

"Enough, Darya," says Red, and there's an edge to her voice I haven't heard before that makes me close my mouth. She lifts her gourd, takes a swig of liquor. The warmth has drained right out of her, leaving her all business. "Yu Hao, we're going to have to talk about how we're doing this."

Yu Hao tightens the ch'in string a fraction and plucks it once, twice, three times. He sighs, sadly it seems to me. "Yes."

She takes another drink; even for a lush like her, she's hitting the bottle pretty hard for someone who's supposed to be getting into a fight to the death in a few hours. "Okay. We wait for Crow to come at the Assassin, they wear each other out, we go after what's left. But you're going to need a weapon. All that close-up southern-style joint-and-tendon stuff isn't going to do too well against two sabres in the hands of a chen-niao. You need some reach—can you at least use, I don't know, a staff or something—"

His ch'in suddenly sings out, a fast ripple of notes, cutting Red off. His fingers blur over the strings, picking out an intricate melody, very different from the meditative music he's played before. Red looks at him with real irritation, which then vanishes completely as he plays the song's final note and a dull *clunk* sounds from inside the wooden frame.

Yu Hao tightens his fingers on the strings and lifts the ch'in's top board right off its body. In the hollow inside, in a cavity shaped to fit it, nestles a sword in its scabbard, a straight-bladed 'chien' like the one Yang Jing was using in the warehouse. The handle is of carved hardwood, dull with use.

"No wonder it was flat," says Red mildly.

He takes the sword and stands up smoothly, fastening the scabbard around his waist. With an equally smooth motion he draws the sword and executes a flourish, the tip tracing sinuous squiggles in the air, impossible to follow with my eye, and the sword is in its scabbard again almost before I've fully realized he took it out.

"So what's that?" asks Red, her voice betraying nothing.

"Dragon-Serpent Sword Style," says Yu Hao.

She shakes her head, looking him right in the eye. "Don't know it."

He looks away. "You wouldn't. It isn't taught outside the Academy."

"You didn't fail your exams," she says softly.

He shakes his head. "Quite the opposite."

"You work for the Emperor."

"Not exactly."

"Oh, Yu Hao." Her voice is full of sadness and disappointment. It's the voice of someone who's seeing for the first time not just how things are, but how they've been for a long time. Someone saying goodbye to a host of treasured memories that now mean something altogether different.

"Red?" asks Yu Hao.

She doesn't reply right away. Instead she upends her bottle and drains it, coughs, wipes her mouth. "Later for this. For all of this. Assuming we're still alive later. Now let's get this damn box."

They look at each other for a moment more, then they both stand up. Red flips her spear into the air with her foot, grabs it and snaps it upright. I have no idea what I've just seen, but when they leap down from the roof I leap right after them, although I go skidding on the ground and fall in a heap and it takes me a minute to struggle to my feet again. They don't stop me. Right now it looks like they've got too much on their minds.

CHAPTER THIRTY-THREE

T hose," says Red, "are some great horses."

"I wouldn't know," says Yu Hao.

"No, you wouldn't, you boat-riding southerner. But take it from me."

We're on the roof of the caravanserai, looking out at the corral of Ferghana horses. Behind us, the caravanserai courtyard is dark—a caravan must have just left, and another hasn't yet arrived to fill the building. I look for their yurt, with the hole in the roof where Red cut it open, but of course it's not there. It'll have been broken down, rolled up, the pieces carried by camel hundreds of miles by now.

That first day, it was a grinding hour-long slog to get here. Just now it only took us a few minutes, whipping along the darkened road, our feet barely touching the ground, although using ch'ing-kung in my current state gives me an awful hollow feeling, like sprinting across a street when you've had nothing to eat all day. Nevertheless, I feel like my world has shrunk, that I barely even fit inside it any more.

The sun has well and truly set. Below us, the corral gate is open and the herd of Ferghana horses is streaming out and collecting in a stamping, neighing cluster in the road, their noise easily covering any we might make.

I see the Khwarezmian, the Assassin da'i, sitting imperiously on his own horse, and I hunch down, sure those piercing eyes of his are going to see me. But he's counting off the horses as they come out the gate, not even looking in our direction. Masoud's bag with the box inside is slung over one broad shoulder.

Flanking him are twelve horsemen in Persian riding gear, swords at their belts, holding up flaming torches. They must be his outriders; they'll keep the herd together as they lead it around the city walls to the west and onto the Shah's Road to Bukhara, and then along the long route to Persia and finally Alamut.

"Who are those guys?" murmurs Red, echoing my own thoughts. "More Assassins?"

"Maybe," I say doubtfully. The horses are all out of the gate now and the da'i and the others are drawn up in a line on our side of the road. I dread his eyes falling on our position, but no one's even looking up, just talking with each other, pointing out different parts of the herd.

Red shrugs. "Only one way to find out, I guess. Any sign of Crow?" Yu Hao has been scanning the terrain, and he shakes his head slightly. "Well if she doesn't get here before they start moving, we're going to have to go for it, plan or no plan. We're never going to able to pick them off without everyone seeing and piling onto us, so we'll just have to rush them."

"You can't just 'rush' twelve men!"

"Darya—either shut up or go back to the city. Either way, you're out of this. Okay, Yu Hao—either these guys are rabble, in which case we'll take them down easy, or they're not, in which case, well, we'll figure that out when we get there." I open my mouth and she holds up a hand. "Shut up, Darya. Yu Hao, the six on the right are yours. I'll take the others and the fat man—with a spear I've got the reach, so I can keep him at a distance until you finish yours off. I hope. I—huh?"

One of the riders is cursing and slapping at his throat, trying to kill whatever's stung him. His hand comes away bloody, and in the light of the torch he's holding I see a shallow gash along his neck, a couple of inches long.

Before he's brought his hand to his face to look at it, two more men have flinched in their saddles and are looking down stupidly at the slender wooden stalks that seem to have sprouted from their chests and thighs. Then I finally hear the rhythmic hollow clacking coming from beneath us, in the caravanserai's gateway.

Crow strides out of the darkness. She's holding a bulky weapon in her hands, like a crossbow but with a wooden box built over the catch. I recognize that box, and the darts she filled it with. Instead of a trigger the crossbow has a lever which she slams down over and over again, *clackclackclack* as she fires from the hip, and with each *clack* one of those wooden darts flies out and pierces a horseman's flesh.

"*Chu-ke nu*," murmurs Yu beside me, just as Red murmurs, "Crap."

Crow never breaks step, and she's filling the air with darts; her rate of fire is unbelievable, but the darts are small and not even travelling that fast, not as fast as an arrow from a bow for sure. They're not even doing any damage, it seems. The horsemen stare, wondering what she's doing, but I know. I remember the crushed centipede leaking black ichor, Crow dipping the darts in it one by one.

Now the horsemen slump in their saddles, eyes glazed and bodies jerking randomly. The Assassin hasn't been hit; he's slid from his saddle and taken his curved sword from his belt. Crow lifts the strange crossbow and brings the lever down one more time. He tilts his head, quick as a bird does, and his free hand whips up faster than I can follow, and suddenly it's holding the bolt by its wooden shaft.

He caught it out of the air. My heart plummets into my guts. There's no way Yu Hao and Red can take on one of these lunatics, let alone both. There's no way. But if Red was right…if they end up killing each other…it's the only chance we've got.

"Poison-tipped," says the da'i, examining the dart. His Khitai is flawless. "Some would consider this unsporting."

Winter throws the crossbow away and draws one of her long sabres as she bears down on him. "Poison on the shaft too. Idiot."

The Assassin drops the dart like it's hot. His expression doesn't change but as he takes a step I see his muscles seize up. He tries to take another and falls to his knees. With a tremendous effort he raises his hand, and Crow slices it off, along with his head, in one sweeping stroke. On her way past the corpse she snags the bag from its shoulder. She still hasn't broken step once. Only then does the Assassin's headless corpse topple into the dust.

"Well shit," says Red conversationally, "there goes that idea."

Crow throws the bag onto the ground beside her and draws her other sabre. Raising her voice, she calls out "Let's get this over with."

That's it, we're done. The only thing left is for the three of us to run, and hope that Crow will be happy with her treasure, that she won't hunt us down. I turn to Yu Hao to tell him this. He's not there. I whip my head around. Neither is Red. Both of them are soaring gently to the ground in front of the caravanserai, landing either side of Crow, who looks from Yu Hao to Red, and back to Yu Hao again.

"Just like the girl said," she says. "How old are you? Eighteen? The girl said you were about eighteen."

Red sets her spearpoint to moving, whipping back and forth on the flexible wooden shaft, horsetail swirling behind it. A fierce grin spreads on her face. "You don't think the two-sabres thing is a little played out? I mean, we all wanted to be Hu San-Niang when we were little girls, but some of us grew up."

As she speaks, she and Yu Hao sidestep and circle Crow, keeping her between them. If Crow even hears Red she gives no sign, just keeps her sabres outstretched and angled down, one of them pointing at each of her opponents, tracking them perfectly even when she's not looking.

The grin doesn't falter, but I can tell it's taking Red effort to maintain. Still, she hasn't lost that confidence. I don't know if Red's ever been beaten in a fight, but despite her words of caution to Yu Hao yesterday, she can't quite imagine herself losing this one.

"I just want to go *home*, do you understand that?" says Crow, frustration creeping into her voice. "I am *so tired* of this. The *Yin-yün Chen-ching* is ours. It belongs to us. All you little thieves, skulking around like rats…if the Wulin want to take us on, let them elect a Meng-Chu and fight us."

"Like you did when you poisoned the Blades?" says Red. Her voice is still flippant but there's a tightness to it that betrays her tension. Yu Hao shoots her a warning glance.

"Like they did when they burned our temple down?" replies Crow. She shakes her head. "Enough of this. If you want it, come and get it, bitch."

Red's spear is already moving, slithering through her hands like a lightning bolt, aimed dead at Crow's breastbone. For a second I think it's going to hit home, that this is over, and my heart leaps—then plummets as Crow twists her torso almost lazily, and Red's spear point sizzles past a hair's-breadth from her chest. She brings her sabres up, one either side of the spear's shaft, and crosses the blades, trapping Red's weapon between hers. Red yanks at her spear. It doesn't move at all. The two women's eyes meet. Red's go wide.

A moment later Yu Hao steps smoothly into battle, his chien swooping at Crow's head. She parts her sabres and spins in place, bringing one up to block his sword while the other cuts at his legs. Red pulls her spear back as Yu Hao leaps backwards. She spins her spear in the air and snaps it upright, and the two of them resume circling around Crow, who again raises her swords.

The whole exchange has taken less than a breath, but once it's over everything's changed. Red's strut is gone; she holds her spear close to her, ready to fend off a blow rather than deliver one with a flourish, and her eyes are still wide, like a dazzled animal. She's outclassed, and she knows it. They both do; Yu Hao's stance is almost entirely defensive too. This fight is going to end in exactly one way, and all three of them know what it is.

With a roar, Red leaps at Crow, circling the point of her spear, the horsetail flaring out. She thrusts once, twice; Crow blocks, once, twice, and the second time shoves the spear-shaft with the flat of her blade, forcing it back across Red's chest. Instantly Red leaps back and in the same motion flings the spear at Crow sideways. The wooden shaft smacks into her chest and she staggers a little as it rebounds into Red's hands again. For the second time my heart is in my throat as I see the opening in Crow's defences—Yu Hao is already pressing the advantage, his chien twirling in his hand, and I'm praying to Allah and Tengri and Buddha and Christ for this to work—

But Crow's already recovered, and she blocks him effortlessly in a flurry of shining steel...and they're circling again, Crow waiting patiently between Red and Yu Hao as they search for an opening that's not going to come.

Steel meets steel again, and again. Red's moves are increasingly outrageous, crazy leaps and twirls, the spear seemingly in a dozen places at once, but she's not showing off—she's desperate, trying to do something Crow won't anticipate, anything to give her an edge. Until, inevitably, she leaves herself open for a moment too long.

Crow's sabres are occupied with Yu Hao's sword, or else she'd cut Red's head off. Instead, without even looking, she lashes out with the point of her boot and it catches Red in the chest, throwing her back. Red raises twin clouds of dust as she skids backwards on her heels, and she drops to one knee, head hanging. She spits on the ground— it's bright red—and looks up at Crow, and I see her bloody chin and the naked fear in her eyes.

Crow launches the next attack, Yu Hao on the receiving end, parrying her lightning-fast slashes, wielding his chien like a musician's instrument or the brush of a painter. Red comes to his aid, thrusting and slashing, but Crow dodges her without effort while she keeps up the attack...and I see something terrible:

Red is holding back. She's keeping her distance, not pressing. Whether it's from calculated caution or unreasoning fear, the result is the same. She's not the unstoppable force that left the Teuton face-down on the dusty bricks. She looks like what she is, a girl only a little older than I am, facing off against an opponent who's faster, stronger and with more experience than her. Meanwhile Crow bears down remorselessly on Yu Hao. And Yu Hao's quick as hell, but he'd have to be twice as quick just to hold Crow at bay. And he's not. This is going to be over soon.

I realize that I've slipped into ch'i breathing without even knowing it. My fingers tense on the caravanserai roof, ready to launch me into the night. *Your wei-ch'i is depleted*, Yu Hao says in my head. *A strong breeze would finish you off.*

Screw it.

Chapter Thirty-Four

I leap from the caravanserai roof, soaring in a gentle arc over the melee below. If Crow looks up I'm done. If Yu Hao or Red catch a glimpse of me and it distracts them from Crow, *they're* done. But the three of them are intent on killing each other, and I clear the circle of torchlight they're fighting in and land just on the other side. As soon as my weight lands on my legs they fold like wet noodles, dumping me face-first into dust and dry horseshit, but I manage to roll and heave myself to my feet again. If I wasn't convinced just now I was in no shape to fight, I am now. But I've got something else in mind.

There's a torch lying on the ground next to the outstretched fingers of a corpse, one of the Assassin's poisoned riders. It's barely stayed lit—weak blue flames crawl over the pitch-soaked cloth, on the verge of going out. I snatch it up anyway and dash for the herd, not bothering to look behind me. If Crow's seen me I'm dead no matter what I do.

The horses, without any outriders to keep them together, have started to spread out, and it takes me a while to get around the other side and by that time I'm wheezing and staggering. I'm afraid it's too late, it's all over—but no, I still hear them, rapid fire clangs and clashes as Crow's twin sabres slash at spear and sword.

The torch is dark and my heart lurches in my chest, but then I see the smoke still rising from the end. I sweep it back and forward, nearly losing my grip on it; the first couple of times have no effect but on the third a pale flame flares into life. I swing the torch wildly, feeding the fire with air, and soon it's blazing merrily. Then I approach the horses.

Ferghana horses are the best in the world. They're bred for speed and for war, and they don't spook easily. Even fire doesn't bother them much, compared to other horses. Unless you're waving a flaming torch directly under their noses. That'll do it.

I keep swinging, getting as close as I dare. The horses are still in a tight enough group that they can't easily shy away from the fire, and I can see the panic ripple through the herd, like a pond someone's dropped a stone into. I lunge back and forth, flanking them with the torch, making sure there's only one way for them to go.

Finally, the horses on the far edge of the herd must get the message and make some room, because the ones on my side begin to shy away, slowly at first and then at a trot. When they're moving fast enough that momentum will carry them forward, I drop the torch and start to run.

Ch'ing-kung carries me level with the front of the herd and I run beside them for a moment, judging my next move—then I leap, soar, and come down on a horse's back on the herd's left flank. The horse, caught up in the stampede, barely notices. Panic has taken the herd— they probably don't even remember the fire just that they're running and they need to keep running. It's not trying to buck me off, but its back still heaves and shakes as it gallops madly.

My foot slips, and I nearly fall off right into the middle of the herd to be trampled to death, but I manage to stay upright long enough to drop onto the horse's back, digging my heels into its flanks, grabbing a double fistful of mane and holding on for dear life.

I don't think I've ever moved this fast. I lift my head, hoping the herd is going in something like the direction I want. And it is—we're heading straight for Crow and Red and Yu Hao. They're so intent on the fight they don't even notice us at first. Then, as I watch, Yu Hao sees us and pauses, just for a second, then goes stumbling backwards, bright red blooming on the sleeve of his white robe. Crow doesn't press the attach though, because she's looking at us now too, all of them are..

Crow is looking right at me, those glittering eyes boring into mine. Red has time to scream *"Darya God damn it what did I fucking SAY—"* and then we're on them. The three of them leap aside effortlessly— Crow, almost lazily. Any hope I had of trampling her is gone. And worse—I'm not coming in at the right angle. I'm going to miss my chance.

In my fury I drive my right heel into the flank of the horse I'm on, trying to drive it where I want it. This is a Ferghana horse, and even in the midst of its fear it responds to its rider, and we angle to the left as the herd pounds past the caravanserai. I'm so surprised that it worked that I nearly forget to slide down its left flank, one hand still holding its mane so I don't fall, and reach down with the other, and grab the bag with the box inside. I nearly fall anyway, but a convulsive effort hauls me back up onto the horse's back.

I have time for a split second of elation, and then I hear Crow's scream. It cuts through the sound of hoofbeats and the blood roaring in my ears. It cuts through the whole world. A scream of pure rage. I suddenly want very badly not to look behind me, but the skin between my shoulder blades is crawling, expecting a sabre-blade to pierce it any second now, and I can't help turning my head.

Crow is standing on the back of a horse at the rear of the herd. The horse rears—even as panicked as it was, Crow must have spooked it even worse—but the white-haired warrior might as well be standing on solid ground. Now, as I watch, she steps lightly forward onto another horse's back, and then another, almost strolling. Her ch'ing-kung is phenomenal, better by a mile than anything I've seen Yu Hao or Red do, let alone what I'm capable of.

"Remember when I said I was done killing children?" Crow says. She speaks softly, so softly, but her words carry all the force of her ch'i and they hammer at me until I think my eardrums are going to burst. "I take it back. But give me the box and it'll be quick."

For the second time today I'm absolutely, utterly certain that I'm going to die now. But I have one trick left and I might as well play this out to the end. I manage to sit up, then crouch on the back of my horse. Even with ch'ing-kung I feel like I'll be bucked off any minute and trampled beneath its hooves, or else it'll throw me clear and I'll land on the ground head-first.

"You want it?" I say, holding up the bag, "take it—" and hurl it at her.

I'm moving before I've finished saying it, leaping past Crow to the back of the herd—or trying to. Because suddenly there's a sabre blade held up to my neck, so suddenly that I have to yank my head back to avoid throwing myself on it and burying it in my throat.

I stand there awkwardly, on the back of yet another horse thundering along the plain outside the city walls. Crow's blade doesn't move. I see the other one has snagged the bag I threw on the tip of its blade. The bag flaps emptily. She twists her sabre and the bag flies off and back into the darkness.

"Enough tricks," says Crow wearily, and the sabre travels down to the black lacquered box I hug to my chest. The horses are galloping through a stand of trees. Black branches whip past us in the darkness. Crow ducks one effortlessly.

"You got it," I say, and let the box fall out of my hands. For the first time I see a look of surprise—just simple, wide eyed surprise—on Crow's face as she dives for the box—

—And then she sees what I've done, of course she sees it, it's the oldest trick in the book, and she begins to pull back, but she's almost at the tipping point and it takes her just a moment—

—and the ground drops away as the herd thunders over the steep bank of the canal.

I'm ready for it, and even I nearly lose my footing. Crow, already overbalanced, follows the box down between the horses. For just a moment I see her face, not angry or frightened, simply surprised, and then it's lost in the churning water of the canal as hundreds of hooves pound it into muddy froth.

I don't remember leaping from the herd as it splashes through the canal, or landing in a heap among the trees. The first thing I remember is firelight, Red and Yu Hao holding torches and rushing towards me, crouching next to me as I lift myself up on my elbows.

"Are you okay?" Red asks.

"You did well, Darya. Very well," says Yu Hao.

"Yeah, she only took out a chen-niao single handed, that's one way to put it, sure," says Red. "Darya?"

"I'm okay," I say. "The manual—"

"Forget it," says Red. "You did the right thing, letting it go—"

"No," I say, "that's just it…" I reach into my kameez and bring out the scroll, crumpled and water-splattered.

Yu sees me holding it with my bare hands and he goes pale. Red chokes back a sob.

"Oldest trick," I say, "in the book…" and then everything goes black.

CHAPTER THIRTY-FIVE

The darkness recedes by degrees, replaced by a sullen red glow lighting up the insides of my eyelids. I squeeze my eyes shut against it, then become aware of how cold it is. All at once I'm shivering convulsively.

I'm lying on the ground, a thin felt blanket the only thing between me and the almost-frozen earth. The sun has risen but I can't see it— the light is shining through a great cloud of dust. Somewhere within the cloud, I can hear a commotion like a dozen battles being fought at once, a yelling, bleating clattering chaos. I roll over. The caravanserai wall looms over me, lit up red with the sunrise. From right underneath it seems as high as the city wall.

"Welcome back," says Red. I sit up. She and Yu Hao are sitting next to me with their backs against the wall. Yu Hao's robe is off and he's wearing that sleeveless tunic, and Red is stitching up a deep cut in his bicep. "You were out two days, this time," says Red. She jerks the thread taut. Yu Hao doesn't react. "Going for a record?"

A gust of wind thins the dust cloud out a little, and I can see what's going on around us. A caravan is getting ready to depart. Camels and donkeys stand around as porters lash tottering piles of boxes and bundles to their backs. The animals stamp the ground, loosening the earth, kicking great plumes of it into the air until I can't even see Samarkand any more. Other men stand around piles of yet-to-be-loaded stuff, doing last-minute deals before it's on the way to…

"Someone wanted to meet you," says Red, "once you were back in the land of the living." She looks around, while her hand continues to run the needle through Yu Hao's arm. "He's—ah." She give a piercing whistle. "Da'ud!"

A tall and harassed-looking Arab with a forbiddingly long beard emerges from the dust. "If this is about an advance, I don't want to hear it," he says in Khitai.

Red jerks her head at me. He squints at me. "This is her?" he says.

"This is she," says Red.

To me, he says in Arabic, "You speak Pathani?"

My Pathani is shakier than my Arabic, but I nod.

"Because I've got a prick of a Pathan who keeps yelling at me about something. Now he can yell at you, instead. I—"

Crash from somewhere in the dust cloud, followed by the sound of porcelain shattering on the ground. The caravanbashi looks over my shoulder and spits a curse in Arabic. "*Hey! Hey! Don't touch that!*" And away he strides into the dust.

Red grins. "I think you made a good impression." She punches the needle through Yu Hao's skin, draws the thread through. Yu Hao looks at me thoughtfully.

"How are you feeling?"

"Better," I say, and it's the truth. He nods seriously and reaches out for my hand. I almost let him do it, then gasp and snatch it back. I remember the feel of the scroll in my hand, smooth silk paper but somehow also slimy, rotten. My fingers tingle and buzz, and I'm afraid to look at them, to see the first hints of corruption spreading. Tears blur my vision as I look at Yu Hao, but when I blink them away I see he's smiling. He still holds his hand out for mine.

"It's okay, Darya," says Red. I hesitate, but then extend my hand and he wraps his fingers around my wrist, resting on my skin where it pulses in time with my heartbeat.

"No trace," he says, "of the Scorpions' ku poison that I can find. Possibly you never touched it. Possibly the...unorthodox...way you overcame the truth drug gave you limited immunity."

"Very limited," says Red. "After you blacked out, your heart stopped for half a minute."

Yu Hao nods. "I would not be in a hurry to repeat the experiment." He smiles at me.

Now I know I'm not going to fall to bits, I have plenty of room to worry about the kissing-Yu-Hao thing, so I freeze, not knowing whether to smile back or not. He doesn't seem standoffish or strained, though, which suits me fine. If he's not going to mention it I won't either. Although do I really want us to pretend it never happened? The silence stretches out until it starts to get uncomfortable, then Red pushes the needle through his skin again. "Mm," he says.

"You are such a giant baby, Yu Hao," she says as she runs the needle through a loop in the thread and pulls the knot tight, tugging at his skin. She leans in, snaps the thread with her teeth. "There. Hope we cleaned it out okay. Who knows what kind of nasty shit a White Scorpion could have on her blade?"

Crow. "Is she…"

Red shrugs. "I went over that canal a mile each way," she says, "and no sign of her. In bits, probably, or got pounded into the bottom so deep she never came up again, but anyway she isn't going to be in any shape to follow us for a while, and the world's a big place." She looks at me. "A chen-niao. Single-handed. Not bad for your first day, wandering chiang-hu. And you're going to have something to remember her by." My incomprehension must show in my face, because she reaches out gently and touches my hairline, where the stubble is turning to fuzz. "It's coming in white."

I don't know how to feel about that and I don't want to figure it out right now. "And the manual?"

"Safe." Yu Hao taps his ch'in, leaning against the caravanserai wall beside him. "No one's going to be touching it, until we get to China."

The dust cloud thins again, and I see a sweaty Pathan coming through the crowd, looking around. "I have to go."

"We're on the move, Darya," says Yu Hao. "We leave in an hour."

"I know," I say. "This won't take long."

Red nods. "Go for it. And good luck." She smiles, a little sadly. "Goodbyes never go the way you want them to, in my experience."

One of the guys on the warehouse door I don't know. The other one is Kazan, muscle for the Martens. Or he used to be—both of them are dressed like household guards, in the colours of a trading clan. Looks like our merchant figured out the Martens were over, and he's made his own security arrangements, and Kazan at least has jumped ship and signed up. Someone's probably already taken away Oleg's and Nina's bodies and for a moment I wonder what's happened to them. Then I realize I don't care.

I don't bother saying hello, asking Kazan where everyone is. There's only one place they could be, anyway. I feel the impulse to give the warehouse one last look before I turn my back on it forever. I don't give in to it.

They're gathered just inside the door of the squat, in a shaft of sunlight from the street. Farid kneels on the ground in front of a bunch of pebbles laid out on the floor. Nasr stands beside him, and a gaggle of pickpockets and thieves—not all of them Martens—line the walls, listening to him. And Mahnaz is here too, arms folded, face hard.

Farid is moving the pebbles around as he talks. "We hold the corners here," he says. Nasr starts to object, and Farid raises a hand. "Just for a couple of days. Ahdath are still cracking down after the thing with the qadi, so we have some breathing room anyway. We have feelers out to the Bears, as soon as they get their muscle organized they can take over without anyone else getting any ideas. That's a favour the Bears will owe us."

"Who says the Bears will see it that way?" pipes up one of the pickpockets. I've never seen him before. "If they say, okay, we can't hold our corners now, and they move in on everything we have—"

"If they go one step further than we're letting them go," Farid says, "we show them why that's a real bad idea." The pickpocket sniffs, but he doesn't push it. Farid taps another pebble. "This one, though," he says, "by the bazaar, that's good traffic. We hold that one."

"You'll need a runner on the roof, then," I say. Sudden, oppressive silence, as everyone turns to look at me and just as quickly finds somewhere else to look. I keep talking anyway. "There's an alley around the back heads straight into the Perfumers' Souk, and that's Fox country. You don't have eyes on it, they'll be able to rush you any time they want." Silence. A moment of that silence is enough to tell me that if I ever really was a Marten, I'm not one now.

Farid stands. He leans over to murmur something to Mahnaz, then steps over the pebble-map towards me as she turns to Nasr. She doesn't even glance at me. He walks past me into the Street of Pepper-Sellers, making me follow him.

"You're still running beggars?" I ask, when we're outside.

He shrugs. "If we can hold the corners, sure. No one's moved on the orphanage yet, and those kids need to be looked after. Mahnaz will run it. And it's somewhere for us to stay."

"You're not staying here?"

He shakes his head. "Can't defend this place, if someone wants to finish us off. Not going to miss it, either. Or the courtyard. No tree anymore. No poker."

"No doubt," I say, just to say something. I look back through the doorway of the squat. "They're not all Martens."

"I'm not sure *we're* Martens. Maybe we're something new. But yeah. Some Wolves—the bottom kind of fell out of them after Ali died. Lot of kids who want a fresh start. Some are just curious; Nasr's trying to convince them to stay."

"He's good at that. That rat before, the one who sassed you about the Bears? He said 'we'. Not 'you'. He's already bought in. I think you can—"

"What do you *want*, Darya?" I meet his gaze, and say nothing. I'm going to make him say it. So he says it. "You can't stay." He looks away long enough to say it, then back at me. "It just wouldn't work out."

"Fine."

"What *happened* that night? Did you even stick to the plan you sold me on? Were you ever going to? Because it looks like it went pretty far off script."

"That wasn't me." I want to get that clear at least. "Masoud—"

"I know about him and the Wolves." He nods at the Wolves among his new crew. "They told me all about it, and yeah, we're gonna have a word with Masoud. If we find him. Sneaky little shit's gone to ground. That's not what I meant."

"So then what?"

"Get Crow's box. Get a place in some other crew. Get out from under Oleg. That was the plan. Now Oleg's dead, Nina's dead, Ali's dead, the *Teuton's* supposed to be dead, the *qadi's* dead, no one's seen Crow at all but who knows when she'll be back to finish us off—"

"She won't."

"Yeah? How do you know, Darya? How much have you known, all along? How long have you had this plan of yours, to just, just sit back and let everybody murder each other?"

"That wasn't—" I begin, then stop. What's the point?

"You've got a bigger body count than Ali did. And who's going to be next? That's not how I'm going to run things." He glances back at Nasr and Mahnaz and his tiny bunch of pickpockets and burglars. "This is going to be damn rough going for a while. Everyone is going to be pushing us hard, looking to bust us up. I need people I can trust. People who are who they say they are, and you're not. You're not who I thought you were."

There it is. So what did he think I was? A helpless little girl for him to save? A lieutenant, a queen? It doesn't even matter. I'm not the murderous puppet master he thinks I am, but I'm still not what he wants me to be, and he's not going to accept who I am. It's that dress he's made for me in his head; he's finally holding it up to me and seeing it doesn't fit. And worse, that he can't alter me to fit it.

I carefully look inside myself, seeing what I feel. Not a thing. I let him off the hook. "I just came to say goodbye. I'm getting out of Samarkand for a while."

His face doesn't change but I see him relax. "I think that's a good idea." He doesn't ask how, or where to. "Good luck."

"You too." And there's nothing more to say. Well. One more thing. Mahnaz looks down at me as I step up to her. Mahnaz, who's running the orphanage now. "I'm going to be out of town," I say. "Way out." She glances at Farid. He's not looking at me, and that tells her all she needs to know. She smirks. She thinks I'm off the board, not something she needs to worry about any more. She's wrong about that.

"But every time I run into somebody coming from Samarkand," I say, "I'm going to ask about the orphanage, about how you're treating those kids. Probably they won't even know what I'm talking about. But if they do, and they tell me something I don't like, then I'm coming right back here. Get it?" Something she sees in my face makes the smirk die away. She gives the barest nod.

On the way out I glance down the lane to the warehouse. From here I can just see that crack in the wall. The climb. I could run up it now, with my eyes closed. I don't bother.

I'm almost at China Gate when I hear a gravel voice I know. It's the Ahdath corporal, the one with the moustache and the scar. He's not a corporal any more; a captain's badge gleams on his cap. I wonder if it's the same one Uthman wore. He's got a trio of pickpockets up against a wall, and he's patting them down. As I watch, he pulls a coin-purse from one's kameez, and deftly slides it into his own belt.

I don't know if the ahdath still want me for burglary, or for being ten feet away from the qadi's murder, but just in case I duck into an alley. I lean to peer around the corner, wait until he's gone, and that's when a hand clutches my ankle.

I whirl, yanking my leg free. It's a beggar, squatting on the ground. Bloody tumours sprout from his grimy face. He holds out a shaking hand, wordlessly seeking alms. A moment later, though, I see the growths on his skin are fake, offal stuck on with glue. I look beneath them as he looks up at my face, and just like that we know each other. He goes grey under the dirt and dried gore.

"Darya," he croaks.

"Masoud," I say.

"You have to help me," he says. "You have to tell them all that I *had* to do it. I need back in, Darya. I can't..." His voice changes. "Darya? Darya—"

The caravan moves slow, and with ch'ing-kung, catching up to it is easy. It's only a little past the caravanserai, but it's still the furthest outside of Samarkand I've ever been. That cloud of dust is now following on its heels, a long wake strung out behind it. Behind *us*. I guess it'll follow us all the way to China, as will the steady background noise of hoofbeats, the calls of the animal handlers, the creaking and swaying of the camels' loads.

As I approach, I gently touch down and jog the rest of the way. Red and Yu Hao are out on the caravan's right flank, cantering along on a pair of horses. Yu Hao's wounded arm is bound across his chest but he raises the other in greeting.

"Everything all right?" says Red.

"Fine," I say, "let's go."

Red doesn't push it. "Hop up," she says, and I boost myself onto the horse behind her. "That Pathan was looking for you—"

"Not right now."

She shrugs. "Plenty of time, I guess. Long way to China." Yu Hao has fallen back a little and she pulls on her horse's reins to keep pace. "Thought about a name yet?"

"A name for what?"

"C'mon, Darya. If you're going to be wandering chiang-hu, you need something to go by, something with a bit of snap. 'Crimson Whirlwind', for example." She shakes her head. "It still sounds crap in Khitai."

I know the answer already. It's a name I fought for my whole life, even if it turned out not to mean much. Now it can mean whatever I want it to mean. And I've earned it. I've more than earned it."

"Marten," I say. "It's Marten."

"Little Marten," says Red, tasting the words. "*Hsiao-tiao.*"

"I didn't say—"

"I like it." She laughs, that rich throaty chuckle again. "I do."

I don't push it. I think of Farid, for the last time in a long time. I'm not who he thought I was. Red and Yu Hao probably think they know me too, but they're wrong. Nobody knows who I am. I'm not even sure I do. But, it occurs to me, I might have some say in that, from now on. And a smile begins to spread on my face.

I turn for a final look at Samarkand, but the dust hides it from view. So I turn, squinting against the rising sun that glares over Red's shoulder, and face East.

THE END

Acknowledgements

This book is a clumsy tribute to the wuxia ("martial hero", kind of) genre. In wuxia you will find the best two-fisted adventure stories ever created by anyone, anywhere on earth. Thanks to every wuxia writer out there, from the legends of the genre to everyone grinding out a two-thousand-chapter monster on Qidian right now.

Very, very few wuxia novels have been translated into English (they didn't even bother to translate Wang Dulu's Crouching Tiger, Hidden Dragon after the movie won four Oscars for Christ's sake), so a big thank-you to Pleco and Skritter for giving me enough Chinese ability to read them at all.

My deepest thanks to Leife Shallcross, who read this as I was writing it and whose encouragement kept me going.

About the Author

Robin grew up in Canberra and lives in Vancouver. His stories have appeared in Andromeda Spaceways Inflight Magazine and the Canberra Speculative Fiction Guild anthology Winds of Change. His wildly original debut novel Wellside was shortlisted for the Aurealis award. You can follow the author online at: @robinshortt2

The ADVENTURE
CONTINUES ONLINE!

Visit the Candlemark & Gleam website to

Find out about new releases

Read free sample chapters

Catch up on the latest news
and author events

Buy books! All purchases on the
Candlemark & Gleam site are DRM-free
and paperbacks come with a free digital version!

Meet flying monkey-creatures
from beyond the stars!*

www.candlemarkandgleam.com

*Space monkeys may not be available in your area. Some restrictions may apply.
This offer is only available for a limited time and is in fact a complete lie.

NOV 1 5 2019